A Dance With Obsession

THE SCOTTISH BILLIONAIRES

M. S. PARKER

BELMONTE PUBLISHING, LLC

This book is a work of fiction. The names, characters, places and incidents are products of the writer's imagination or have been used fictitiously and are not to be construed as real. Any resemblance to persons, living or dead, actual events, locales or organizations is entirely coincidental. V1

Copyright © 2024 Belmonte Publishing LLC

Published by Belmonte Publishing LLC

FURY

THE BALLROOM WAS PACKED, a sea of faces staring at me like I was about to drop the mic on the performance of a lifetime. Except I felt more like throwing up. The champagne in my hand was warm, the bubbles long gone. Just like my enthusiasm for this whole farewell party. The fake smiles and forced laughter grated on me. I was ready to get the hell out of there.

"Fury!" Cory's voice sliced through the noisy crowd. "Dude, where have you been? I've been searching everywhere for you."

I turned to see my best friend and business partner weaving through the crowd, Rylee in tow. Their idiotic grins made me smile.

"Jesus, Cory. You'd think I was dying, not moving to New York," I said, gesturing at the extravagant decorations. "This is a bit much, don't you think?"

Cory's dimples deepened as he laughed. "Are you kidding? This is barely enough to celebrate the great Fury Gracen, co-founder of Gracen & McCrae, conqueror of Wall Street!"

I rolled my eyes. "I haven't conquered shit yet, you moron."

"Details, details," Cory waved his hand dismissively. "You will, though. That's what matters."

Rylee elbowed him playfully. "Don't let it go to his head, babe. His ego's big enough as it is."

I snorted. "Says the woman who once described me as 'sex on legs'."

"Hey!" Rylee's cheeks flushed. "That was before I knew you. And I was drunk."

"Keep telling yourself that, sweetheart." I winked at her, and she stuck her tongue out at me.

Cory wrapped an arm around her waist, pulling her close. "Alright, alright. Let's not rehash ancient history. Tonight's about looking forward, right?"

His words hit me. Forward. Right. To New York. To a whole new life. Suddenly, the room felt too small, too hot.

"You okay, man?" Cory's brow furrowed. "You look a little pale."

I forced a smile. "Yeah, just... it's a lot, you know?"

"I get it," he nodded, his eyes softening. "Listen, Fury. I know we've talked about this a million times, but I want you to know... I'm one hundred percent behind you. This is a big move, and I know it wasn't an easy decision."

I swallowed hard, fighting back the lump in my throat. "Thanks, Cory. That... that means a lot."

He clapped me on the shoulder. "You're gonna kill it in New York. And hey, if it all goes to shit, you can always come crawling back to sunny California."

I barked out a laugh. "Gee, thanks for the vote of confidence."

"Anytime, buddy," he grinned. "Now come on, it's time for your big speech."

My stomach dropped. "A speech. Really?"

Rylee snickered. "Sorry, big guy. Price of fame and all that."

Before I could protest further, Cory was dragging me towards the makeshift stage. The room quieted as we approached, all eyes turning to me. Christ, I'd rather face down an angry mob than this adoring crowd.

Cory tapped the microphone, feedback screeching through the speakers. "Ladies and gentlemen, may I have your attention please?" His voice boomed across the ballroom. "We're here tonight to celebrate a man who needs no introduction. My best friend, my business partner, and the reason half of you have jobs - Fury Gracen!"

The crowd erupted in applause and cheers. I plastered on my best smile and stepped up to the mic.

"Thank you, thank you," I said, waiting for the noise to die down. "I gotta say, when Cory told me he was throwing a going-away party, I pictured lukewarm pizza and flat beer in the conference room. Guess I underestimated how much you all love me." I paused, letting a self-deprecating chuckle escape. "Or maybe you're just happy to see me go."

Laughter rippled through the audience. I took a deep breath, scanning the faces before me. Colleagues, friends, a few exes... six years of my life condensed into one room.

"Seriously, though," I continued, my voice softening slightly, "I'm not great at these mushy speeches, but I do want to say thank you. To every single one of you. Gracen & McCrae wouldn't be what it is today without your hard work and dedication. And to Cory..." I turned to my friend, who was beaming at me from the side of the stage. "I couldn't have asked for a better partner in crime. You've always had my back, even when I was being a stubborn ass. And hey, thanks for finally letting me ditch the tie." I loosened the offending neckwear, earning a few appreciative whistles from the crowd.

"As most of you know, I'm heading to New York to

oversee our expansion there. It's a big step, and if I'm being honest, it's a little terrifying. But I'm also excited. It's time for a new challenge, a new adventure." I paused, my gaze sweeping across the familiar faces. "I'm leaving a piece of my heart here in California, but I know I'm leaving things in good hands." I raised my glass. "To Gracen, McCrae & Palmer, to new beginnings, and to all of you. Cheers!"

The crowd echoed my toast, glasses clinking. I downed my champagne in one gulp, desperate to get off this stage and away from all these expectant faces.

As soon as I stepped down, I was mobbed. Handshakes, backslaps, tearful hugs from the secretaries. It was overwhelming, suffocating. I pasted on a smile and nodded along to their well-wishes, all the while searching for an escape route.

Finally, I spotted a gap in the crowd and made a beeline for the balcony. The cool night air hit me like a blessing, and I gulped it down greedily.

"Needed some air?" A familiar voice made me turn.

Natalie Bishop leaned against the railing, looking stunning in a slinky black dress. My breath caught in my throat.

"Nat," I managed. "I didn't know you were here."

She shrugged, a small smile playing on her lips. "Rylee invited me. Hope that's okay."

"Of course," I nodded, moving to stand beside her. "It's good to see you."

We stood in silence for a moment, looking out over the twinkling lights of Palo Alto. It was a view I'd seen a thousand times, but tonight it felt different. Bittersweet.

"So," Natalie said finally. "New York, huh? Big change."

I chuckled humorlessly. "You could say that."

She turned to face me, her hazel eyes searching mine. "Are you excited? Nervous?"

"Both," I admitted. "Terrified, actually. But don't tell anyone in there that."

Natalie laughed softly. "Your secret's safe with me, Fury Gracen."

There was a warmth in her voice that made my chest ache. We'd had a brief thing last year, nothing serious. Just two lonely people finding comfort in each other. But standing here with her now, I wondered what might have been if I'd let myself fall.

I watched Natalie's face in the moonlight, noticing a flicker of sadness in her eyes. It hit me then – she wasn't just here as Rylee's friend. She was here for me.

"Fury," she said softly, her hand brushing against mine on the railing. "I know we said it was just casual, but…"

I tensed, knowing where this was headed. "Nat…"

She leaned in closer, her perfume enveloping me.

"Maybe we were too quick to write it off. I've been thinking about you, about us."

My heart raced, a mix of desire and panic. Part of me wanted to pull her close, to lose myself in her warmth one last time. But I knew better. I took a step back, putting some distance between us.

"Natalie, I can't," I said, my voice rougher than I intended. "I'm leaving for New York in two days. It wouldn't be fair to either of us."

She bit her lip, looking away. "Right. Of course. I just thought... never mind."

The disappointment in her voice was like a punch to the gut. I ran a hand through my hair, frustrated with myself and the situation.

"Look, Nat, what we had was great. But it was what it was. I'm not in a place for anything more, especially now."

She nodded, forcing a smile that didn't reach her eyes. "I get it. Really, I do. I guess I just wanted to see if there was still something there before you left."

I sighed, leaning back against the railing. "I'm sorry. I never meant to hurt you."

"You didn't," she said quickly, then paused. "Well, maybe a little. But that's on me, not you."

We stood in awkward silence for a moment, the sounds of the party drifting out to us.

"Fury..." she started, but I was already backing away.

"I should get back inside," I muttered. "Thanks for coming, Nat. Take care of yourself."

I fled back into the noise and heat of the ballroom, my head spinning when Cory appeared at my elbow. "There you are! Come on, man. It's time to cut the cake."

I let him lead me towards a monstrosity of sugar and fondant, shaped like the New York skyline. It was ridiculous and over-the-top and so perfectly Cory.

"You're insane," I told him as he handed me a knife.

He grinned. "You love it."

And damn it, I did. Despite everything, despite the fear and doubt gnawing at my gut, I loved this crazy bastard and the life we'd built together.

As I raised the knife to cut into Lady Liberty's head, my phone buzzed in my pocket. I fished it out, frowning at the unknown number.

"Fury Gracen," a smooth voice purred when I answered. "Gavin Manning here. Hope I'm not interrupting anything important."

I blinked, surprised. I'd heard of Gavin Manning, of course. The infamous owner of Club Privé. Who hadn't? The man was a legend in certain circles. We even crossed paths once years ago.

"Mr. Manning," I said, stepping away from the cake and the confused looks from Cory and Rylee. "No, not interrupting at all. What can I do for you?"

"Gavin, please," he chuckled. "I hear you're setting up shop in my city, Fury. I have a business proposition for you."

My heart rate kicked up a notch. "I'm listening."

"Not over the phone," Gavin said. "But I'll have a car waiting for you at JFK. The driver will bring you straight to me. What do you say? Interested in hearing me out?"

I hesitated for a split second, then grinned. "Mr. Manning - Gavin. You've got yourself a deal."

As I hung up, I felt a surge of excitement coursing through my veins. This, right here, was why I was going to New York. For opportunities like this. For the chance to prove myself on a whole new playing field.

I turned back to the party, to Cory and Rylee and the ridiculous cake and all these people who believed in me. And for the first time that night, my smile was genuine.

"Alright, folks," I announced, brandishing the knife. "Who wants a piece of the Big Apple?"

Laughter and cheers erupted around me, a familiar symphony that I knew I'd soon leave behind. I plunged the knife into the cake, severing the ties to my past and embracing the unknown future that awaited me.

New York, here I come.

SIENNA

I GRITTED my teeth as Dana stumbled again, this time nearly crashing into Venus. "Jesus, Dana! Get it together before you break our star attraction!"

The music screeched to a halt, leaving us hanging in a thick silence. All I could hear was the dancers' ragged breathing. *Great.* I rubbed my temples, fighting the urge to scream. These girls were supposed to be the best of the best, but today they were moving like they'd been hitting the tequila since sunrise.

"I'm sorry, Sienna," Dana mumbled, her cheeks flushed with embarrassment. "I'll do better, I promise."

Yeah, you better. I sighed, my irritation battling with a flicker of sympathy. Dana was our oldest dancer, pushing thirty, and usually one of our most reliable. But today? She looked like she'd rather be anywhere but here.

I pulled her aside. "What's going on with you?" I asked, softening my tone just a touch. "You're a million miles away."

Dana's eyes welled up, and I braced myself for the waterworks. "It's Lily," she said, referring to her daughter. "She had a really rough night. The autism... sometimes it's just..."

"Shit," I muttered, feeling like an asshole. Of course, it was about her kid. I ran a hand through my hair, buying myself a moment to switch gears. "Look, I get it. Being a mom is tough. But when you're here, you've got to be here, you know? We can't afford any injuries, especially not to Venus."

Venus piped up from the back. "It's okay, Sienna. We're all just a little off today."

I shot her a look that said 'not helping,' but appreciated the attempt at smoothing things over. "Alright, ladies, listen up," I said, clapping my hands to get everyone's attention. "I know we're all tired, I know we all have shit going on outside these walls. But in here? In here, we're goddamn professionals. This routine needs to be perfect for tomorrow night's debut, and right now, it's looking about as coordinated as a drunk octopus trying to put on rollerskates."

A few giggles rippled through the group, and I felt the tension ease a bit. Good. I needed them focused, not terrified.

"Now, I want to see this routine one more time, start to finish, no mistakes. After that, we'll take a water break. Got it?"

A chorus of "Yes, Sienna" echoed back at me. I nodded to Darcy, our sound tech, and she cued up the music.

As the first beats pulsed through the speakers, I watched the girls snap into formation. Dana's movements were still a bit sluggish, but at least she was hitting her marks. Venus moved like liquid sex, as always, drawing the eye even in rehearsal clothes.

Just as they were hitting their stride, my phone buzzed in my pocket. I ignored it, eyes glued to the dancers. It buzzed again, more insistently this time. With a growl of frustration, I pulled it out, ready to silence it.

Gavin's name flashed on the screen.

"Shit," I muttered. I don't ignore a call from the boss. "Keep going!" I shouted to the girls as I answered the phone. "Gavin, what's up?"

"Sienna, darling," Gavin's smooth voice flowed through the speaker. "I need a favor."

I felt my eyebrow arch involuntarily. Gavin Manning didn't ask for favors. He gave orders and expected them to be followed. "What kind of favor?"

"I need you to pick someone up from JFK. A friend. Name's Fury Gracen."

I blinked, momentarily thrown. "I'm sorry, you want me to do what? Gavin, I'm in the middle of rehearsal. We've got the new routine debuting tomorrow night, and—"

"I'm aware," Gavin cut me off, his tone brooking no argument. "But this is important. Fury's flight lands in two hours. I need you to pick him up, take him to the club, make him feel welcome. Consider it part of your job description for the day."

I bit back a sigh. "Fine. But who's Fury Gracen, and why is he so important?"

Gavin chuckled, a sound that always sent a shiver down my spine. "He's our new money manager, darling. Treat him well."

The line went dead before I could respond. I stared at my phone for a moment, trying to process what just happened. Since when did we need a money manager?

A crash from the stage snapped me back to reality. I looked up to see Dana sprawled on the floor, Venus helping her up with a concerned look.

"Alright, that's it!" I barked, striding back to the stage. "Water break, five minutes. Then we're running this thing until it's perfect or we all drop dead. Understood?"

The girls scattered, grateful for the reprieve. I pulled Dana aside, lowering my voice. "You okay?"

She nodded, looking miserable. "I'm so sorry, Sienna. I swear, I'll get it together."

I squeezed her shoulder. "I know you will. Look, take ten minutes, call home, check on Lily. But when you come back, I need you one hundred percent here, got it?"

Relief washed over her face. "Thank you," she whispered before darting off to make her call.

I watched her go, then turned to survey the rest of the dancers. They were all chugging water and stretching, stealing glances at me like I might explode at any moment.

"Listen up, ladies," I called out, drawing their attention. "Change of plans. We've got exactly one hour to nail this routine before I have to leave on a... special assignment." I ignored their curious looks. "That means no more screw-ups, no more distractions. We're going to run this thing until it's perfect, even if that means you're all puking in the wings tomorrow night. Clear?"

A chorus of determined "Yes, Sienna" echoed back at me. I nodded, satisfied. They might hate me right now, but they'd thank me when the crowd was screaming for more tomorrow night.

"Alright, ladies!" I shouted as the dancers took their positions. "From the top. And this time, make me believe you actually want to be here!"

An hour later, I sighed as I stepped into the dressing room, kicking off my heels and savoring the cool floor against my aching feet. The rehearsal had been a nightmare, but we'd finally nailed the routine. Now, a whole new headache was waiting for me.

"Fury Gracen," I muttered, testing the name on my tongue as I made my way to my private closet. "What kind of name is that anyway?"

As I stripped off my dance clothes, my mind wandered back to how I'd ended up here. From struggling dancer to talent coordinator at one of New York's most exclusive clubs. It was a hell of a journey, and I owed it all to Gavin Manning.

I remembered the night he'd saved me from a handsy client, offering me a job on the spot. "You've got fire, darling," he'd said, those piercing eyes seeing right through me. "I could use someone like you."

And used me he had. But not in a lewd way. Gavin had been a mentor, a challenge, a force that pushed me beyond my limits. He'd molded me into the woman I was today - a woman who could handle entitled rich boys and temperamental dancers with equal ease. A woman who commanded respect, not just admiration.

Standing in front of my closet, I frowned at the rows of clothes. What the hell do you wear to pick up a money manager? I settled on a dark forest green silk blouse, pairing it with a modest black pencil skirt. Professional, but with just enough edge to remind this Fury guy that he was entering my world.

I slipped on a pair of three-inch heels, checking my reflection in the full-length mirror. The outfit hugged my curves without being too provocative. Perfect for representing Club Privé.

The drive to JFK was a nightmare, as usual. Stuck in traffic, I pulled up Fury's profile on my phone, curious about the man who'd thrown my day into chaos.

"Well, well," I murmured, scrolling through his impressive resume. Stanford grad, co-founder of a successful marketing and investment firm, now expanding to New York. But how did he know Gavin?

By the time I reached the airport, I'd worked myself into a state of nervous irritation. I stood in the arrivals area, holding a sign with "F. Gracen" written in my neat script, feeling like a damn chauffeur.

And then I saw him. He looked even hotter than in his online picture.

Fury Gracen was, well, fury personified. Tall, with a build that screamed 'I work out but I'm not a meathead about it.' His bronze hair was artfully tousled, like he'd just rolled out of bed, yet looking like a model. But it was his eyes that caught me off guard – dark brown, intense, with a hint of something dangerous lurking beneath the surface.

I straightened my spine, plastering on my best professional smile as he approached. "Mr. Gracen? I'm Sienna Marquez from Club Privé. Welcome to New York."

He looked me up and down, a slow smile spreading across his face. "Well, this is a pleasant surprise. I didn't expect Gavin to send one of his entertainers to pick me up."

And just like that, my irritation flared back to life. I kept my smile firmly in place, but I knew my eyes had gone frosty. "I'm the talent coordinator for Club Privé, Mr. Gracen. Not your 'entertainer'."

To his credit, Fury had the decency to look embarrassed. "I'm sorry, I didn't mean to offend—"

"No offense taken," I cut him off, my tone making it clear that offense had very much been taken. "Shall we get your bags?"

As we made our way to baggage claim, Fury tried to salvage the conversation. "So, talent coordinator? That sounds like an interesting job."

"It has its moments," I replied, my eyes scanning the carousel for his luggage. "What brings you to New York, Mr. Gracen? Besides the obvious allure of our charming traffic and overpriced real estate?"

He chuckled, a warm sound that I refused to find attractive. "Expanding our business, actually. Gavin mentioned he could use someone with my financial expertise."

I arched an eyebrow. "Did he now? And what exactly does a high-flying investment guru know about running a club?"

"About as much as I know about coordinating talent, I'd imagine," Fury shot back, his eyes twinkling with amusement. "But I'm a quick study."

I bit back a smirk. Okay, so maybe he wasn't completely insufferable. "You're ready?"

"Lead the way, Ms. Marquez," Fury said, grabbing a sleek black suitcase from the carousel. "I'm eager to find out what all the fuss is about."

As we walked to the parking garage, I felt Fury's eyes on me. It wasn't the usual leering I was used to from men—this felt more... assessing. Like he was trying to figure me out.

"So," he said as we reached my car, "how long have you worked for Gavin?"

I popped the trunk, gesturing for him to load his bag. "Five years. Started as a dancer, worked my way up."

Fury nodded, looking impressed. "That's quite a climb. Gavin must think highly of you."

"Gavin knows talent when he sees it," I replied, sliding into the driver's seat. "Just like he seems to think you're some kind of financial messiah."

Fury laughed as he buckled up. "Hardly. But I do know my way around a balance sheet. And I'm always up for a new challenge."

I gripped the steering wheel tighter, my knuckles turning white as we inched forward in the gridlock. "You've got to be kidding me," I muttered, glaring at the sea of red brake lights stretching out before us.

Fury shifted in the passenger seat, his long legs cramped in the confines of my modest car. "I thought California had bad traffic, but this is something else."

I snorted. "Welcome to New York, honey. Where dreams come to die in a traffic jam."

He chuckled, and I felt a little surge of pride at making him laugh. *Wait, what? No. Focus, Sienna.*

"Any idea what's causing this?" Fury asked, craning his neck to see ahead.

I pulled out my phone, scrolling through the traffic alerts. "Looks like a perfect storm. Road work on 5th, and apparently there's some kind of demonstration near Times Square." I groaned. "We're not moving anytime soon."

Fury checked his watch, then glanced at me. "How far are we from the club?"

"About ten blocks," I said, already knowing where this was going.

He grinned, a mischievous glint in his eye. "Up for a walk?"

I weighed our options. Sit in this hellish traffic for who knows how long, or stretch our legs and get there faster? I figured I could have Gus, our bouncer, pick up my car later and drop off Gavin's luggage. It would save me hours.

"Alright, Gracen," I said, already scanning for a place to park. "Hope those fancy shoes are made for walking."

We found a spot in a nearby garage, and soon we were on the sidewalk, dodging harried New Yorkers and tourists alike.

"So," Fury said as we walked, matching my brisk pace, "what's the deal with Club Privé?"

I smirked. "Let's just say it's not your average nightclub. We cater to a... discerning clientele."

"Discerning, huh?" He raised an eyebrow. "That's a fancy way of saying 'rich as hell,' isn't it?"

A burst of laughter escaped from my lips. "Among other things. But don't worry, you'll fit right in with your fancy suit and big city swagger."

Fury clutched his chest in mock offense. "I'll have you know this swagger is one-hundred percent genuine, small-town boy charm."

"Oh please." I rolled my eyes. "I've met plenty of 'small-town boys' in this city. They usually last about a week before running home with their tails between their legs."

He leaned in closer, his voice dropping to a whisper. "Wanna bet I'll last longer than a week?"

I was about to fire back when I felt the first drop hit my nose. "Shit," I muttered, looking up at the suddenly ominous sky.

And then, because the universe clearly had it out for me today, the heavens opened up.

"Run!" I yelled, grabbing Fury's hand without thinking and darting towards the nearest awning. We made it about half a block before the rain really started coming down in sheets.

"There!" Fury pointed to a cozy-looking café across the street. "Come on!"

We dashed across, narrowly avoiding a taxi, and burst through the café door, breathless and dripping.

The place was packed with other rain refugees, but Fury snagged us the last empty table in the corner. I collapsed into the chair, pushing my wet hair out of my face.

"Well," Fury said, looking at me with an amused grin, "that was refreshing."

I couldn't help it. I burst out laughing. "Oh yeah, nothing like a New York shower to really welcome you to the city."

He joined in, and for a moment, we were just two people laughing at the absurdity of it all.

A waitress appeared, looking frazzled but friendly. "What can I get you two?"

"Large black coffee, please," Fury said, then looked at me.

"Make that two," I said, then added, "And a blueberry muffin, please."

As the waitress left, Fury raised an eyebrow. "Blueberry, huh? I pegged you more as a chocolate chip girl."

I leaned back, crossing my arms. "Oh really? And what else have you 'pegged' about me, Mr. Gracen?"

He grinned, accepting the challenge. "Well, let's see. You're tough as nails on the outside, but I bet there's a softy in there somewhere. You probably have a secret stash of rom-coms you'd never admit to watching. And..." he paused for dramatic effect, "you definitely have a cat."

I blinked, thrown off by how close he'd gotten. "Okay, Sherlock. How'd you figure all that?"

Fury leaned forward, his eyes twinkling. "The tough part's obvious. You've got your hands full handling dancers and dealing with Gavin Manning. The rom-com thing? Just a hunch based on that little smile you got when we walked past that movie poster earlier. And the cat?" He pointed to my black skirt. "You've got some telltale fur on your clothes."

I brushed at my skirt, cursing internally. *Damn it,*

Whiskers. "Not bad, Gracen. But don't go thinking you've got me all figured out."

The waitress returned with our coffees and my muffin. I took a sip, savoring the bitter warmth.

"So," Fury said, wrapping his hands around his mug, "since we're stuck here, why don't you tell me something about yourself that I couldn't guess?"

I took another sip of my coffee, buying time as I considered my response. Fury's eyes were still on me, patient but expectant. I couldn't deny the pull I felt towards him - the way his smile made my stomach do a little flip, how his gaze seemed to see right through my carefully constructed walls. But I'd been down this road before, and I wasn't about to make the same mistakes again.

"Something you couldn't guess?" I finally said, a coy smile playing on my lips. "How about the fact that I can juggle knives?"

Fury's eyebrows shot up. "Now that I'd like to see."

I laughed, the sound surprisingly genuine. "Maybe if you're lucky. It's not exactly a skill I break out at parties."

"I'll have to make sure I'm at the right party then," he replied, his voice low and warm.

I felt a flush creep up my neck and cursed internally. Despite my best efforts, there was definitely a spark there. And in my experience, sparks usually led to fires.

And I'd been burned enough times to know better than to play with matches.

Chapter Three

FURY

"Welcome to Club Privé, Mr. Gracen," Sienna said, her voice barely audible over the music. She was close enough that I could smell her perfume - something spicy and exotic that made my head spin.

Knife-juggling, huh? What other secrets are you hiding, Sienna Marquez?

I tried to take it all in at once - the opulent decor, the mirrored walls, the crystal chandeliers that seemed to dance in time with the music. But my eyes kept being drawn back to Sienna. She moved through the space with the confidence of someone who owned it, and I wondered what it would be like to see her dance.

"Impressive," I managed, hoping I didn't sound as overwhelmed as I felt.

Sienna smirked, clearly seeing right through me. "You ain't seen nothing yet, Gracen."

She led me deeper into the club, past the main bar where bartenders were prepping for the night ahead. As we rounded a corner, I nearly collided with a group of scantily clad dancers rushing by.

"Watch it!" Sienna snapped, her hand shooting out to steady me. The moment her fingers grabbed my arm, a shiver traced its way down my back.

Our eyes met, and for a split second, I saw something flicker in those emerald depths. Desire? Annoyance? Maybe both?

She pulled her hand away like she'd been burned. "Rehearsals," she muttered. "Come on, Gavin's office is this way."

We weaved through the backstage area, dodging more dancers and a small army of makeup artists and costume designers. The energy was frenetic, everyone laser-focused on their tasks. It reminded me of the trading floor back in my early days on Wall Street, but with a lot more glitter.

Finally, we reached a door marked 'Private'. Sienna knocked once, then pushed it open without waiting for a response.

"Gavin? Your new boy wonder is here."

I bristled at being called a boy, but before I could say anything, she left.

As the door closed behind me, I focused on the man rising from his chair. At thirty-seven, Gavin Manning had been through hell and emerged, and I was sure I didn't even know half of it. He smiled as he circled his desk, extending his hand to me.

"Fury, damn good to see you, again. What's it been? 5-6 years?"

"I believe so," I said. His handshake was firm, no macho posturing to prove he was more manly than me by trying to crush my fingers. Glancing around his office and observing the way he carried himself as he sauntered over to a bar along one wall, I realized what was different.

He was relaxed.

In the past, when I'd seen him, he hadn't been high-strung, but he had been serious and focused—a detail-oriented person who demanded perfection in every aspect of his business. Now, he seemed completely at ease, even though Sienna and I had arrived much later than expected.

"You want a drink?" he asked, holding up a glass bottle half full of amber liquid. "It's Shannon's."

I grinned at the familiar logo. My step-cousin slash brother, Brody, had named his latest whiskey after his late mother. It was fantastic.

"Just a bit," I said. "I don't like to drink too much when I'm discussing business."

Gavin poured us each a couple of fingers and set mine in front of me before returning to his chair. "I know you didn't have much time to observe downstairs, but from what you did see, what do you think?"

"It's different," I replied, taking a sip of the whiskey and savoring its rich depth. "I gotta ask. You're out of the life? Is that why you changed this place from a BDSM club?"

Gavin grinned, the kind of grin that hinted at secrets. "Hell, no. But I'm not sharing what goes on between me and my very hot—and pregnant—wife."

"Pregnant? Your first?" I asked, genuine curiosity sparking.

"This'll be the third for me and Carrie," he said, picking up a frame on his desk and turning it around to show me a family portrait featuring a blonde in her early thirties, a dark-haired teenager, a little dark-haired boy, and a toddler sporting her mother's golden curls.

"Congratulations." I lifted my glass in a toast. "To family."

"Family."

We drank, then I answered his original question. "The place has a good vibe. Very modern and sophisticated."

"That's what we're going for ," Gavin explained. "We

dress the servers in sexy outfits, put on dance routines like something out of *Moulin Rouge*. We still have private rooms, some with the same sort of toys we had before, but others designed to allow members to invite multiple partners to join them."

"I noticed several male performers here as well."

Gavin nodded. "I've got enough powerful women in my life to know better than to cater only to men, even if I'd considered it. No, I'm all about ensuring every member's desires are met in a safe, consensual way, regardless of gender."

I nodded, took another sip, then asked, "When you say dance routines. That'd be what Sienna does?"

"It is," Gavin said slowly.

"What's her story?" I finally let myself ask the question that had been bouncing around in my head.

"Hired her as a dancer, and she worked her way up to where she is now, talent coordinator." Gavin's eyes narrowed slightly. "But she's off-limits."

"Off-limits?" I echoed, curiosity piqued.

"Members are allowed to ask most employees to join them, but it's always up to the employee whether or not they want to participate. We have different colored wristbands that they choose each day when they start their shift, and the colors show what they're open to." Gavin reached into his desk and pulled out a piece of paper.

"Take a look at that. You're welcome to invite anyone wearing the appropriate wristband to spend time with you."

"What color does Sienna usually choose?" I asked, not willing to let her go so easily.

"None. Sienna's usually best left alone," Gavin said. "But there are plenty of other women in our club who are just as beautiful."

I didn't doubt that, but my curiosity about her went beyond mere looks. I set her aside for the moment, though; I was here for business. Pushing that would be both rude and unprofessional. I had time, so I changed the subject. "Shall we get down to business?"

Gavin shook his head. "How about I give you a full tour and we grab something to eat from the bar? We don't have a wide selection, but it's delicious." He stood. "Tonight's about friends catching up. We'll talk about business tomorrow."

I agreed, partly because the thought of going downstairs meant I might catch another glimpse of Sienna. I kept that desire to myself, simply standing and telling Gavin to lead the way.

For the next hour, I trailed him as he arranged for us to grab a bite and then took me on an extensive tour of the club, always keeping the conversation light and personal.

We returned to Gavin's office when his phone buzzed.

"My wife," he said with a smile. "I think that's enough for today. Sienna will show you out. And Fury?" He fixed me with a serious look. "Remember what I said about off-limits?"

I nodded, not trusting myself to say a word. Just then, as if on cue, there was a knock at the door, and Sienna poked her head in.

"Ready to go, Gracen?" she asked, her tone all business.

I followed her out of the office, my mind still spinning from everything Gavin had shared. What was Sienna's story? Why was she considered "off-limits"?

Suddenly, a blur of glitter and perfume crashed into me.

"Oh my god, I'm so sorry!" A sultry voice purred. I looked down to find myself face to face with a stunningly beautiful woman. She had curves for days, golden skin, and eyes that seemed to change color in the light.

"No harm done," I managed, trying to regain my composure.

The woman's full lips curved into a smile. "I'm Venus," she said, extending a perfectly manicured hand.

I shook her hand, acutely aware of how soft her skin was. "Fury Gracen. Nice to meet you, Venus."

Venus's smile widened. "Oh, the pleasure is all mine, Mr. Gracen."

I heard Sienna clear her throat loudly. "Venus, don't you have a costume fitting?"

Venus pouted, but her eyes never left mine. "Always the taskmaster, Sienna. Fine, fine. But Fury?" She leaned in close, her breath hot on my ear. "If you ever want a private tour of the club, just let me know."

As Venus sashayed away, I turned to find Sienna glaring at me. "What?" I asked, feeling defensive.

She shook her head, her expression unreadable. "Nothing. Come on, let's get you out of here before you cause any more trouble."

As we reached the exit, I couldn't resist one last attempt at connecting. "You know, Sienna, I feel like we got off on the wrong foot. Maybe we could—"

"Stop right there, Gracen," she cut me off, her voice sharp. "Whatever you're thinking, whatever you're planning, just don't. You're here to do a job, nothing more. Got it?"

I held her gaze, feeling that same electric tension from earlier. "Got it," I said finally.

Sienna nodded, then pushed open the door. "Good. See you around, Mr. Gracen."

The condo Cory and I kept in Manhattan was fairly small, but it'd just been for us to stay in when we were in town on business. Now that I'd be living here for the foreseeable future, I wanted to get something of my own, something bigger.

Moving to New York City was my chance for a fresh start. I had family here, but this was the first time I'd really been this much on my own. After my parents had died, my brother and sister and I had gone straight to our Aunt Theresa and her new husband ... and all of their kids. Being alone in the McCrae-Carideo-Gracen family wasn't really possible. I went to college and Cory joined me. We started our business together. Yeah, we'd kept separate homes, but we spent a lot of time together as we built our empire.

And now I was here. Alone.

My phone buzzed, snapping me out of my reverie. A text from Cory:

"Landed safely? How's the Big Apple treating you?"

I smirked, typing back: "Landed and survived my first NYC rainstorm. Met some... interesting people."

The response was immediate: "Interesting, huh? Do tell!"

Before I could reply, my phone started ringing. Cory's face popped up on the screen, grinning like an idiot.

"Alright, spill it," he said as soon as I answered.

"What's this about 'interesting people'? Did you meet the Kardashians or something?"

I chuckled, moving away from the window to collapse onto the leather sofa. "Not quite. But man, Cory, Club Privé, that place... it's something else."

"Club Privé? I looked it up after you told me about the meeting. Looks pretty swanky."

"Swanky doesn't begin to cover it," I said, running a hand through my hair. "Remember that BDSM club we snuck into sophomore year?"

Cory snorted. "How could I forget? I couldn't look at a pair of handcuffs for months without blushing."

"Yeah, well, picture that, but make it a thousand times classier and add a few million dollars worth of crystal chandeliers."

"Holy shit," Cory breathed. "That's impressive. So, aside from the club, how's the city treating you? Met any cute New Yorkers yet?"

My mind immediately flashed to Sienna - her fierce green eyes, the way she moved through the club like she owned it. But maybe it was Gavin's warning, or maybe it was that hint of vulnerability she tried so hard to hide. Whatever it was, I wasn't ready to share that particular detail with Cory just yet.

"Nah, nothing to report on that front," I lied, hoping my voice sounded casual. "Been too busy getting settled."

"Uh-huh," Cory said, and I could practically hear his eyebrow raising. "Well, don't work too hard. Remember to actually enjoy the city, yeah?"

"Yes, dear," I said, rolling my eyes.

As we said our goodbyes, I walked to the window, staring out at the city. Somewhere out there, Sienna was probably still at the club, running rehearsals or dealing with some crisis. I wondered what she was like when she wasn't in work mode. Did she ever let her guard down? And why was I so damn curious to find out?

Chapter Four

SIENNA

I SLUMPED INTO MY CHAIR, pushing off my high heels with a groan. My feet were killing me, but at least I'd finally caught up on all the work I'd missed. Who knew picking up someone from the airport would throw my whole day off?

Glancing at the mirror, I saw the toll of the long day etched on my face. My perfectly applied eyeliner had smudged, giving me a slightly raccoon-like appearance. Great. Just great.

As I cleaned my face, my mind drifted to the cause of my chaotic day - Fury Gracen.

I snorted. Fury? That's a ridiculous name, but damn if he didn't wear it well.

"Stop it," I scolded my reflection. "He's just another suit. Nothing special."

But even as I said it, I knew it wasn't true. There was something about him that got under my skin. The way his eyes crinkled when he smiled.

I shook my head, trying to dislodge the image of his broad shoulders and warm brown eyes. "It's just been too long since you got laid," I told myself firmly. "That's all this is."

A knock at the door saved me from my spiraling thoughts. "Come in!" I called, grateful for the distraction.

The door swung open, and Gavin strode in, looking as impeccable as ever in his tailored suit.

"Sienna, darling," he greeted, flashing that million-dollar smile. "How are you holding up?"

I quirked an eyebrow. "I'm fine, Gavin. What's up? You don't usually come checking on me this late."

He settled into the chair across from me, crossing one leg over the other. "Can't a boss check on his favorite employee?"

"Sure, when hell freezes over," I retorted, earning a chuckle from him. "Spill it, Manning. What do you want?"

His eyes twinkled with amusement. "Always so direct. I like that about you, Sienna." He leaned forward, resting his elbows on his knees. "I wanted to get your thoughts on our new friend, Mr. Gracen."

I fought to keep my expression neutral, even as my heart did a little flip at the mention of Fury's name. "What about him?"

"Oh, come now. You spent quite a bit of time with him today. What's your read on him?"

I shrugged, aiming for nonchalance. "He seems... competent enough. Why the sudden interest in a money manager, Gavin? Is everything okay with the club?"

His smile faltered for a split second before sliding back into place. If I hadn't been watching closely, I might have missed it. "Everything's fine, Sienna. Just looking to diversify our investments a bit. You know, stay ahead of the curve."

I narrowed my eyes, not buying it for a second. "Uh-huh. But you've never needed outside financial help before. Why now?"

He stood up, straightening his jacket. "Sometimes it's good to get a fresh perspective, that's all. Now, if you'll excuse me, I have a few calls to make before heading home."

As he reached the door, he paused and looked back at me. "You know you can always come to me if something's bothering you, right? About anything... or anyone."

I nodded, forcing a smile. "Of course, Gavin. Goodnight."

As the door closed behind him, I couldn't shake the feeling that there was more going on than he was letting on. And why did he seem so interested in my opinion of Fury?

Squaring my shoulders, I stepped out of the dressing room and into the controlled chaos of the club.

I weaved through the crowd, nodding at the security guards and ignoring the drunken come-ons from patrons. Just as I made it to the exit unscathed, I locked eyes with Venus. She was perched on the lap of some Wall Street type, her golden skin glowing under the lights. She gave me a wink and a little wave, and I smiled back. For all her faults, Venus was a sweetheart.

I was so distracted by Venus that I didn't see the man until I practically ran into him.

"Well, hello there, beautiful," he slurred, his meaty hand landing on my arm. "Where are you running off to? The party's just getting started!"

I plastered on my best fake smile, the one that showed too many teeth to be friendly. "I'm afraid the party's over for me, sir. Perhaps you'd like to order another drink?"

He leered at me, his breath reeking of expensive scotch. "Only if you'll join me, sweetheart. Come on, let me buy you a nightcap."

I opened my mouth to deliver a scathing retort when Dana appeared at my side like an avenging angel.

"Mr. Carmichael!" she exclaimed, all bubbly enthusiasm. "I've been looking everywhere for you! Your wife's waiting for you in the VIP lounge."

The man's face paled, and he released my arm like it had burned him. "Ah, yes, of course. Thank you, my dear."

As Dana led him away, she threw a wink over her shoulder at me. I mouthed a silent 'thank you' and made my escape.

The blast of cold air as I stepped outside was a shock to the system, but a welcome one. I took a deep breath, letting the icy air clear my head. The streets were relatively quiet at this hour, but I kept my guard up as I made my way to the subway station. New York might never sleep, but it got a hell of a lot more dangerous after midnight.

I carefully picked my way across the sidewalk, cursing myself for not splurging on a cab. But old habits die hard, and the memory of scraping by on tips and cheap noodles was still too fresh.

The subway platform was mercifully empty, save for a group of teenagers huddled in the corner. They eyed me warily, and I returned the favor, keeping one hand on the pepper spray in my pocket. The tension didn't leave my body until I was safely on the train, the doors closing behind me with a hiss.

As the subway car rattled through the tunnels, I let my mind wander. It drifted, annoyingly, back to Fury. What was his deal? Why was Gavin so interested in him? And why couldn't I shake the feeling that his arrival was going to change everything?

The walk from the subway to my apartment was blessedly uneventful, and by the time I reached my building, my feet were screaming in protest. I dragged myself up the three flights of stairs, cursing the broken elevator for the millionth time.

As I fumbled with my keys, Mrs. Goldstein from 3B poked her head out. "Late night, dear?" she asked, concern etched on her wrinkled face.

I mustered up a smile. "You know how it is, Mrs. G. The glamorous life of a talent coordinator never sleeps."

She tutted disapprovingly before smiling and retreating back into her apartment. I finally got my door open and tiptoed into my place, praying that the click of the lock wouldn't wake Vanessa. My roommate had a sleep schedule opposite of me, working early mornings at the hospital while I was busy wrangling drunk VIPs and entitled dancers afternoons and evenings. It was a miracle we ever saw each other.

My cat, Whiskers (shut up, I was going through a literal phase when I named him), meowed a greeting from his perch on the windowsill.

"Hey, buddy," I murmured, scratching him behind the ears. "At least someone's happy to see me."

I kicked off my heels, wincing at the blisters that had formed. Note to self: break in new shoes before wearing them for a 16-hour workday.

I contemplated a long, hot bath, but the thought of falling asleep and drowning in my own tub wasn't exactly appealing. Shower it was.

The hot water cascaded over me, washing away the stench of overpriced cologne. I closed my eyes, letting the steam envelop me, but instead of relaxing, my mind drifted to Fury. Those dark eyes, that crooked smile. The way his hand felt in mine as we ran through the rain.

It was stupid, but I couldn't help it.

I palmed my breasts, squeezing gently as I tweaked my nipples. My breath caught as I imagined it was his hands on me. That stupid grin of his as he teased my peaks to tight buds.

I tilted my head back, letting the water pour over my face. My hands roamed lower, caressing my thighs and hips. In my mind, it was Fury's tongue exploring every inch. I toyed with one nipple while my other hand ventured south, delving into slick heat.

It felt so real. Fury's mouth on me, his fingers plunging inside as I arched into his touch. I bit my lip, craving more.

I grabbed the showerhead, angling it to blast my clit.

My legs trembled as the hot jets pummeled my sweet spot. I pumped my fingers in and out, wishing it was Fury's cock instead - thick and hard, buried to the hilt. I pictured how he'd move, starting slow then building to a frenzied pace as he lost control. The thought made me clench, and I surrendered to the rising wave of pleasure.

My inner walls pulsed around my fingers as I cried out, panting heavily. The shower rained down on my flushed skin, but all I saw was Fury's face, all I heard was his name on my lips.

"Fuck," I muttered, cranking the cold water to snap out of it. What was wrong with me? I barely knew the guy, yet here I was getting off to fantasies about him in the shower.

I was a mess, and it was all his fault. Sienna Marquez did not get attached. Sienna Marquez did not fantasize about stupid grins and handsome faces.

Sucking in a deep breath, I vowed to get my shit together. Fury Gracen might be good-looking and charming, but he wasn't for me. And I wasn't about to let him mess with my head, no matter how good he made me feel.

I turned off the water with a decisive twist and stepped out of the shower with a renewed sense of determination. Fury Gracen might be sexy as sin, but I was done thinking about him.

Clean and marginally more relaxed, I had thrown on

an oversized t-shirt and settled into bed with my latest guilty pleasure—a reverse harem romance featuring a human girl who somehow ended up mated to an entire pack of werewolves. It was ridiculous, it was over-the-top, and it was exactly the kind of mindless entertainment I needed right now.

Except I couldn't seem to focus on the words. I'd read the same sentence about Alpha Brock's "smoldering amber eyes" at least five times now. Every time I tried to picture the brooding werewolf, he morphed into Fury, with those warm brown eyes that seemed to see right through me.

I tossed the book aside with a frustrated groan. This was getting downright pathetic.

I padded to the kitchen for a much-needed glass of wine, and I nearly jumped out of my skin at the sound of Vanessa's voice. She was leaning against the doorframe, already dressed in her yoga gear, a knowing smirk on her face.

"Jesus, Vanessa. Wear a bell or something, would you?" I clutched my chest, willing my heart rate to return to normal.

"Sorry, didn't mean to startle you. You're usually passed out by now. Everything okay?"

I waved a hand dismissively. "Yeah, yeah. Just a long night at the club. New VIP in town, had to play tour guide."

Vanessa's eyebrows shot up. "Oh? Anyone interesting?"

I tried to keep my face neutral, but I could feel the heat creeping up my neck. "Just some finance guy Gavin's bringing on board. No big deal."

"Uh-huh," Vanessa said, clearly not buying it. "And does this 'no big deal' finance guy have a name?"

I sighed, knowing I wasn't getting out of this. "Fury. Fury Gracen."

"Fury?" Vanessa repeated, a grin spreading across her face. "Well, that's certainly a name. What's he like? Handsome? Charming? A total asshole?"

"He's..." I trailed off, searching for the right words. "He's different. Not like the usual guys we get at the club. He's smart, funny in a dry sort of way. And yeah, I guess he's not bad to look at."

Vanessa's grin widened. "Not bad to look at, huh? Coming from you, that's practically a marriage proposal."

I grabbed an oven mitt and chucked it at her head. "Shut up. It's not like that."

She dodged it with practiced ease. "Oh, come on, Sienna. I haven't seen you this worked up over a guy since... well, ever. Spill."

I groaned. "There's nothing to spill. He's Gavin's new money manager, end of story."

Vanessa snorted. "Yeah, right. Come on, give me

details. What does he look like? What did you guys talk about?"

I closed my eyes, knowing resistance was futile. When Vanessa got like this, she was like a dog with a bone. "Fine. He's tall, built, but not in that gross steroid way. Dark hair, brown eyes. And he's got this... I don't know, this intensity about him. Like he's really listening when you talk."

"Mmhmm," Vanessa hummed encouragingly. "And? What else?"

"And nothing," I insisted, but even I could hear the lack of conviction in my voice. "We just talked about work stuff. And... okay, we got caught in the rain and had to duck into this little café. It was... nice."

Vanessa squealed, actually squealed, like we were teenagers at a slumber party. "Oh my God, Sienna! This is huge! When was the last time you actually enjoyed spending time with a guy?"

I sat up, suddenly defensive. "It's not a big deal, V. So what if he's kind of attractive and not a complete asshole? It doesn't change anything. He's still a client, and I'm still... me."

Vanessa's face softened. She reached out, squeezing my hand. "Hey, I know you've got your past. But not every guy is like Ralf, you know?"

I pulled my hand away, a familiar knot forming in my stomach at the mention of Ralf's name. "It doesn't matter if he's not some asshole. I can't... How would I ever be able to open up to a guy after...? I just can't."

"Sienna," Vanessa said gently, "I know you're scared. But you can't let one total scumbag ruin your chance at happiness forever. And hey, if Gavin trusts this Fury guy enough to bring him on board, he can't be all bad, right?"

I chewed my lip, considering her words. She wasn't wrong. Gavin was a lot of things, but he was an excellent judge of character. He wouldn't bring someone into the fold if he didn't trust them implicitly.

"Maybe," I conceded. "But it doesn't change the fact that he's part of the club. And I have a strict 'no mixing business with pleasure' policy."

Vanessa rolled her eyes. "Yeah, because that's worked out so well for you so far. When was the last time you even went on a date?"

I opened my mouth to argue, then closed it again. She had me there.

"Look," Vanessa said, her tone softening. "I'm not saying you need to jump his bones or anything. Just... don't close yourself off completely, okay? It's okay to be interested in someone. It's okay to let yourself feel things."

I nodded, not trusting myself to speak. Vanessa pulled me into a hug, and I let myself relax into her embrace. Sometimes I forgot how much I needed this – this unconditional support, this gentle push out of my comfort zone.

"Thanks, V," I mumbled into her shoulder.

She pulled back, grinning. "Anytime. Now, get some sleep. You look like you need it."

I stuck my tongue out at her, but I could feel exhaustion creeping in. "Yeah, yeah. Go do your pretzel poses or whatever."

Vanessa laughed as she headed for the door. "It's called yoga, you heathen. Sweet dreams. Maybe about a certain tall, dark, and handsome finance guy?"

I threw another oven mitt at her retreating form, but a smile was tugging at my lips.

As I settled into my bed, I could feel my defenses crumbling just a little. Maybe Vanessa was right. Maybe it was okay to let myself feel something . Maybe I could let go of the past for once.

Chapter Five

FURY

I STEPPED out of the cab, straightening my tie as I took in the gleaming facade of Hartley & Associates. The building towered above me, all glass and steel, a monument to New York's real estate royalty. I'd done my homework on this place, but seeing it in person was something else entirely.

"Here goes nothing," I muttered, striding through the revolving doors with as much confidence as I could muster. The lobby was a masterpiece of modern design - all clean lines and subtle luxury.

As I approached the reception desk, a statuesque blonde looked up, her smile practiced and professional. "Welcome to Hartley & Associates. How may I assist you?"

"Fury Gracen, here to see Olivia Hartley."

Her eyes widened slightly at my name - whether from recognition or surprise, I couldn't tell. "Of course, Mr. Gracen. Ms. Hartley is expecting you. Please, take the express elevator to the 50th floor."

I nodded my thanks and made my way to the elevator, my mind racing. Finding the right location for Gracen & McCrae's expansion into New York was crucial. No pressure, right?

The elevator ride was mercifully short, and as the doors slid open, I came face to face with Olivia Hartley herself.

"Mr. Gracen," she said, extending a delicate hand. "Welcome to Hartley & Associates."

I took her hand, noting the firm grip. "Ms. Hartley. Thank you for meeting with me on such short notice."

She smiled, a flash of white teeth that could probably close deals on its own. "Please, call me Olivia. And it's my pleasure. We pride ourselves on being responsive to our clients' needs."

I immediately noticed the way her tailored suit hugged her curves in utterly delicious ways. *Focus, Fury. You're here on business.*

"I hope you don't mind," Olivia said, breaking into my thoughts, "but I thought we might take a little field trip.

The space I have in mind for Gracen & McCrae is best appreciated in person."

I raised an eyebrow. "Let's do it."

We stepped into the elevator, and on our way down to the garage, Olivia briefed me on the property we were about to view.

She led me to a gleaming black Audi, its lines so sharp you could probably cut yourself on them.

"Nice ride," I commented as Olivia unlocked the doors.

She flashed me another smile. "One of the perks of the job. Hop in."

As we pulled out into the busy New York traffic, Olivia expertly maneuvered through the chaos.

"So, Fury," she said, glancing at me. "That's an unusual name. There must be a story there."

I chuckled. "My mother had a flair for the dramatic. Said I came into the world kicking and screaming, full of fury. The name stuck."

Olivia laughed, a warm, genuine sound. "Well, it certainly makes an impression. I bet it comes in handy in the boardroom."

"It has its moments," I admitted. "Though sometimes I think people expect me to start flipping tables or breathing fire."

"And do you?" she asked, a teasing glint in her eye.

"Only on Tuesdays," I deadpanned.

She laughed again, a refreshing sound.

We fell into an easy conversation about New York real estate, the challenges of expanding a business, and the differences between the East and West coasts. Before I knew it, we were pulling up to a sleek, modern building in Midtown.

"Here we are," Olivia announced, parking the car. "Ready to see your future office?"

I nodded, feeling a mix of excitement and nerves. This was it - the first tangible step towards making Gracen, McCrae & Palmer a New York powerhouse.

As we entered the building, Olivia guided me through the lobby, chatting with the security guard like an old friend. The elevator ride was quick, and soon we were stepping out onto what could only be described as a blank canvas of potential.

"Wow," I breathed, taking in the open floor plan, the floor-to-ceiling windows, the stunning views of the city.

Olivia smiled, clearly pleased with my reaction. "I thought you might like it. The entire floor is available, which gives you plenty of room to grow. And the building has some of the best amenities in the city."

She led me through the space, pointing out features and possibilities. I could see it all coming to life in my mind - the sleek conference rooms, the bustling trading floor, my office overlooking the park.

"And here's the crown jewel," Olivia said, leading me towards a set of glass doors. She pushed them open with a flourish, revealing a stunning rooftop garden.

I stepped out, momentarily speechless. The garden was an oasis in the middle of the concrete jungle, with lush greenery, comfortable seating areas, and panoramic views of the city.

"This is incredible," I said, turning to face Olivia. The sunlight caught her hair, turning it to spun gold. "You've outdone yourself, Olivia."

She beamed, clearly in her element. "I'm glad you like it. I thought this might be a delightful spot for client meetings or team gatherings. It's a great way to impress without being ostentatious."

I nodded, already imagining the possibilities. "It's perfect. Though I have to admit, it makes my current living situation seem pretty lackluster in comparison."

Olivia raised an eyebrow. "Oh? Where are you staying?"

I grimaced. "An old condo my partner and I acquired years ago. It's fine for now, but..."

"But not exactly home," Olivia finished for me. She seemed to consider something for a moment, then smiled. "You know, I might have a solution for that, too."

I looked at her, intrigued. "I'm listening."

"There's a penthouse that's not officially on the market yet," Olivia purred, her voice dripping with temptation. "It's in a prime location, fully furnished, and available soon. I could show it to you, if you're interested."

The way she looked at me, her eyes smoldering with unspoken promise, made me hesitate for a moment. This was veering dangerously close to mixing business with pleasure, and my pulse quickened at the thought. Unbidden, an image of Sienna flashed through my mind - her fierce green eyes blazing with passion, that challenging smirk that always set my blood on fire. But then I looked at Olivia, all professional charm and subtle allure, her body language screaming of possibilities. This was just business, right? My mind raced with the tantalizing prospects, both professional and decidedly not.

"That sounds great," I heard myself say. "I'd love to see it."

Olivia's smile widened. "Excellent. Why don't we head over there now, and then afterwards grab dinner to discuss the details?"

I nodded, pushing aside any lingering doubts. "Lead the way."

The drive to the penthouse was filled with more easy conversation, but I could feel a subtle shift in the air. The professional veneer was slipping, replaced by something more... personal.

"So, Fury," Olivia said as we navigated through the bustling streets, "what made you decide to expand to New York? I mean, besides the obvious allure of our charming traffic and overpriced real estate."

"Opportunity, mainly. Cory—my business partner—and I have been discussing this for years. With the merger with Palmer Management, which is Cory's fiancé's firm, the timing for me to seize this chance just felt right."

She nodded, a knowing smile playing on her lips. "And I'm sure the challenge doesn't hurt. From what I've heard, you're not one to back down from a fight."

"You've been doing your homework," I observed, impressed despite myself.

Olivia shrugged, but there was a glint of pride in her eyes. "I like to know who I'm dealing with. It's served me well in this business."

"I bet it has," I murmured, studying her profile. In the fading light of the day, she looked almost ethereal - all golden hair and sharp angles. A far cry from Sienna's dark intensity.

Stop it, I chided myself. Why was I even comparing them?

We pulled up to a towering building that screamed

'exclusive'. As we stepped out of the car, I let out a low whistle. "This is quite the place."

Olivia beamed. "Wait until you see inside."

The lobby was a marvel of marble and modern art, with a concierge desk that looked like it belonged in a five-star hotel. Olivia greeted the staff by name, further cementing my impression of her as someone who knew everyone and everything in this city.

As the elevator came to a stop at the top floor, the doors slid open, and Olivia turned to me with a smile that was equal parts professional and provocative. "Ready to see your potential new home?"

I nodded, not trusting myself to speak. She led me into the penthouse, and I felt my jaw drop.

The space was stunning - all clean lines and panoramic views, with touches of warmth that kept it from feeling sterile. Floor-to-ceiling windows showcased the glittering city skyline, making me feel like I was floating above New York. Far away from the condo I was currently occupying.

"This is... wow," I managed, turning in a slow circle to take it all in.

Olivia's laugh was low and pleased. "I thought you might like it. Come, let me give you the tour."

She led me through the penthouse, pointing out features with the expertise of someone who knew exactly what her client wanted - sometimes before they even knew it themselves. The kitchen was a chef's dream, all state-of-the-art appliances and sleek countertops. The living room was spacious yet cozy, with a fireplace that I could easily imagine curling up in front of on a cold winter night.

But it was the master bedroom that really took my breath away. The bed was enormous, covered in what looked like the softest sheets I'd ever seen. And the view... well, let's just say waking up to that every morning would make even the toughest day bearable.

"So," Olivia said, leaning against the doorframe with a smile that could only be described as seductive, "what do you think?"

I swallowed hard, suddenly very aware of how alone we were. "It's incredible. But I have to ask - why isn't this on the market yet? It seems like it would be snapped up in a heartbeat."

She shrugged, pushing off the doorframe and sauntering towards me. "The owner is... particular about who lives here. They want someone who will appreciate the space, not just use it as a status symbol."

"And you think I fit the bill?" I asked, raising an eyebrow.

Olivia stopped just inches from me, close enough that I could smell her perfume - something expensive and intoxicating. "I think you're exactly what they're looking for. But obviously, they'll have to approve of you first. However, I can't imagine they wouldn't."

The double meaning in her words wasn't lost on me. This was a crossroads, and I knew it. On one hand, there was the promise of something exciting and new with Olivia. On the other... well, there was Sienna, and all the complicated feelings that came with her.

Sienna had made it clear that nothing could happen between us. Gavin likewise. And here was Olivia, offering not just a beautiful home but a chance at something more.

"I think," I said slowly, meeting her gaze, "that I'd like to discuss the details over dinner."

Olivia's smile widened, a predatory gleam in her eye. "I was hoping you'd say that. I know just the place - intimate, impressive wine list, perfect for... negotiations."

The restaurant Olivia chose was exactly as she'd described - intimate and elegant, with soft lighting that made everything look more alluring. As we settled into our booth, it felt like I was stepping into a whole new world.

"So," Olivia said, perusing the wine list with the air of a connoisseur, "shall we start with a toast to new beginnings?"

I nodded, trying to ignore the way her foot had somehow found its way to my calf under the table. "Sounds perfect."

She ordered a bottle of something that probably cost

more than my first car, then turned her full attention to me. "Now, Fury, tell me - what do you really think of New York so far? And don't give me the polite answer. I want the truth."

I chuckled, leaning back in my seat. "The truth? It's overwhelming. Exciting. A bit terrifying, if I'm being honest. But also... invigorating. There's an energy here that you can't find anywhere else."

Olivia nodded, a smile playing on her lips. "That's what I love about this city. It pushes you, challenges you. But if you can make it here..."

"You can make it anywhere," I finished, raising my glass in a mock toast. "Bit of a cliché, but I'm starting to see the truth in it."

Our wine arrived, and as Olivia swirled her glass, inhaling the bouquet with practiced ease, my eyes were drawn to her. She was beautiful, no doubt about it. But there was something else there too - a sharp intelligence, a hunger for success that mirrored my own.

"So," she said, setting down her glass, "shall we discuss the penthouse? Or would you prefer to talk about the office space first?"

I hesitated for a moment. "Why don't we start with the office? After all, that's what is the most pressing."

If Olivia was disappointed by my choice, she didn't show it. Instead, she launched into a detailed breakdown of the lease terms, potential build-out options, and the various amenities included in the package.

As we worked our way through our entrees - a perfectly cooked steak for me, some kind of fancy fish for her - the conversation flowed easily from business to more personal topics. We swapped stories about our worst clients and found common ground in our shared love of classic films.

It was... nice. Comfortable, even. But as the evening wore on, I realized that something was missing. Or maybe someone.

"Penny for your thoughts?" Olivia's voice broke through my reverie.

I blinked, realizing I'd been staring off into space. "Sorry, just... processing everything, I guess. It's been quite a day."

She smiled, reaching across the table to lay her hand on mine. "I hope I haven't overwhelmed you. I know I can be a bit... intense when it comes to business."

I turned my hand over, giving hers a gentle squeeze. "Not at all. I appreciate your thoroughness. It's refreshing, actually."

Olivia's smile widened, and I could see the invitation in her eyes. "Well, if you're not too overwhelmed... perhaps we could continue this conversation somewhere more private? Say, back at the penthouse?"

And there it was. The moment of truth. I looked at Olivia - beautiful, successful, clearly interested. Everything I should want. But as I opened my mouth to respond, all I could think about was a pair of fierce green eyes and a challenge issued in a rain-soaked café.

"Olivia," I said softly, "I'm flattered, truly. And under different circumstances... But I think it's best if we keep this professional. At least for now."

To her credit, Olivia took the rejection gracefully. She leaned back, a rueful smile on her face. "Can't blame a girl for trying. But I understand. And I respect your decision."

I nodded, grateful for her understanding. "Thank you. And I hope this doesn't affect our business relationship. I really am interested in the office space, and potentially the penthouse, as well."

"Of course not," she said, waving a hand dismissively. "I'm a professional, Fury. I don't mix business with pleasure... often."

We shared a laugh at that, and just like that, the tension dissipated. We spent the rest of the evening ironing out details for the office lease, with Olivia promising to send over the paperwork for both the office and the penthouse in the morning.

We said our goodbyes outside the restaurant when Olivia fixed me with a knowing look. "She must be something special, whoever she is."

I started to protest, but Olivia held up a hand. "Don't bother denying it. I've been in this game long enough to know when a man's heart is already spoken for, even if he doesn't realize it yet."

The valet brought her car around and, as I watched her disappear into the night, I realized one thing. I needed to figure out what the hell was going on with Sienna and me. Because if I was turning down someone like Olivia Hartley, there had to be a damn good reason.

Chapter Six

SIENNA

I PUSHED through the revolving door of Bistro Moderne, the tantalizing aroma of freshly baked bread and sizzling garlic hitting me like a wave. Vanessa was right behind me, chattering excitedly about finally having a day off from the hospital.

"I swear, if I have to look at another chart or deal with one more entitled patient, I might—oof!"

I stumbled backward, colliding with Vanessa as I ran smack into what felt like a brick wall. A familiar, cologne-scented brick wall.

"Sienna?" Fury's deep voice sent an unwelcome shiver down my spine. I looked up, meeting those warm brown eyes that had been haunting my dreams lately.

"Fury," I managed, trying to keep my voice neutral. "Fancy bumping into you here."

He chuckled, steadying me with a hand on my arm. The touch sent sparks shooting through my body, and I jerked away like I'd been burned.

It was then that I noticed the woman standing next to him. Tall, blonde, and gorgeous in a way that made me want to crawl under a rock and hide. She looked like she'd just stepped off a runway, all legs and perfect hair and a smile that could probably stop traffic.

"Oh, uh, let me introduce you," Fury said, clearing his throat. Was it my imagination, or did he sound a bit flustered? "Sienna, this is Olivia Hartley, my real estate agent. Olivia, this is Sienna Marquez, talent coordinator at Club Privé. "

Olivia extended a perfectly manicured hand, her smile never wavering. "Pleasure to meet you, Sienna."

An awkward silence fell over us, broken only by Vanessa clearing her throat behind me. "Oh! Sorry," I said, stepping aside. "This is my roommate and best friend, Vanessa Rodriguez."

More pleasantries were exchanged, but I barely heard them. My mind was too busy spinning, trying to make sense of the scene before me. Fury and Olivia, looking like the perfect power couple. The way they stood just a little too close to each other. The slight rumple in Fury's shirt that suggested it had spent the night on a floor somewhere.

"Well, we should get going. I'm about to sign the rental agreement for our new office building," Fury said, breaking into my thoughts. "It was great running into you, Sienna. Vanessa, nice to meet you."

"You too," Vanessa replied, her tone warm, but her eyes narrowed slightly as she glanced between Fury and me.

As they walked away, I noticed how Olivia's hand rested on the small of Fury's back, guiding him through the door. It was such a slight gesture, but it spoke volumes.

"Earth to Sienna," Vanessa's voice cut through my haze. "You okay there? You look like you've seen a ghost."

I shook my head, plastering on a smile that felt more like a grimace. "I'm fine. Just hungry. Let's get a table."

We were seated quickly, the bustling lunchtime crowd providing a welcome distraction from my tumultuous thoughts. I buried my nose in the menu, pretending to be deeply invested in the difference between the Niçoise and Cobb salads.

"So," Vanessa said, her tone deceptively casual, "that was the famous Fury, huh?"

I looked up, meeting her knowing gaze. "Famous? Hardly. He's just Gavin's new money guy."

Vanessa raised an eyebrow. "Uh-huh. And I suppose

that's why you looked like you wanted to claw that Olivia woman's eyes out?"

"I did not!" I protested, but even I could hear the lack of conviction in my voice. "She seems... nice."

"Nice," Vanessa repeated flatly. "Right."

I sighed, setting down my menu. "What do you want me to say, V? That I'm jealous? That seeing Fury with some leggy blonde bothers me? Because it doesn't. It can't."

Vanessa reached across the table, placing her hand over mine. "Sweetie, it's okay if it bothers you. You're allowed to have feelings, you know."

I pulled my hand away, suddenly finding the tablecloth fascinating. "I don't have feelings. Not for Fury, not for anyone. I can't afford to."

"Sienna," Vanessa said softly, "we've been over this. You can't keep punishing yourself for what happened with Ralf. It wasn't your fault."

"Can we not do this right now? Please? I thought this was supposed to be a fun lunch to celebrate your day off."

Vanessa sighed, but nodded. "Okay, okay. I'll drop it. For now. But we're not done talking about this, missy."

I rolled my eyes, grateful for the reprieve. "Yes, mom."

Our waiter arrived then, a welcome distraction. We placed our orders—a Cobb salad for me, the duck confit for Vanessa—and settled into easier conversation. Vanessa regaled me with tales from the ER, each story more outrageous than the last.

"And then," she said, barely containing her laughter, "the guy says, 'But doc, I swear, I just slipped and fell on it!'"

I choked on my water, laughing despite myself. "No way. People actually say that?"

Vanessa nodded solemnly. "More often than you'd think. It's like they forget we've heard every excuse in the book."

As our food arrived, the conversation drifted to safer topics – Vanessa's latest yoga obsession, my ongoing battle with the ancient coffee maker in our apartment. But even as I laughed at her impression of our sweet neighbor, Mrs. Goldstein, I couldn't shake the image of Fury and Olivia from my mind.

Why did it bother me so much? It's not like I had any claim on him. Hell, I barely knew the guy. And yet...

"Sienna?" Vanessa's voice broke through my reverie. "You still with me?"

I blinked, realizing I'd been pushing the same piece of chicken around my plate for the past five minutes. "Yeah, sorry. Just... thinking."

Vanessa's expression softened. "About Fury?"

I opened my mouth to deny it, but the words wouldn't come. Instead, I nodded. "I just... I don't get it, V. Why does it bother me so much? I've seen plenty of guys come and go at the club. Why is he different?"

Vanessa reached across the table, squeezing my hand. "Maybe because he's the first guy in a long time who's gotten past those walls you've built up. And honey, that's not a bad thing."

I shook my head, pulling my hand away. "It is a bad thing. You know what happened. I can't do this."

Deep down, I knew she was right, but admitting it felt like opening Pandora's box. If I acknowledged these feelings for Fury, where would it end? I'd spent years building up my defenses, carefully cultivating an image of the tough, no-nonsense talent coordinator who didn't need anyone. Could I really risk all that for a guy I barely knew?

"It doesn't matter anyway," I said, forcing a lightness into my tone that I didn't feel. "He's clearly moved on to greener pastures. Did you see that Olivia woman? She looked like she stepped out of a Victoria's Secret catalog."

Vanessa rolled her eyes. "Please. That woman had 'high maintenance' written all over her. Besides, didn't Fury introduce her as his real estate agent?"

I shrugged, stabbing a piece of avocado with more force than necessary. "So? Doesn't mean they're not sleeping together. You saw how cozy they looked."

"Uh-huh," Vanessa said, her tone skeptical. "And I'm sure that's why Fury looked like he wanted the ground to swallow him up when he saw you. Because he was so proud of his conquest."

I blinked, replaying the encounter in my mind. Now that she mentioned it, Fury had seemed… uncomfortable. Embarrassed, even. But why would he be embarrassed unless…

No. I shook my head, banishing the thought before it could take root. It didn't matter. Whatever Fury did or didn't do with Olivia was none of my business.

"Can we please talk about something else?" I pleaded. "How's that cute doctor you were telling me about? The one with the dimples?"

Vanessa's eyes lit up, and she launched into a detailed account of her latest interaction with Dr. Dimples. I let her words wash over me, grateful for the distraction.

But as I sipped my water, my mind wandered back to Fury. The way his eyes had widened when he saw me, the slight flush that had crept up his neck. And underneath it all, that undeniable spark of… something between us.

What if Vanessa was right? What if I was reading too much into things? And even if I wasn't, did I have the courage to do something about it?

Chapter Seven

FURY

I stepped out of the elevator, the polished marble floor reflecting the morning sunlight streaming through the floor-to-ceiling windows. The air was thick with the scent of new carpet and fresh paint, a tangible reminder of the new beginning that awaited me. As I approached the reception area, a bright smile and an enthusiastic wave greeted me.

"Good morning, Mr. Gracen! Welcome to your new office!" Sarah, my receptionist, chirped, her green eyes sparkling with excitement.

I returned her smile. "Good morning, Sarah. And please, call me Fury. Mr. Gracen makes me feel old."

She nodded, a slight blush coloring her cheeks. "Of

course, Fury. Your office is ready, and I've set up the conference room for your team meeting at 10."

I paused, drinking in the sleek, modern design of the space. My eyes traced the clean lines of the furniture and the minimalist decor, a sense of pride swelling in my chest. Olivia had outdone herself, her network of top-notch contractors transforming this blank canvas into a cutting-edge workspace in what felt like the blink of an eye. The office hummed with potential, ready for the challenges that lay ahead.

"Perfect, thank you," I said as I savored the moment.

As I made my way to my office, my mind drifted to Sienna. It had only been a couple of weeks since I met her, but her impact on me was undeniable. The way her eyes flashed when she was challenged, the sound of her laughter echoing through Club Privé... I shook my head, trying to focus on the task at hand. There was no time for distractions, not when I was about to lead my first team meeting in our new Manhattan office.

Before I could dwell on it too much, there was a knock at the door. "Come in," I called, turning to see Jules, my executive assistant, striding in, a stack of files in her arms. Jules, the only employee who had followed me from Palo Alto, brought a sense of continuity and familiarity that I desperately needed right now.

"Morning, boss," she said, her tone businesslike but with a hint of warmth. "Ready to face the troops?"

I chuckled, grateful for her familiar presence in this sea of newness. "As ready as I'll ever be. What've you got for me?"

Jules handed me the files. "Everything you need to know about our current projects, including your new client, Gavin Manning. I've highlighted the key points, but we can go over it in more detail later."

I flipped through the pages, impressed, as always, by Jules's thoroughness. "Thanks, Jules. You're a lifesaver."

She smirked. "Tell me something I don't know. Now, let's go knock the socks off your new team."

The conference room was already full when we arrived. A dozen pairs of eyes turned to me, a mix of curiosity and apprehension clear in their gazes. I took a deep breath, channeling all the confidence I could muster.

"Good morning, everyone," I began, my voice steady despite the nerves fluttering in my stomach. "I'm Fury Gracen, and I'm excited to have you all be part of launching the Gracen, McCrae & Palmer office here in New York. I know new startups can be unsettling, but I want you all to know that I'm confident we can grow and succeed together."

As I launched into my vision for the company, I could see some of the tension in the room ease. A few people even nodded along, their expressions shifting from wariness to cautious optimism.

The numbers and charts flashed by as I rattled off our plans, but my brain kept circling back to Sienna. I hadn't seen her since that moment at the restaurant, bumping into her with Olivia clinging to me like she owned me. What the hell had Sienna thought? My heart clenched, picturing her face when she saw us together.

"Mr. Gracen?" A voice cut through my thoughts. I blinked, realizing I'd paused mid-sentence.

"Sorry," I said, clearing my throat. "As I was saying, our focus for the next quarter will be..."

I got through the rest of the meeting with no more slip-ups, but I could tell Jules had noticed my momentary lapse. As the team filed out, she hung back, her eyebrow raised in a silent question.

"Just lingering jet lag," I lied, not meeting her eyes. "Nothing to worry about."

Jules snorted, clearly not buying it. "Right. Want to try that again?"

I sighed, running a hand through my hair. "It's nothing, really. Just... adjusting to the new environment."

"Uh-huh," Jules said, crossing her arms as she leaned against the doorframe. "Adjusting or avoiding? Come on, Fury, spit it out. What's really eating at you?"

I felt my face heat up. "Really. It's nothing."

Jules rolled her eyes. "Please. I've known you for years, Fury. I can tell when something's got you twisted up. Or should I say, someone?"

Before I could respond, my phone buzzed. I glanced down to see a text from my cousin Carson: *"Hey man, Vix and I are grabbing dinner tonight. Want to join? Promise we won't make you feel like a third wheel."*

I hesitated, my thumb hovering over the screen. A part of me wanted to say yes, to forget about work for a night and just enjoy some time with family. But the responsible part of my brain, the part that had gotten me this far, reminded me of the mountain of work waiting on my desk.

"Sorry, can't tonight. Raincheck?" I typed back, ignoring the pang of regret in my chest.

Carson's response came quickly: *"All work, and no play, makes Fury a dull boy. Don't forget to live a little."*

I pocketed my phone, trying to shake off the feeling that I was missing out on something important. When I looked up, Jules was watching me with a mixture of concern and exasperation.

"Let me guess," she said. "You just turned down plans with friends to work late?"

I shrugged, not meeting her eyes. "There's a lot to do if we want to hit the ground running."

Jules sighed. "Fury, I get it. This is a big move, and you

want to prove yourself. But you can't pour from an empty cup. You need to find some balance."

Her words hit a little too close to home, echoing the nagging doubts I'd been trying to ignore. "I know, I know. I just... I need to focus right now. Get everything settled."

Jules looked like she wanted to argue, but instead, she just shook her head. "Alright, boss. But don't say I didn't warn you when you burn out before the end of the month."

"Right. Let's get back to work, shall we?"

Jules gave me a look that said she knew exactly what I was doing, but she sat down without comment, spreading out a series of charts and graphs.

As we dove into the numbers, I felt some of the tension ease from my shoulders. This, at least, was familiar territory. I could lose myself in market trends and growth strategies, push aside the complicated tangle of emotions for a while.

A few hours later, I stepped into my condo, the stark contrast between its modest furnishings and the opulent penthouse Olivia had shown me hitting me like a slap to the face. The beige walls seemed to close in on me, the impersonal decor giving off the vibe of a temporary crash pad rather than a home. The silence was almost deafening, broken only by the hum of the refrigerator.

God, I couldn't wait to move. This place felt more like a hotel room than a home, and the sooner I could settle into that swanky new pad, the better.

I tossed my keys onto the kitchen counter with a clatter, shrugging off my jacket and loosening my tie. The silence of the place was deafening. Back in Palo Alto, I'd always had people around - Cory dropping by unannounced, colleagues crashing on my couch after late-night brainstorming sessions. Here, it was just me and my thoughts. And let me tell you, my thoughts weren't exactly splendid company at the moment.

I grabbed a beer from the fridge and flopped onto the couch, kicking off my shoes. The TV remote felt heavy in my hand as I flicked through channels, not really seeing anything. My mind kept drifting back to Sienna, to Olivia, to the mess I'd created in such a short time.

"Get it together, Gracen," I muttered to myself, taking a long swig of beer. "You're here to work, not get tangled up in some rom-com plot."

But even as I said it, I knew it was too late. I was already neck-deep in exactly that kind of situation. And the worst part? A tiny part of me was kind of enjoying the ride.

Suddenly my phone buzzed and I tossed the TV remote onto the couch.

It was Gavin Manning.

"Fury," his voice crackled through the speaker, tension clear even through the phone. "I need you at Club Privé. Now."

My eyebrows shot up. "Everything okay, Gavin?"

"No," he said bluntly. "I'll explain when you get here. How fast can you make it?"

I glanced at the clock. It was just past 9 PM. "I can be there in twenty minutes."

"Make it fifteen," Gavin said, then hung up.

Well, shit. So much for a quiet night in. I threw on a fresh shirt and slacks, not bothering with a tie. Whatever was going on, it sounded serious.

As I hailed a cab, my mind raced. What could be so urgent? Was the club in trouble? And then a thought crept in: Would Sienna be there?

I shook my head, trying to focus. This was business, not some teenage crush.

Arriving at Club Privé, I nodded to the bouncer, who let me in without a word. The club was in full swing, the bass thumping through my chest as I made my way to Gavin's office. I scanned the crowd, looking for a familiar face, but there was no sign of Sienna.

Gavin's assistant ushered me in without any introduction. The man himself was pacing behind his desk, looking more disheveled than I'd ever seen him.

"Fury," he said, relief evident in his voice. "Thanks for coming so quickly."

I nodded, taking a seat. "What's going on, Gavin? You look like you've seen a ghost."

He ran a hand through his hair, messing it up even further. "Worse than a ghost. I found out who's behind the buyout offers."

I leaned forward, intrigued. "And?"

"Arthur Dalton."

The name left a sour taste in my mouth. Arthur Dalton, the Wall Street shark with a reputation for hostile takeovers and shady dealings. I'd had my own run-in with him a few years back, and it hadn't been pretty.

"Shit," I muttered. "Are you sure?"

Gavin nodded grimly. "Positive. He approached me directly today. Made quite a generous new offer, too."

I let out a low whistle. "How generous are we talking?"

"Double what the club's worth on paper."

My eyebrows shot up. "That's... suspicious."

"Exactly," Gavin said, collapsing into his chair. "From what I hear, Dalton doesn't overpay for anything unless he thinks he can squeeze ten times the value out of it."

I nodded, my mind already racing through possibilities. "What do you think he's really after?"

Gavin shrugged, looking more defeated than I'd ever seen him. "Could be anything. The real estate, the client list, hell, maybe he just wants a fancy playground for his rich friends."

"Or worse," I said quietly, memories of my past encounter with Dalton flooding back.

Gavin's head snapped up, his eyes narrowing. "What do you know about Dalton?"

I sighed, leaning back in my chair. "A few years ago, he approached Gracen & McCrae about managing some of his 'special' investment portfolios. It didn't take long to realize that 'special' meant 'illegal.' We turned him down flat."

"And?" Gavin prompted.

"And suddenly, we started losing clients. Big ones. Contracts that were all but signed fell through at the last minute. It was like someone was whispering in their ears, turning them against us."

Gavin cursed under his breath. "So he's not above playing dirty."

"Not even close," I confirmed. "It took us months to recover from the damage he did. And that was just because we said no to working with him. I can't imagine what he'd do if he actually got rejected from a business he wanted this badly."

I watched as Gavin abruptly shot to his feet, resuming

his agitated pacing. "So what the fuck do we do?" he growled, running his hands through his hair for the umpteenth time. "I can't sell to that dirty crook, Fury. This club..." His voice cracked. "It's more than just a business. It's family."

I nodded, understanding all too well. In the short time I'd been involved with Club Privé, I'd seen how much it meant to everyone who worked here. Especially Sienna.

"We fight," I said simply. "We look for ways to shore up the club's finances without compromising its integrity. Maybe we can find some legitimate investors to counter Dalton's offer."

Gavin stopped pacing, a thoughtful look on his face. "That could work. But we'd need to move fast. Dalton gave me forty-eight hours to respond to his offer."

I whistled low. "That's not much time."

"No, it's not," Gavin agreed. "But with your financial expertise and my connections, we might just pull it off."

We spent the next hour brainstorming ideas, from restructuring the club's debt to reaching out to potential friendly investors.

"Gavin," I said during a lull in the conversation. "What about the employees? Sienna, the dancers... how do we protect them if Dalton decides to play really dirty?"

Gavin gave me a long, hard look. "I thought I told you

to keep things professional with Sienna. You better be careful, Fury."

I felt my face heat up. "This isn't about that. I'm just concerned about everyone who works here. They deserve to know what's going on."

Gavin sighed, rubbing his temples. "You're right, of course. But we need to be careful about how we handle this. The last thing we need is a panic."

I nodded, trying to ignore the way my heart raced at the mere mention of Sienna's name.

As I stood to leave, Gavin's words echoed in my head. Be careful with Sienna. If only he knew how careful I was trying to be. How hard I was fighting against this pull I felt towards her.

I stepped out of Gavin's office, my mind a whirlwind of conflicting thoughts and emotions. On one hand, I was energized by the challenge ahead. Taking on Arthur Dalton wouldn't be easy, but it was the kind of high-stakes situation that got my blood pumping. On the other hand, the thought of what might happen to Club Privé—and more specifically, to Sienna—if we failed made my stomach churn.

I made my way through the club, my mind a whirlwind from the conversation with Gavin. A flash of movement on stage snagged my attention, and I glanced up. My lungs seized, refusing to draw breath.

Sienna moved on stage, her body a living sculpture of grace and sensuality. She undulated to the pulsing beat, each motion so perfectly timed and executed it transcended mere dancing. This was art in its purest form.

Our eyes locked across the sea of bodies, and the world around me blurred into insignificance. The thundering music faded to a whisper, the crowd dissolved into mist, even the looming specter of Arthur Dalton evaporated. There was only Sienna, her gaze burning into mine, the ghost of a smile teasing at the corners of her lips.

My heart hammered against my ribs as sweat beaded on my palms. Christ, she was breathtaking. Talented. Brilliant. And completely, utterly off-limits.

Gavin's warning reverberated in my skull: "Be careful with Sienna." Right. Professional. I had to keep things professional. But as I stood there, rooted to the spot, I wondered if I was fighting a losing battle.

With a herculean effort, I tore my gaze away from her just as a group of rowdy patrons stumbled between us, blocking my view. It was probably for the best. I needed to focus on saving the club, not on my growing attraction to one of its employees.

I had a job to do, a club to save, and a lot of complicated feelings to sort out.

Chapter Eight

SIENNA

I squinted at the mirror, adjusting the sequined top of Venus's costume. It was snug in all the wrong places, designed for her petite frame rather than my taller, curvier one. Sighing, I reached for the double-sided tape. This wasn't my first rodeo with wardrobe emergencies, but it had been a while since I'd had to MacGyver an outfit quite like this.

"Dammit, Venus," I muttered, securing the top in place. "You couldn't have given me a little more notice?"

The text from Venus still burned in my mind. No explanation, no warning—just a terse message saying she quit and wouldn't be back. It was so unlike her that alarm bells were ringing in my head, but I pushed them aside for now. I had a show to save. I glanced at the clock. Ten minutes until the curtain rises.

I slipped into my heels and gave myself one last once-over in the mirror. It would do. It had to.

A pang of disappointment twisted in my chest as I made my way to the stage. Venus was my ace, my star performer. Losing her was like losing my right arm. But I'd been in this business long enough to know that the show must go on, with or without my star.

I nodded at Darcy as I took my position on stage. She gave me a thumbs up and the music started.

My body moved on autopilot, muscle memory kicking in as I lost myself in the routine. For a moment, I forgot about Venus, about the chaos of the day, about everything except the music and the movement.

Then I felt it. A gaze so intense it was almost physical. I turned, mid-spin, and locked eyes with Fury Gracen.

Time seemed to stand still. His eyes were dark, unreadable, but there was something in the air between us that made my skin tingle. For a heartbeat, I forgot to breathe.

Then he looked away, and the spell was broken. I stumbled slightly, cursing under my breath as I forced myself back into the rhythm of the dance.

When the music ended, I was breathing hard, and not just from the exertion. I grabbed a water bottle, chugging it down as I tried to shake off the lingering effects of Fury's gaze.

"Alright, ladies," I called out as the dancers filed in. "We've got some changes to discuss for this next performance."

I briefed them on Venus's resignation, watching their faces for any signs of wavering. But these girls were made of stronger stuff. They nodded, determined, ready to step up and fill the gap.

Pride swelled in my chest. They were survivors, every one of them. Just like me.

"Okay, let's do our best," I said, clapping my hands.

As the dancers lined up, I heard a familiar voice behind me. "Sienna, darling. I didn't know you were back on stage."

I turned to find Gavin approaching, his eyebrows raised in surprise. "I'm not," I said, suddenly very aware of how little Venus's costume covered. "It's just... Venus quit. No notice, no explanation. She just sent a text saying she was done."

Gavin's face darkened. "Venus quit? Why wasn't I informed immediately?"

I shrugged, feeling a twinge of guilt. "It just happened, Gavin. I was trying to sort out the routine before bringing it to you."

He sighed, running a hand through his hair. "This is... unfortunate. Venus was one of our top draws."

"I know," I said, the weight of the situation settling on my shoulders. "I'm handling it, Gavin. We'll make it work."

He nodded, but I could see the wheels turning behind his eyes. "If you need anything—resources, extra staff, whatever—just let me know. We can't afford any hiccups right now."

There was something in his tone that set off alarm bells in my head. "Gavin? Is everything okay?"

He waved off my concern, but I could see the tension in his shoulders. "Nothing for you to worry about, darling. Just focus on the show."

As he turned to leave, I felt a surge of determination. Something wasn't right here—with Venus, with Gavin, with this whole situation. And I was going to get to the bottom of it.

After our performance, I headed back to the dressing room, my mind racing. As soon as the door closed behind me, I was pulling out my phone, dialing Venus's number. It went straight to voicemail.

"Venus, it's Sienna. Call me back as soon as you get this. We need to talk."

I hung up and immediately sent a text: "Venus, what's going on? Are you okay? Please call me."

No response. I tried again. And again. Each unanswered call, each unread text, ratcheted up my anxiety. This wasn't like Venus. She'd always been reliable, always answered when I called. Something was definitely wrong.

I paced the room, my mind whirling with possibilities. Did something happen to her? Was she in trouble? Or did she just decide she'd had enough of this life and wanted out?

Venus wasn't just my star dancer—she was my friend. And I'd be damned if I was going to let her leave without a fight.

My mind was already formulating a plan. I knew her usual haunts, her favorite spots in the city. If she was out there, I'd find her. And if she was in trouble... well, I had connections in this town. People who owed me favors. I'd call them in if I had to.

A knock at my door made me jump. "Come in."

It was Darcy, looking worried. "Hey, Sienna. I just wanted to check if you um, heard from Venus?"

I forced a smile, trying to keep my voice steady. "No, I haven't heard anything. But I'm sure she's fine."

Darcy nodded, but I could see the doubt in her eyes. She'd known Venus almost as long as I had. She knew this wasn't like her.

"Okay, well, if you need anything..." she trailed off, fidgeting with her headphones.

"I'll let you know," I finished for her. "Thanks, Darcy."

I took a deep breath, steeling myself for what was to come. Venus's address burned in my mind like a neon sign, flashing and impossible to ignore. I needed to find Venus, make sure she was okay. The worry gnawing at my gut wouldn't let me do anything else.

The taxi ride to Venus's neighborhood was a blur of signs and honking horns. As we pulled up to her building, my heart sank. The place was a dump, all crumbling brick and graffiti-covered walls. It was a stark reminder of how hard it was to make it in this city, even for someone as talented as Venus.

"You sure this is the right place, lady?" the cabbie asked, eyeing the building warily.

I nodded, handing him a twenty. "Unfortunately, yeah. Thanks for the ride."

As I stepped out onto the cracked sidewalk, the smell of garbage and stale urine assaulted my nostrils. God, how did Venus live like this? I made a mental note to talk to Gavin about raising salaries. Our girls deserved better than this.

I pushed through the front door, wincing at the

groan of rusty hinges. A sign on the elevator declared it "OUT OF ORDER" in angry red letters. Of course it was. With a sigh, I started the long climb up five flights of stairs.

By the time I reached Venus's floor, I was breathing hard, my calves burning. The hallway was dimly lit, the flickering fluorescent lights casting eerie shadows. I pulled out my phone, double-checking the apartment number before approaching the door.

My heart thundered against my ribs as I lifted my fist to the peeling paint of Venus's door. I hesitated for a moment, my hand hovering inches from the surface. What if she wasn't there? What if something had happened to her? I pushed the thoughts aside and rapped my knuckles against the worn wood.

"Hold on!" a voice called from inside. It wasn't Venus, but it was something. I waited, shifting my weight from foot to foot, anxiety coiling in my stomach.

The door swung open, revealing a woman I recognized as Chelsea, Venus's roommate. She looked like hell, dark circles under her eyes and her hair a mess. Her eyes narrowed as she took me in.

"Can I help you?" she asked, her tone making it clear that she'd rather not.

I pasted on my most charming smile. "Hi, Chelsea. I'm Sienna, Venus's manager from Club Privé. Is she here?"

Chelsea's face hardened. "No, she ain't. And I don't know where she is, so you can just—"

"Wait," I interrupted, holding up a hand. "Please. I'm worried about her. She quit without any notice, and that's not like her. When was the last time you saw her?"

Chelsea leaned against the doorframe, crossing her arms. "Why should I tell you anything? Venus owes me rent, and now she's gone and disappeared. I've got my own problems."

I bit back a frustrated sigh. This wasn't getting me anywhere. Time to change tactics.

"Look," I said, reaching into my purse. "I get it. You're pissed, and you have every right to be. But I'm just trying to find out if Venus is okay." I pulled out a twenty-dollar bill. "How about this? You tell me when you last saw her, and this is yours."

Chelsea's eyes flicked to the money, then back to me. For a moment, I thought she was going to slam the door in my face. But then she sighed, holding out her hand.

"Fine," she said as I handed over the cash. "Last time I saw her was Tuesday night. She came home late from work, looking all stressed out. I was heading out for my shift at Little Kitty—that's the club where I dance," she added, a hint of defensiveness in her tone.

I felt a chill run down my spine. Little Kitty had a

reputation, and it wasn't a good one. "Did anyone follow you home? Any clients giving you trouble?"

Chelsea's eyes flashed. "Hey, I'm out of that life. I just dance now, that's it."

I held up my hands in a placating gesture. "I get it, believe me. I used to escort, back in the day. I know how hard it can be to get out."

Something in Chelsea's face softened at that. She studied me for a moment, as if seeing me for the first time. "Yeah, well... it ain't easy, that's for sure."

I nodded, feeling a moment of connection. "No, it's not. But you're doing it, and that's what matters." I paused, then added, "I'm just worried about Venus. It's not like her to quit without saying anything. Are you sure there wasn't anything unusual that night?"

Chelsea shook her head, a flicker of concern crossing her face. "Nah, nothing I noticed. I mean, she seemed stressed, but that's not exactly new around here. I figured she'd just moved on to something better, you know? Not... whatever this is."

"Yeah," I mumbled. "Me too." I pulled out one of my business cards, holding it out to her. "Look, if you hear from her, or if you remember anything else, can you call me? Day or night, it doesn't matter."

Chelsea took the card, turning it over in her hands. "Yeah, sure. I hope she's okay."

As she closed the door, I felt a mix of frustration and determination. It wasn't much to go on, but it was something. I turned to the next apartment, steeling myself to keep knocking on doors. Someone in this building had to know something.

An hour and countless doors later, I was no closer to finding Venus than when I had started. The sun was setting, casting long shadows across the dingy hallway. I had to head to the club soon to get ready for tonight's show. But the thought of leaving, of giving up, made my stomach churn.

I pushed through the front door of the building, the cool evening air a welcome relief after the stuffy hallways. My phone buzzed in my pocket—probably Gavin, wondering where the hell I was. I ignored it for now, needing a moment to collect my thoughts.

As I hailed a cab to Club Privé, I made a mental list of the next steps. I'd need to talk to the other dancers, see if any of them had noticed anything off about Venus lately. And I'd have to do some digging into Little Kitty. If that place was as shady as its reputation suggested, it might be the key to all of this.

The cab weaved through traffic as I checked my phone, wincing at the string of missed calls and texts from Gavin. I'd deal with him when I got back. Right now, all I could think about was Venus.

Where are you, girl? What kind of trouble are you in?

As the familiar facade of Club Privé came into view, I straightened my shoulders and took a deep breath. I had a show to run and a missing friend to find.

The moment I stepped into Club Privé, the pre-show buzz was electric, dancers rushing back and forth, the muffled thump of music from the main floor vibrating through the walls.

"Sienna!" Darcy's voice cut through the chaos. She was rushing towards me, a headset dangling around her neck and panic in her eyes. "Where have you been? Gavin's been looking for you everywhere!"

I took a deep breath, steeling myself. "I know. I was following a lead on Venus. Any word from her?"

Darcy shook her head, her expression a mix of worry and frustration. "Nothing. And we're down two more girls tonight. Jasmine's got food poisoning, and Trixie sprained her ankle during rehearsal."

"Shit." I ran a hand through my hair, trying to process this latest disaster. "Okay, we can work with this. We'll have to adjust the choreography, maybe pull in some of the waitstaff who know the routines. It's not ideal, but—"

"Sienna," Darcy interrupted, her voice dropping low. "There's something else. There's a woman here asking for Fury. She says it's urgent."

My heart skipped a beat. "Olivia?" I asked, thinking of

the leggy blonde real estate agent I'd seen him with at the restaurant.

Darcy shrugged. "I don't know. She's waiting by the bar."

Great. Just what I needed tonight. Another complication.

"Alright, I'll handle it," I sighed. "Can you start working on the new lineup? I'll be there as soon as I can."

I made my way to the bar, spotting a woman I didn't recognize perched on a stool. She was pretty, with long brown hair and wide, anxious eyes. My stomach clenched. This had to be Fury's girlfriend.

"Can I help you?" I asked, keeping my voice neutral despite the irrational anger bubbling up inside me.

She stood quickly, smoothing down her dress. "Yes, I'm looking for Fury Gracen. It's important that I speak with him."

I forced a smile. "He's in a meeting with the owner right now. I can take you to the office."

She nodded gratefully, and I led her through the club, my mind racing. Who was this woman? Why was she here? And why did I care so damn much?

Chapter Nine

FURY

I HAD JUST FINISHED GIVING Gavin a more detailed picture of the Arthur Dalton I had known when someone knocked on the door. Gavin went to open it, and for a moment, I only saw Sienna; then my brain registered the other woman with her.

"Rose?" I moved past Gavin to hug my sister. I heard Sienna say something before leaving, but I was too caught up with my sister showing up here to pay much attention to anything else. I led her into the office. "Gavin, this is my little sister, Rose. Rose, this is Gavin Manning. He owns the club."

"It's nice to meet you." Rose smiled as she shook his

hand. "I'm sorry to interrupt. I needed to talk to my brother and couldn't get a hold of him at his office."

"Jules told you I was here," I said.

"I'll give the two of you some time," Gavin said as he headed back to the door. "I have a few things I need to do out of the office, anyway."

I waited until Gavin closed the door behind him before turning to my sister, my curiosity burning. "What are you doing in New York?" I asked, following up with an equally pressing question. "Is everyone alright back home?"

"Yeah, everyone's fine," Rose replied hastily. "At least, as far as I know. I've only spoken to Maggie."

"Tell me," I urged, sinking onto the plush leather couch and patting the spot next to me. "What's going on? More shit hitting the fan at the ranch?"

Rose had bought a horse ranch in Colorado over a year ago, and initially, things seemed to go smoothly. But this past March, she'd called me in a panic, needing help. When I'd shown up at her place, she'd cryptically told me something felt off, but she didn't have the skills to investigate properly. I did.

She'd handed over the books and asked me to take a look, not wanting to plant any preconceived notions. It hadn't taken long for me to uncover the truth. One of her employees had been embezzling funds from the ranch.

They'd done a piss-poor job of covering their tracks, which is how Rose had noticed the discrepancies. I'd offered to stick around and help her deal with the fallout, but she'd thanked me for my help and sent me packing back to Palo Alto.

"I fired that thieving son of a...," Rose said, her gaze fixed on her hands, unable to meet my eyes. "But there have been some... unsavory rumors circulating about me and the real reason I fired him. Between what he stole and the gossip in town, I sold the ranch a couple of weeks ago."

It took a moment for her words to sink in. She'd sold her ranch? The place she'd dreamed of owning her entire life? The horses she adored?

"Shit. Why?"

She started twisting her fingers together nervously, a habit I recognized from childhood. Whenever she was trying to keep her emotions in check, she'd do that, even as a little girl.

"I knew someone interested in the property, and it just seemed like the best solution for everyone involved."

I reached out and placed my hand over hers. "Why didn't you come to me? Or Blaze, or anyone else in the family? Any of us would've been more than happy to float you the cash to cover whatever you needed."

Honestly, I couldn't fathom how, even with the embezzlement, she hadn't been able to keep the ranch. All of us, regardless of how we fit into the bizarre McCrae-Carideo-Gracen family tree, were worth an obscene amount of money. And we'd all been taught how to handle our finances responsibly.

She shook her head. "It was more about the rumors than the money. And before you ask why I didn't seek help with that, I wanted to handle things on my own. I needed to prove that I wasn't just the baby of the family who needed everyone to coddle her."

"No one thinks that about you," I protested.

She finally met my gaze, her expression speaking volumes. "Everyone else has these big, important careers, and I just wanted to work with horses. No one has to say that out loud."

"Rose," I began.

"I didn't want anyone to know," she interrupted. "That's why I came here instead of going back to California or heading to Baltimore to see Blaze. People would start asking questions, meaning well, but making me feel like a complete idiot."

I wanted to argue and tell her that our family would never do that, but I knew, as well as anyone, that sometimes people tried to be helpful, yet it just made everything worse. I could easily imagine our older brother, Blaze, grilling her about why she hadn't hired a competent bookkeeper who could have caught the embezzling sooner or why she hadn't done more thorough background checks on her employees. He'd be trying to understand, but she'd feel like those were things she should have thought of from the start.

"I knew Maggie would get it," Rose continued. "And the last time we talked, she mentioned wanting to hire some help with the twins. So, I called her. She and Drake said I could stay with them as long as I want."

"You know you could stay with me too," I offered. "The condo isn't massive, but there's a guest room."

"I know," Rose replied. "But Maggie understands what it's like to not want to air your dirty laundry to the family. And since I'm not in any danger, she supports me by keeping things under wraps for now."

"I won't breathe a word," I promised. "But I think it's probably going to come out at some point."

"Thank you," Rose said, offering me a smile that almost reached her eyes. "And I know. I just need some time. I'll probably tell Carson since he lives in the city too, but I wanted you to know before I even got settled at Maggie's, since you were already in the loop about the ranch drama."

"Well, if you need a break from screaming babies or from a sickeningly sweet couple, you know where to find me," I said.

Her phone chimed with an incoming text. "That's

Maggie. I asked her to pick me up here instead of at the airport."

I glanced at the time. "Let me walk you out, since the club's just opening. It shouldn't be too crazy yet, but I don't want anyone mistaking you for an employee or a member."

Rose rolled her eyes. "You do remember that I'm twenty-six, right? More than old enough to drink or have sex, even the kinky stuff that goes on here."

I winced. "Come on, kiddo. I really don't want to hear my baby sister talking about sex."

She chuckled, and I decided it would be worth feeling uncomfortable if it got her to laugh like that.

"You know, now that I'm here for who knows how long, maybe I should look into getting a membership. It'd give me something to do," she teased.

"You're killing me, Rose," I groaned. "Please, don't do that. I know you're old enough, but I really don't want to risk coming here and running into you grinding on some leather-clad stud."

Now she let out that loud, boisterous laugh that I had always loved, and I felt some of the tightness in my chest ease. She was going through a rough patch, but she would be okay.

"Come on," I said, opening the door.

The music when the elevator door opened on the

ground floor was deafening, so we didn't talk as I escorted her through the club to the front entrance. To my relief, nothing too wild was happening, though I had to shoot a couple of 'big brother' death glares at a few guys who were clearly eye-fucking Rose. I knew that, technically, she was old enough to make her own choices about who she dated, and if she chose someone from here, I'd accept it.

Well, after a very thorough background check and a conversation where I made my intentions crystal clear for her potential suitor, then I'd accept it.

Maggie's car was pulled up to the curb right in front of the club, so we headed straight for it. The driver opened the door for Rose while I leaned down to greet my step-cousin. It didn't surprise me that Drake had Maggie using a driver, but I was a little shocked that she'd given in. We didn't chat long since this wasn't an actual parking spot, but it was enough for me to tell both women that we needed to get together soon and to ask how the little rugrats were doing.

By the time I headed back into the club, I was smiling despite still being slightly worried about Rose. I was halfway to the elevator, completely intending to go back to Gavin's office to finish what we had started, when I saw Sienna standing next to the door to a private room. That strange magnetic pull I always seemed to feel around her came back with too much force for me to resist.

I changed direction and headed straight for her, running over possible conversation starters in my head. However, I didn't even have a chance to say a word before she snapped at me.

"What do you want?" She glared at me, folding her arms across her chest.

I pretended not to notice how her particular stance pushed up her breasts into a cleavage that was even more mouth-watering than normal.

"I just wanted to say hello, but apparently today's not a good day for that," I shot back. "Though I would like to know if you're biting the heads off of every guy that talks to you like you're some sort of praying mantis, or am I just special?"

Her mouth twisted into a scowl, and she turned on me with a finger already out to jab into my chest, but froze when a tall guy in a 'Security' shirt walked by. A snide remark was on the tip of my tongue when she grabbed my arm and dragged me into the private room next to where she was standing.

When it closed behind me, all the noise from the club cut off, making her next words crystal clear.

"You are such a pain in my ass!"

"Is that what you're into?" I stepped closer into her personal space. "Because spanking your ass until you can't sit without thinking of me is awfully appealing."

Color crept into her cheeks, and I wondered if her ass would turn that same pretty shade of red under my hand. She didn't, however, back down. Instead, she closed the last of the distance between us, leaving barely an inch of space. Looking up at me, her eyes flashed, heat mixed in with the anger there. That electricity between us was stronger than ever, and my blood rushed south.

"You've got a high opinion of yourself," she said. "Want to put your money where your mouth is?"

I smirked at her. "I'd rather put my mouth somewhere else and show you why I can think highly of myself."

There was a beat, and then she was pulling my head down and crushing her mouth against mine. It only took a second for my brain to catch up, and then I was pushing her up against the wall and taking control of the kiss.

Chapter Ten

SIENNA

What had I been thinking, letting this happen? No, that wasn't right. I knew exactly what I'd been thinking when I kissed him: I wanted this. Him. Now. And I wasn't about to let a little thing like sanity get in my way.

Fury's lips on mine sent a jolt through my body, short-circuiting any rational thought. All I knew was that I needed more of that electric touch. I wound my arms around his neck, feeling the flex and shift of powerful muscles beneath my palms. His hands roamed eagerly, sending flames licking across my skin even through the thin barrier of my dress.

A sharp intake of breath as he lifted me, my legs

locking around his waist. I could feel the hard planes of his body, every ridge and contour, as he pressed against me. My core clenched, aching for more contact, and I squirmed, desperate for relief from the building tension.

He must have felt my need because he suddenly ground his hips into mine, the considerable bulge in his pants igniting a fire. I wanted to feel all of him now. My fingers dug into his shoulders, urging him closer as I arched my back, seeking more friction.

Then his hands were on me, slipping beneath my dress to stroke my overheated skin. With a growl, he hauled me against him, his fingers teasing their way under my panties. The touch of his calloused fingers on my sensitive flesh made me gasp.

"Damn," he muttered, his breath hot against my mouth. "You're soaked."

Soaked? I was a goddamn waterfall. My body was screaming for release, and this delicious man was taking his sweet time. Enough was enough.

"Quit teasing," I demanded, my voice hoarse. "I need you now."

A split-second pause, and then he was fumbling with his pants, his eyes dark with desire. "Condom?"

"I'm clean and on birth control. You?" If he wasn't, I was going to be even more pissed than I already was.

"All good," he promised as he buried himself to the hilt in one hard thrust.

My head slammed back against the wall from the sudden pressure of him filling me completely. Pleasure and pain blurred together.

"Like a fucking vice," Fury muttered, every muscle in his body as tight as his voice.

"Talk less," I managed to get out. "Fuck more."

He raised his head, his eyes meeting mine. One eyebrow went up.

I clenched around him, feeling his girth, and he growled, the deep, rumbling sound vibrating through me. I'd only ever read about guys doing that, and damn, it was so much hotter in person.

"Fuck me," I ordered, my voice husky with need. "Or I swear, I'll go find someone who will."

The threat died on my lips as he withdrew and then slammed back into me, harder this time. The force of it took my breath away, and I arched my back, pressing myself against him.

He did it again, setting a relentless pace, each thrust pushing me further into the wall.

"Yes, right there," I hissed, pleasure coiling tight inside me.

Fury said nothing more, clearly taking my instructions to heart. He slammed into me like a man possessed, his body a blur of motion as he drove us both towards the edge. Our grunts and moans filled the room, a carnal symphony that would make a porn star proud.

It was overwhelming, having all his attention, all that raw, primal energy focused on me. I could feel the pressure building, a delicious tension coiling in my core. Fury reached down, cupping my breast in his large hand, squeezing gently at first, and then harder until I cried out. He released my breast, only to pinch and twist my nipple between his thumb and finger, sending a sharp jolt of pain through me. That little bite of pain, mixed with the intense pleasure, was my undoing.

I exploded around him, crying out as my body shattered into a million pieces. I clung to him, my fingers digging into his back as I rode out the waves of my orgasm. Fury buried his face in the curve of my neck, his breath hot against my skin as he found his release. His groan vibrated through me, extending my climax, leaving me boneless and sated.

We stood there, fused together, our hearts beating in unison.

Damn. This was exactly what I needed.

We stayed there for a minute, Fury's body pinning me to the wall even as his cock softened inside me. Gradually, as the high from my orgasm wore off, I realized what'd happened and was furious at myself for it.

I was furious with him, too. Not for fucking me. Not when I'd initiated the kiss, and then I'd demanded that he fuck me. I'd gotten caught up in the heat of the moment and my stupid, stupid attraction to him. No, I was pissed because I remembered what'd made me mad at him in the first place.

Rose. That gorgeous woman he'd been wrapped around.

I shoved at his chest, and he stepped back, helping me find my feet, both of us suddenly fascinated by our shoes.

"You don't need to worry, by the way," I finally bit out, slicing through the quiet.

He looked at me, all genuine confusion, and it was like dumping gasoline on a fire. "Worry about what?"

"I won't spill the beans to your lady who came to see you about us getting down and dirty."

His eyebrows shot up. "My lady—wait, you think Rose is my girlfriend?" He touched my arm, and I had no choice but to meet his gaze. "You actually believe I'd walk my girl out of the club and then, what, five minutes later, I'm balls deep in you?"

A cold dread seeped in, suggesting maybe I'd jumped the gun here. But I stiffened my spine and folded my arms. "Enlighten me."

"Rose is my sister."

Well, fuck.

Fury shook his head, both disappointment and anger showing on his face. "Maybe Gavin was right about me needing to stay away from you."

Ouch. I hadn't known Gavin had said that to Fury, and it hurt more than I would've thought.

"I'm not a cheater," Fury said quietly. Even though he wasn't shouting, I could see how mad my words had made him.

His reaction, along with everything else that'd just happened, had me off-balance, and that was the only excuse I could think of to explain what came out of my mouth next.

"Yeah, well, most guys don't exactly consider hooking up with someone like me as actual cheating."

As soon as the words were out, I clamped my mouth shut, but it was too late. I'd just handed him a piece of my history, something I kept locked up tight. I saw the question in his eyes and knew that he was going to ask what I meant.

So, like any sensible person with their foot jammed in their mouth, I did the only thing I could do.

I ran. Ran and didn't look back.

I sighed, adjusting the straps on Jasmine's costume. The sequins were digging into her skin, and I made a mental note to have them re-sewn before tomorrow's show. My mind was still reeling from the encounter with Fury earlier, but I pushed those thoughts aside. I had a job to do.

"There you go, hon," I said, patting Jasmine's shoulder. "How does that feel?"

She twisted, checking her reflection in the mirror. "Much better. Thanks, Sienna."

I was about to respond when I caught sight of Dodd in the mirror, hovering in the doorway. Great. What now?

"Dodd," I said, turning to face him. "Everything okay out there?"

He stepped into the dressing room, his eyes darting around nervously. "Yeah, all good. I, uh, actually wanted to talk to you about something."

I raised an eyebrow. "Oh?"

He cleared his throat. "I've been watching the routines, you know? And I've been practicing a bit in my spare time."

I blinked, trying to process what he was saying. "You've been... practicing our performances?"

He nodded eagerly. "Yeah! I mean, I know I'm not a professional or anything, but I think I've got some moves."

I chuckled. "Okay, Dodd. And why exactly have you been practicing?"

He shifted his weight, looking uncomfortable. "Well, the thing is, I'm kind of in a tight spot financially. I was hoping maybe I could audition? You know, to perform in some of the private parties or something?"

I stared at him, momentarily speechless. Dodd, our head of security, wanted to be a performer? It was so absurd I almost laughed, but the desperate look in his eyes stopped me.

"Dodd," I said gently, "I appreciate your... enthusiasm. But you're our head of security. It's not exactly common for security personnel to double as performers."

He nodded quickly. "I know. But hear me out. I'm in really good shape, right? And I've been told I'm not too hard on the eyes." He flashed a grin that I had to admit was pretty charming. "Plus, I already know the club, the clientele. I could be a real asset."

I considered his words. It was true, Dodd was in excellent shape and undeniably attractive. And with Venus gone and two other performers out of commission, we were seriously short-staffed. If he could actually perform...

"Look," Dodd continued, sensing my hesitation, "there's a private party this weekend, right? I helped arrange it. Why don't you let me be a part of it? Consider it my audition. If I suck, no harm done. But if I'm good..." He trailed off, leaving the possibility hanging in the air.

I bit my lip, weighing the pros and cons. On one hand, it was a risky move. Dodd had no professional experience, and letting him perform at a private party might damage our reputation. On the other hand, we were desperate for performers, and if he was even halfway decent, it could be a temporary solution to our staffing problem.

"Alright," I said finally, holding up a hand to stop his excited response. "But let's get one thing straight. This is a one-time thing, got it? If you're terrible, that's it. No second chances."

Dodd nodded eagerly. "Of course, of course. Thank you, Sienna. You won't regret this."

As he turned to leave, practically bouncing with excitement, I called after him. "Dodd!"

He turned back, eyebrows raised.

"Be here two hours before the party starts. We need a medical and get you fitted for a costume."

He grinned and gave me a mock salute before disappearing down the hallway.

I turned back to Jasmine, who had been watching the entire exchange with wide eyes.

"Did that really just happen?" she asked, a hint of amusement in her voice.

I shook my head, still not quite believing it myself. "Apparently so."

Chapter Eleven

FURY

Most people wouldn't consider hanging out at a client's house with his family, diving into research, as their idea of a good time, but I was all in. We had taken over the Manning dining room table, our documents scattered across it like a chaotic paper landscape. It was a welcome distraction from the nagging obsession over Sienna ghosting me ever since our hot little encounter at the club two nights ago. That was, of course, until I accidentally opened my mouth about her.

Leaning back in his chair, Gavin fixed me with a steady gaze that felt both serious and unnerving. "Look, man, I know we're all about business here, but we're becoming friends, too. And I've got to be upfront, I was serious about Sienna being off-limits."

"You know I'd never intentionally cause her pain," I replied, the memory of our fiery encounter flashing through my mind—the intensity of my grip, the sting of her nails etching into me, even through the fabric of my shirt. Had I been too forceful? Had she said something to Gavin? The questions lingered in my mind.

"Seriously, Fury, let it go," he urged, his voice calm but laced with genuine concern. "There are literally millions of other women to pursue in this city."

Chuckles from the kitchen caught our ears, and I noticed Gavin's face softened as his daughter, Skylar, twirled past, clutching her younger brother, Micah. Thanks to a series of events I only vaguely understood, her grandparents had raised Skylar from the get-go, but Gavin had always been present and Skylar knew he was her father. These days, she spent at least one weekend per month with Gavin and Carrie's family to nurture bonds with her half-siblings.

Given Gavin's protectiveness over Sienna, I felt sorry for any potential suitors of Skylar. She was well into her teens, and that day was fast approaching. Oh yes. I knew all too well. As a protective brother and cousin myself, I felt the urge to shield my loved ones.

If Skylar possessed even half the spunk and determination I suspected she did, Gavin would have his work cut out for him.

Of course, none of that helped me figure out a way to politely, but firmly, tell my friend to back off the Sienna issue. I appreciated that Gavin would always have her back, but I wasn't some creep. Despite my reputation as a bit of a player, I didn't mistreat women. Sure, things hadn't always ended on good terms with every woman I'd been with, but any animosity usually stemmed from them not believing me when I'd stated upfront that I wasn't looking for anything serious.

Except Sienna had completely thrown me. Having sex with a virtual stranger without clarifying it was a one-time thing was something I never did. Even in college, I'd been smarter than that. But something about Sienna seemed to turn my brain cells to mush.

"Maybe we should only meet here or at your new office for our business dealings," Gavin continued. "Limit your time at the club. Out of sight, out of mind, and all that."

"How are things going in here, boys?" Carrie's question cut into our conversation, and from the look in her chocolate brown eyes, I could tell she'd shifted the subject on purpose. "Figure out what Arthur Dalton is up to yet?"

She came around the couch and leaned down to kiss Gavin's cheek. Pregnant with their third child, she wasn't yet far enough along to be showing, but the way she rested her hand on her stomach said just how aware of it she was.

I smiled as I took in their home, every corner reflecting the importance of family. Toys littered the floor despite Carrie's lovingly exasperated reminders to the kids to pick up after themselves. The younger kids' artwork adorned the fridge, alongside a test Skylar had aced. And pictures. Pictures were everywhere. Of the kids. Gavin and Carrie. The whole family, including Skylar.

It warmed my heart to see just as many pictures of her as there were of Micah and Katy. All the important milestones were captured, without a hint of favoritism from Carrie or Gavin. Coming from a blended family where explaining our connections usually involved charts and PowerPoint presentations, I knew all too well the asinine things people thought and said about 'non-traditional' families. I was glad to see my new friends didn't hold onto any of those notions.

"We're still looking," Gavin said. "It's nothing you need to worry about."

"I'm not worried," she assured him. "Just curious. It's been a while since I've heard either of you mention his name."

The pointed look she gave him clearly confirmed she'd interrupted on purpose to get him to lay off hounding me about Sienna. I wasn't sure if that meant she actually thought Sienna and I would be good for each other or if she just wanted to remind him that his protectiveness over his employees should have limits, but either way, I welcomed the reprieve.

A sound from a nearby baby monitor offered even more distraction. It wasn't exactly a cry, but it definitely sounded like it could become unhappy quickly.

"Katy's awake," Carrie said. "She slept longer than I thought she would with Skylar here."

She started toward the stairs, but Gavin was on his feet in an instant. "Hey, we had an agreement. You need to take it easy, so our compromise was when I'm home, I'll do the heavy lifting, including picking up our toddler from her bed."

Carrie rolled her eyes. "I'm pregnant, Gavin. Not made of glass. And in case you've forgotten, I've done this twice before."

"Yes, but Katy was two years ago and now you're..." His voice trailed off as Carrie's eyes narrowed.

"Finish it," she said. "Finish what you were going to say Gavin Manning, so I can put you in your place."

He ran a hand through his hair and looked at me as if I could save him from his pregnant wife's wrath. I shrugged and gave him a look I hoped conveyed I had no clue what to say, but was rooting for him. He opened and closed his mouth a couple of times before finally just giving up.

Carrie pointed at him, still glaring. "Yes, I am two years older than I was when I was pregnant with Katy, and yes, I am thirty-two, but if you ever use the phrase 'geriatric pregnancy' or 'advanced pregnancy,' I swear you will wake up the next day with your balls in a vice. And not in a good way."

He winced and held up his hands in surrender. "I swear, babe, I wasn't going to say that. I was there when you informed the doctor that you were still a few—um, I mean, several years away from that. I was going to say that two years ago, you just had Micah, and now you have Micah and Katy. Two kids under the age of five are a lot when you're also creating a human being inside your body."

He tentatively put his hands on her hips, his thumbs brushing her stomach in a touch both innocent and intimate enough to make me wonder if I should excuse myself. His voice dropped low enough that I almost didn't hear what he said next, and when I did, I wished I'd followed my instincts.

"Your very perfect and beautiful body that I will definitely spend some time later today worshiping until you forget all about this."

Okay. I was fairly certain they'd both forgotten that they had company.

I cleared my throat at the same time Katy made

another sound in her room, and the moment was broken. Gavin kissed Carrie's forehead and the love that shone on both of their faces filled me with something a lot like wistfulness and envy. I'd seen that look on the faces of more than one member of my family recently, but it'd never been something I'd coveted. Until now, maybe.

"I'll be back in a minute," Gavin said to me before heading for his daughter's room.

Carrie's cheeks were pink, and she had a pleased look on her face as she turned toward me. "Sorry. We got a little carried away."

"It's okay," I said. "I've gotten used to the public displays of affection recently. Half my family seems to have had encounters with Cupid over the last couple of years. It's nice, though, to see a couple who's been together for a while still be like that."

I hoped I didn't sound like I was complaining, because I wasn't. I didn't begrudge my family anything. While my cousins and step-cousins hadn't lost both their parents like my siblings and I had, they'd all lost one parent, and all of us had struggled when we'd first put together our blended family. And then there were the ones who'd had their own individual struggles. Eoin's near-death experience with an IED. Alec's ex leaving their daughter on his doorstep. Maggie's abusive asshole ex-boyfriend. They deserved to be happy, and for many of them, that'd come in the form of the people they'd found to love.

This was just the first time I'd ever thought that the same thing might make me happy.

"I heard what Gavin was saying about Sienna," Carrie said. "I will not tell you he's wrong to be protective of her, but I do think he's wrong to tell you to leave her alone. My gut says the two of you will be good for each other."

"Thanks."

Carrie smiled. "But if you hurt her, Gavin will be the least of your worries. Remember my threat to him?"

"Balls. Vice." I nodded. "Yes, ma'am."

"And I like his balls, so imagine what I'd do to you if you pissed me off."

She said it all so sweetly that my brain didn't want to accept it for the threat that it was.

"Mama!"

Gavin returned, his adorable little girl squirming in his arms as soon as she spotted her mom.

"Hey there, my little Katy girl," Carrie beamed, reaching out for her daughter. "Tell Daddy to let me take you so he and Mr. Fury here can keep doing the work they're supposed to be doing."

"Let Skylar help you," Gavin said. "Please."

"I will," Carrie promised as she settled Katy on her hip. "If you two need anything, holler."

"We will," Gavin said, reclaiming his seat beside me.

For a moment, I thought he'd pick up where he'd left off before Carrie had interrupted us, but he just opened his laptop.

"Ready to go back down the rabbit hole?" he asked.

I nodded, and we dove back into trying to uncover more about Arthur Dalton. Gavin was using his contacts to track down anyone who might know something, while I did what I did best - following the money.

A couple of hours later, I let out a string of curses that I really hoped the kids couldn't hear. Gavin looked over as I leaned back, staring at my screen in disbelief.

"Is that frustration because you keep hitting brick walls, or did you find something?"

"Oh, I found something." I turned my laptop so he could see. "Do you want the details or the overview?"

"Overview," Gavin said. "If I have questions, I'll ask."

"The company Dalton's working with, Pendragon Holdings, is connected to a foreign group known for human trafficking."

"Fuck." Gavin ran his hand through his hair. "Trafficking."

"Indeed. I didn't go deep, but I checked it out to make sure it wasn't merely a handful of isolated rumors," I clarified. "It took me less than fifteen minutes to find enough to be fairly confident that it's not mere hearsay."

"Did I ever tell you that trafficking played a role in Skylar's mother's death?" Gavin asked quietly.

"What? No?"

"The guy I used to work for, the one who originally owned Club Privé, used it as one of his many fronts for one of the biggest trafficking rings in the country. He nearly trafficked Carrie."

I let out a low whistle.

"You said Dalton is shady, so chances are he knows about this company's reputation," Gavin continued. "I won't sell my club to someone who has no scruples about working with traffickers."

"I can't say I disagree," I said. "And I should warn you. As I have said before, I know Arthur Dalton will not be happy to hear he won't get what he wants."

My breath caught as I watched Gavin's eyes darken. "I don't give a damn if he's happy or not. He just needs to keep his hands off my club."

His phone rang, and I glimpsed the name on the screen. Laila Chiles. She was the new manager at the club. Gavin had told me he'd hired her so he could have more flexibility in his schedule now that they had another baby on the way.

Gavin put the call on speaker. "Hey, Laila."

"Gavin, I'm sorry to bug you, but there's an issue with a private party at the club."

The worry in Laila's voice put us both immediately on alert.

"We've got a couple of our girls in there and… I didn't want to call the cops, but…"

"I'm on my way," Gavin said as he ended the call.

"I'm coming with you."

I didn't know if Sienna was one of the women involved, but if she was, I wanted to be there. If she wasn't, well, Gavin might need some extra muscle. No way was I going to let my friend walk into an unknown situation alone.

Chapter Twelve

SIENNA

I mostly enjoyed managing the private parties at the club. The clientele were usually wealthy and generous tippers. It was typically quieter than the main area, and sometimes the guests were fascinating. At worst, they'd be dull and stingy with gratuities.

Occasionally, though, even Gavin's thorough vetting couldn't keep out the jerks, and tonight seemed to be one of those times.

It had begun normally. I was in the room with my performers when Laila texted that the party had arrived. Since they'd requested the routine start immediately, Darcy cued the music, and I positioned everyone. The moment I spotted the first guest in the doorway, I signaled for the dancers to begin.

Five minutes in, I realized this wouldn't be a good night. It wasn't because the men were loudly chatting during the second run-through of the routine. No, it was their crude rating of my dancers' physical attributes and their use of offensive language about both the women and men performing. Their vulgar comments had me itching to call Laila to eject these jerks, but as long as their hands didn't wander too much, I'd let it slide. For now, anyway. I told myself if things escalated, I would take action.

As the routine finished, I quickly motioned for the dancers to exit the stage and went to the front to announce our 'special' performance would start in fifteen minutes. The hungry way the men eyed me now made my guard go up.

"Are you gonna be part of our special performance?" one man near the front asked as I walked away.

When I didn't answer, I heard him call me a stuck-up bitch, but I let the words roll off me. I had more important things to do, like warning the trio who actually were part of the special performance that our audience was... unpleasant.

Before entering the compact dressing room adjacent to the stage, I gently knocked. Waiting inside were JJ and Liza, the female performers scheduled for the evening, and

Dodd, our head of security who normally worked behind the scenes but tonight was making his debut as a performer. I'd been skeptical about his follow-through when he'd said he wanted to do this, but aside from his initial flirting, he'd been professional, completing paperwork and medical clearances. The women hadn't complained about him either, which made me decide to give him a real chance.

"Everyone ready?" I asked. All three wore Club Privé robes to be removed on stage, but I trusted their outfits underneath were the ones we'd discussed.

"We're good," Dodd said enthusiastically.

Liza nodded, but JJ gave me a searching look. She was one of our seasoned performers and knew how to read me better than Liza did.

"What's wrong?" the blonde asked.

"This group is a little cruder than our usual clientele," I said. "I don't think it'll be a problem, but if anyone says or does anything that makes you uncomfortable, use your safe word, and we'll stop things right then. Got it?"

They all nodded, and I confirmed each of their safe words. In all my time at the club, from a server until now, I'd never known of a performance where someone had to use it, but I believed in being prepared for anything. Something in my gut told me that the men at this party were bad news, not just in an 'all talk, no walk' kinda way, either.

After introducing the three performers by their stage names and reiterating the club's consent rules, I moved to the bar. As the trio took the stage, Gus approached me. The tattooed, bald bartender in his mid-forties had started here around the same time I had. He still worked as a bouncer mostly, but handled private party bartending too, providing extra security without seeming distrustful.

"I need to grab more tequila," he said. "The party booker didn't restock."

I nodded, eyes fixed on the stage where Dodd and the women were disrobing and settling in. The party had requested a FFM threesome scene with male domination, so Dodd, wearing only tight black briefs, began by ordering Liza to undress JJ.

As the performance continued, my mind drifted. Usually, some shows here turned me on, but this one left me cold. I wasn't sure if it was the room's vibe or my lack of attraction to Dodd, but I only paid enough attention to intervene if needed.

As the show progressed, the audience grew louder and rowdier, tension building until something had to give.

That something was the guy who'd called me a bitch earlier.

He suddenly lurched up, shouting, "Gonna get me some of that!"

My first thought was *who actually talks like that*, quickly followed by, *oh shit, he's going for the stage.*

Gus had vanished for more alcohol, leaving me the closest non-performer. Without thinking, I ran to intercept the asshole, putting myself between him and the stage. He stumbled to a stop as everything froze for a split second before he leered at me.

"You'll do."

He lunged at me, triggering chaos throughout the room. I focused solely on my immediate threat as pandemonium erupted around us. True to drunken form, Mr. Grabby-hands aimed straight for my chest.

I sidestepped and warned, "Back off."

His flushed face contorted uglily. "No one talks to me like that, 'specially not an uptight cunt whore."

Ignoring his words, I watched his movements. A woman's scream momentarily distracted me, and I paid for it. His fingers clamped onto my upper arm, yanking me against him. The stench of liquor assaulted me as I struggled, pushing away with my free hand, but his grip only tightened. Panic crept in as I jerked sideways. Though still trapped, the new angle revealed another man pulling a gun from his waistband.

Screams filled the air as he waved it, and I suddenly thought I was going to die.

Then, like a scene from an action movie, the door

burst open. Gavin and Fury charged in, Gavin bee-lining for the gunman while Fury rushed toward me, his eyes blazing with unprecedented intensity. My jaw dropped as Fury grabbed my assailant and slammed his fist into the man's face. He crumpled, unconscious, before hitting the floor.

"Get them out of my club," Gavin commanded, his quiet tone belying his anger as security rounded up the men. "They're banned for life. Photograph every one of them. Anyone who lets them in again is fired."

"Are you okay?" Fury's concern drew my attention back to him.

I nodded, my heart still hammering against my ribcage.

"Sienna." Gavin came over. "Are you hurt?"

"I'm okay," I said.

"Sienna, I'm so sorry." Dodd rushed off the stage, clutching a robe in front of him like an afterthought.

"Dodd." Gavin's eyes narrowed. "Is this the private party you rented the room for?"

Dodd's cheeks turned red. "Yeah," he mumbled.

"You want to tell me, then, how my head of security missed someone bringing a gun into my club?" Gavin took a step into Dodd's personal space, enough to make Dodd swallow hard, Adam's apple bobbing as he tried not to retreat. "Not only that, but no doubt those guys are affiliated. Mobsters." Gavin shook his head. "Fucking head of security."

"I'm so sorry," Dodd apologized. "I guess I was just really focused on getting this performance right since it's my first one and I didn't think—"

"It's pretty clear that you didn't think," Gavin cut in.

"Please don't fire me."

Now Dodd was begging, and I had the sudden urge to walk away, so I didn't have to see it, but I was more or less trapped between the three men.

"Sienna, what do you..." Gavin's voice trailed off when he looked down at my arm.

I followed his line of sight and saw that the place where I'd been grabbed was already turning black and blue.

"Dodd, you're fired." The words were ice cold. "Get dressed and get out of my club. And be thankful I'm not throwing your naked ass out on the street."

The color drained from Dodd's face, and I watched half a dozen emotions play across his features.

"Dodd's not the one who hurt me," I mumbled. All eyes were on me now. "And he protected JJ and Liza when the fight broke out. He made a mistake, but there's no permanent damage to anyone. Please don't fire him."

Dodd looked at Gavin hopefully and we all watched as our boss appeared to think things through.

"All right," Gavin said. "You're not fired."

Dodd's relief was short-lived.

"But you're no longer the head of security. I can't have someone making that big of a mistake and staying in charge." Gavin jerked his thumb over his shoulder. "You're working the door until further notice. Starting now. Get some clothes on and get out there."

I caught a flash of anger in Dodd's eyes, but then he nodded and headed toward the dressing room.

"As for the rest of you," Gavin raised his voice, addressing everyone in the room. "Take the night off with pay. If you're still shaken up on Monday, call off. It won't count against your sick days." He looked down at me. "That includes you."

I nodded instead of arguing, which should've told me I was more freaked out than I was showing. I was trying hard to bury everything until I could be alone. I knew once I actually processed what'd happened, I'd need time to pull myself together.

"I'm going to get my things from the office," I said, giving Gavin and Fury each a smile before calmly walking away.

I closed the door to my office and leaned against it, finally letting out the breath I'd been holding. My legs trembled, and I slid down to the floor, wrapping my arms around myself. The reality of what had just happened hit me like a freight train.

"Fuck," I whispered, my voice shaking. "Fuck, fuck, fuck."

A gun. There had been a fucking gun in the club. Inside the room where my dancers were performing. Where I was standing. The image of that asshole waving it around flashed through my mind, and I felt bile rise in my throat.

I scrambled to my feet and barely made it to the trash can before emptying the contents of my stomach. As I wiped my mouth with the back of my hand, I caught sight of the bruise forming on my arm. It was an angry purple, a stark reminder of how close I'd come to... what? Being assaulted? Shot?

I thought about JJ and Liza, how scared they must have been. And Dodd... God, what a mess. He'd fucked up, sure, but he didn't deserve to lose everything over one mistake. At least Gavin had listened to me.

A knock at the door made me jump, my heart racing. I quickly wiped my face, trying to compose myself.

"Come in," I called, hoping my voice didn't betray me.

The door opened, and Fury stepped in, his eyes immediately locking onto mine. I saw concern etched across his face, and something else... anger? No, not anger. Worry.

"Sienna," he said softly, closing the door behind him. "Are you okay?"

I nodded, not trusting my voice. He took a step closer,

and I could see him battling with himself, like he wanted to reach out but wasn't sure if he should.

"I'm sorry," he said suddenly, running a hand through his hair. "I'm sorry if I scared you earlier. When I saw that guy with his hands on you, I just... I saw red. I didn't think, I just acted."

I blinked, surprised. "You're apologizing? Fury, you have nothing to be sorry for. You saved me. You and Gavin... if you hadn't shown up when you did..." I trailed off, unable to finish the thought.

He moved closer, close enough that I could feel the heat radiating off his body. "I've never felt that kind of rage before," he admitted. "The thought of someone hurting you... it made me want to tear him apart."

My breath caught in my throat. The intensity in his eyes was overwhelming, and I leaned towards him, drawn in.

For a moment, it seemed like he was going to kiss me. His eyes flicked down to my lips, and I felt my heart race for an entirely different reason. But then, just as quickly as the moment had come, it passed. Fury stepped back, clearing his throat.

"I should go," he said abruptly. "Gavin probably needs help to deal with the aftermath. You should head home, get some rest."

Before I could respond, he was gone, the door closing

behind him with a soft click. I stared at the space where he'd been standing, more confused than ever.

What the hell just happened? One minute he's looking at me like I'm the only person in the world, and the next he's running out the door like I've got the plague. I couldn't make sense of it.

This had been such a weird day. I needed a drink.

Probably more than one.

Chapter Thirteen

FURY

I stormed out of Sienna's office before I could succumb to my urges and kiss her senseless. Maybe even bend her over her desk and make her forget the past hour. But it was clear that she needed some time to think things through, not for me to act like a Neanderthal, which I definitely would have if I had stayed. Every primal instinct in my body screamed at me to take her, claim her, lose myself in her. To just let everything go and surrender to passionate desire.

And that would've been an even bigger mistake than our impulsive encounter a couple of days ago.

I shoved my hands into my pockets to conceal their trembling and kept my head down as I headed for the exit.

As I hit the cool night air, I realized my usual coping mechanism wasn't an option anymore. The thought of seeking out a casual hookup left me cold. There was only one woman I craved, and she was decidedly off-limits.

Gavin's warning echoed in my mind, and I hated to admit it, but maybe he had a point. I was far from the calm, composed man Sienna needed right now. The way I'd lost control earlier proved that.

I pulled out my phone, thumbing through my contacts until I found Carson's name.

Even though Carson and Cory were twins, I'd always been closer to Cory, even before we'd gone into business together. Still, it wouldn't be weird for me to reach out to him, especially since he'd already invited me over for dinner. I hadn't been able to take him up on it yet, so this could take care of two birds with one stone.

Making my way to my car, I texted Carson, asking if he wanted to meet for a drink. His reply was quick enough that I didn't feel guilty about pulling him away from his gorgeous fiancée, Vix. He gave me the name of the place to meet him and I plugged it into my GPS. Thirty minutes later, I entered the bar and looked around for a familiar face.

While Carson and Cory were fraternal twins and had slightly different coloring, their features were similar enough that it sometimes felt like looking at Cory with baby blue contacts and hair dyed a burnished copper. The pair of them had even pulled off switching once in a while when we were teens, though only if they could wear hats and sunglasses.

I weaved through the crowd, my eyes scanning until they locked onto Carson's familiar form at the bar. My shoulders relaxed a fraction as he caught sight of me, his hand lifting in a welcoming wave.

"I ordered us each a beer," Carson said, sliding a frosty glass toward me as I settled onto the neighboring stool.

"Thanks," I muttered, wrapping my fingers around the cool glass. The condensation dampened my palm as I lifted it to my lips, the bitter taste a welcome distraction.

Carson's brow furrowed, his eyes searching my face. "Everything okay?"

I let out a long, weary breath, feeling the weight of the day pressing down on me. "Not even close," I admitted, my voice rough with frustration and barely contained emotion.

"So is this a 'I want to sit silently with someone and brood over whatever's going on' or a 'I need to talk before I punch someone' kind of thing?" Carson's mouth quirked into a small smile but I couldn't blame him.

"Shit." I shook my head. "Sorry. Seeing you the first time since I got here should have been just because we're family, not because I'm having a shitty day."

"Hey, no need to feel guilty," Carson assured me. "That wasn't my intent. I just wanted to know what you needed."

I raised an eyebrow. "Okay, we weren't raised in an emotional vacuum, but I don't remember you being insightful."

He shrugged. "Wait until you spend more time with Vix. She just brings out that sort of thing in people."

We sat for a couple minutes in silence, nursing our drinks, until I decided to talk.

"Honestly, I'm not sure what I want right now," I admitted. "My head feels like it's about to explode and I knew if I went home, or even if I just did something physical like working out, I'd be too keyed up to sleep at all tonight."

"Well," Carson said, "maybe you need to share some of what's in your head. Talk to me."

I didn't know if it was me missing spending time with Cory, maybe being a little homesick, or knowing Carson was probably right, but after taking another drink of my beer, I opened my mouth and the story poured out. Everything from Sienna picking me up at the airport to me kissing her and walking away tonight. I told him about Gavin warning me off and how I was starting to think he might be right.

When I finished, I took a gulp of my beer and waited

for words of wisdom from my cousin. He had a thoughtful expression on his face as he finished his beer and leaned on the bar.

"Vix didn't have the best time growing up," Carson said slowly. "And it sounds like Gavin's saying that Sienna didn't either, so I understand why he's being protective. But maybe, if she's experienced that much trauma, what she really needs is the freedom to make her own decisions instead of having someone else make them for her—whether it's Gavin telling you to back off or you choosing to follow Gavin's orders instead of asking her what she wants. Sometimes we think we're acting for someone's own good, but in reality, we're hurting them more by treating them like they shouldn't have a say in their own lives."

I took a sip of my beer as I mulled over Carson's words. He was right, of course. In trying to protect Sienna, we might be inadvertently taking away her choice. The thought made me uncomfortable, forcing me to confront my own paternalistic instincts.

"You're right," I admitted. "I've been so caught up in my head, in what I think is best for her, that I never even considered asking what she wants."

Carson nodded. "It's an easy trap to fall into, especially when you care about someone. But Fury, if you really like this woman, you need to treat her as an equal. Let her make her own choices, even if those choices might end up hurting her—or you."

I let out a long breath, feeling some of the tension leave my body. "Thanks, man. I needed to hear that."

"Anytime," Carson replied, raising his glass in a mock toast. "Now, how about we order some food? I'm starving."

Grateful for the change of subject, I flagged down the waitress. We ordered a couple of burgers and another round of drinks. As we waited for our food, I shifted the focus off my love life.

"So, how's the design business going?" I asked, genuinely interested. Carson had always had a genius flair for fashion, and I was proud of how successful he'd become.

Carson's eyes lit up. "It's going great, actually. I just landed a contract to design a line of sustainable, size-inclusive formalwear for a major department store chain."

"That's fantastic!" I said. "Congratulations, man. You've worked hard for this."

He nodded, a mix of pride and excitement on his face. "Thanks. It's been a long time coming, but it feels good to see all that effort paying off. And the best part is, I get to stick to my principles. No compromise on sustainability or inclusivity."

"That's always been important to you," I observed. "I

remember when you first started out, how passionate you were about making fashion accessible to everyone."

Carson chuckled. "Yeah, I was pretty idealistic back then. Still am, I guess. But now I have the clout to actually make it happen on a larger scale."

Our food arrived, and we dug in, the conversation flowing easily between bites. It felt good to catch up with Carson, to talk about something other than my own problems for a while. As I savored the rich flavors of my burger, I finally relaxed. There was something comforting about being with family. It was a reminder that even in the midst of life's challenges, there were still moments of pure joy and connection. And for that, I was grateful.

Chapter Fourteen

SIENNA

I hadn't even considered calling off today. I spent yesterday cleaning my apartment and relaxing with junk food and *Friends* reruns, so I felt together enough to treat Monday normally. The fact that I'd scheduled auditions for a new dancer to replace Venus played a role, too. I didn't want to let Gavin down, especially after what happened with Dodd.

When I arrived at the club, Gus was already outside, looking grim.

"You okay?" he asked. "I should've been there when everything went down."

"It's not your fault," I assured him. "Is Gavin increasing security?"

Gus nodded. "He's not taking chances. Everyone remotely connected to security is doing extra rotations. Except Dodd. He's restricted to door duty, never alone."

I winced. "That must be tough."

I felt bad for Dodd, and I was glad I'd spoken up to keep him from being fired, but I agreed with Gavin that consequences were necessary. Honestly, I wasn't sure if I'd have felt safe at the club if Dodd had remained in charge of security.

"Well, I'm glad you're alright," Gus said, punching in the code and opening the door for me.

I resisted the urge to touch my bruised arm. I usually wore short sleeves with a jacket to adapt to the club's temperature fluctuations, but tonight I'd chosen lace sleeves - light enough if I got hot, but dense enough to conceal the marks. I'd used makeup to cover them, but knew it could wear off, and I didn't want anyone seeing the bruises and recalling what happened. Some employees here had dark pasts, and we'd promised them safety. I wanted them to feel secure again.

Entering the club, I plastered on my brightest smile and greeted everyone I passed en route to my office. The time I spent preparing for the auditions had me ready to set a positive example for my co-workers.

By the second potential dancer, I almost felt like things

were back to normal. That alone should have warned me that trouble was brewing.

"I don't need a fucking escort! I assure you, I'm quite familiar with this club's layout. I'm always thorough regarding my investments."

An unfamiliar male voice, raised in anger, drew my attention to the employee hallway. Moments later, a tall, lean man I didn't recognize appeared, followed closely by a visibly irritated Gus.

"And I told you, I don't care who you are," Gus said tensely. "Unless Mr. Manning explicitly instructs me to allow someone unsupervised access outside operating hours, it's my job to keep eyes on them."

The stranger's lip curled into a sneer. "Well, if I have any say, it won't be your job much longer."

His icy gaze swept over the handful of workers performing their usual tasks, lingering inappropriately on the women. I saw plenty of lust in his expression, but there was something beneath the leering - something calculating and assessing, as if he were mentally cataloging each person he saw.

"It's good to see Gavin still has excellent taste in eye candy," he remarked, seemingly to no one in particular, yet expecting everyone to hang on his every word. "New outfits will need to be issued to maximize everyone's assets."

What the hell was he talking about?

"Of course, the male-to-female ratio will need adjustment. While there's some demand for men in these establishments, women are definitely more lucrative." His eyes fell on Bernie, our head of cleaning, taking in her age and the scar on her cheek. "We'll also need to implement appearance regulations. We can't have a sex club where employees' looks turn men off."

Before any of us could figure out how to respond or who this man even was, Gavin appeared, looking as unhappy as he had on Saturday night. He also looked exhausted, beyond mere sleeplessness.

"Thank you, Gus," Gavin said. "I'll take it from here." He turned to the older man. "Mr. Dalton, if you'll come with me, we'll have our meeting in my office."

Shooting a look over his shoulder at Gus, this Mr. Dalton said, "You know, Mr. Manning, I expected better of your hires, as their continued employment will only be guaranteed if they do their jobs. And I'm sure you'll agree, accosting and harassing their new employer is hardly the way to make a good first impression."

He actually sniffed, like some blue-blood deigning to mingle with commoners. Judging by his clothes and stick-up-his-ass walk, I didn't doubt he had money. But if I'd learned anything about pretentious wealthy people, it was that no amount of money could buy class or respect. I didn't know who this silver-haired man with sharp blue eyes was, but I already disliked him.

As Gavin and Mr. Dalton disappeared toward the elevator, I looked at Gus and asked, "What the fuck was that about?"

Gus shook his head. "No idea. He just showed up claiming he had a meeting with Gavin."

"Given the boss's mood, I expect he'll set that jerk straight," I said before turning my attention back to Rita, today's last auditioning server.

In her early thirties, she looked years younger and had a classic dancer's build. I just didn't know if she had the skills to match.

"You're up," I told her.

When she was in position on stage, I started her music and focused on her rather than whatever was transpiring in Gavin's office.

Or on the more persistent presence in my thoughts.

I'd been replaying Fury's apology and almost kiss before storming out of my office, ever since it happened, still unsure what it meant - or if it meant anything at all. For all I knew, it was a heat-of-the-moment thing, handled differently than our previous heated encounter.

And that, of course, led me to thinking about how he'd literally handled me last week...

I gave myself a mental shake as I realized I'd started

drifting. I had to get a grip. I was at work and needed to be professional. More importantly, it was disrespectful and rude to Rita, who'd clearly put significant time and effort into her routine. My job, my dancer, my co-workers, my friends - those were important. Not some random guy I'd hooked up with, no matter how hot the sex had been.

I jotted down a few notes and, as the music reached its end, prepared to ask some questions. I didn't get the chance because as soon as the music stopped, we could all hear raised voices coming from the direction of the elevator.

"I don't give a damn what Fury Gracen told you about me! We had a verbal agreement and now you're getting cold feet. I won't stand for it," Mr. Dalton shouted, his tanned skin flushed as he entered the room. "Do you understand me? I will ruin you."

Even from where I stood, I could see the muscles in Gavin's jaw clenching, but his voice remained calm as ever when he spoke.

"We made no deals. Nothing was signed. I said I'd consider your offer, and I did."

"You went to Fury Gracen and believed whatever lies he's telling about me." Mr. Dalton turned and pointed at Gavin, but his hand dropped almost immediately, as if he'd suddenly realized how much larger my boss was.

I didn't need to know Mr. Dalton to recognize that he

was used to being the biggest bully in the playground. Gavin, however, had the sort of presence that commanded attention.

"Fury and I discussed your offer," Gavin said. "And then I decided to decline it."

"You can't do that," Mr. Dalton protested, sounding more like a sulking child than a man in his late fifties.

Gavin raised an eyebrow. "I just did. And now you're going to leave before I have my security escort you out."

Mr. Dalton was practically shaking, but he turned on his heel and stormed toward the exit. Only at the door did he pause to throw one last parting remark over his shoulder.

"You'll be hearing from my lawyer!"

A moment of silence followed the slamming door, and everyone looked expectantly at Gavin. Instead of an explanation, he offered a single statement.

"The club's not going anywhere."

As he turned and walked away, my co-workers formed groups, their voices hushed as they discussed what had just transpired. I didn't join them. While I wanted details about that argument and reassurance that not only was the club staying but Gavin as well, something else in the exchange between the two men had caught my attention and wouldn't let go.

Fury had known about the offer, had discussed it with

Gavin... and hadn't said a word to me about it. Even though he knew how important my job was to me, he didn't even hint at the possibility that I could end up unemployed soon.

The anger churning inside me, however, was nothing compared to the unexpected hurt I felt.

This was exactly why I didn't trust men. Or anyone, really. I was the only one who looked out for me. That was how it had always been and how it would continue to be.

Chapter Fifteen

FURY

My heart raced as I stepped into Club Privé, silently praying that Gavin wouldn't be here. He'd be livid if he found out why I was at the club. I hadn't breathed a word about Sienna during our earlier discussion about Arthur, nor had I revealed my conversation with Carson about letting Sienna choose for herself who she wanted to see. Honestly, I hadn't planned on coming here at all, but Sienna still consumed my thoughts, and I couldn't shake her from my mind.

Her body moving against mine, her fierce strength, the fire in her eyes as she stood up to me. I recalled her compassion for Dodd, despite the danger he'd put her in, and how vulnerable she'd looked in her office. The taste of her kiss lingered on my lips. Most of all, I couldn't shake how I felt being inside of her.

My carefully constructed arguments for staying away had crumbled in the face of Carson's simple logic. The more I mulled it over, the more I agreed - it should be Sienna's choice. When the thought of waiting any longer to see her became unbearable, I gave in and hailed a car for the club.

The absence of a line outside told me it was a private night. After the recent incident, I couldn't blame Gavin for being cautious. I felt a wave of relief wash over me when I saw Dodd wasn't at the door. The urge to deck him for his negligence, which had put everyone in danger, simmered just beneath the surface, ready to boil over at any moment.

Inside, I paused, letting my eyes adjust to the dim lighting before scanning the room for Sienna. Though I wasn't certain she was working tonight after what happened, I had a hunch she'd want to set an example for her performers by being here.

The Monday night crowd was thin, making it easy to spot her tall, slender figure by the bar. She was chatting with two men, and I felt a stab of jealousy as I approached. It faded when I saw the shorter, muscular man wrap his arm around his partner's waist.

Their conversation seemed light, so I sidled up to the

bar nearby, close enough to eavesdrop while I ordered a drink. Sienna didn't notice me as I positioned myself behind the couple.

"This is only our second time here," the shorter one was saying. "So we're still getting used to the system you guys use to show who's up for what."

His partner jumped in, "What my partner is trying to say, and doing it poorly, is that we weren't sure if you're one of the employees we're allowed to ask to join us in a private room."

I felt my body tense, jealousy flaring anew.

Sienna's eyes widened. "Oh, okay, I wasn't expecting that."

The taller man continued, "We get that a lot. Everyone sees two men together and they assume homosexual, but we're actually both bisexual. We're not interested in having a polyamorous relationship or an open relationship, but every once in a while, we get in the mood for something ... different, you know?"

His partner chimed in, "That's why when we moved here, we were so excited to find Club Privé. Knowing we could come here to a safe place, find someone to play with, and not have to worry about messy fallout, well, it just made us love the Big Apple even more."

My patience wore thin as they rambled on. I fought the urge to interrupt, to claim Sienna as mine. I knew that would be a dick move, one she would hate. So I held my tongue, waiting for her response. If she wanted to go with them, it had to be her choice. I wasn't about to let my possessiveness ruin things before they even started, but holding back my temper was a struggle.

"So, what do you say, gorgeous? Want to spend the rest of the night being thoroughly pleasured by two men at the same time?"

I couldn't take it anymore. I straightened, turning towards them. All three looked my way. I caught a glimpse of the men's faces as they glanced between Sienna and me, but my focus was on her. Her eyes met mine for a split second before darting away, a blush creeping up her cheeks. I could sense the men shifting uncomfortably, suddenly aware they'd stepped into something they hadn't expected.

I watched the shorter man's face fall as he broke the awkward silence. "Um, I guess we really did read things wrong," he mumbled, shifting his weight from foot to foot. "Didn't mean to step on any toes."

Sienna's chin lifted, her eyes flashing with defiance. "You didn't," she shot back, her tone daring me to contradict her.

I swallowed hard, forcing myself to stay calm. "She doesn't answer to me," I managed, my voice rougher than I intended. "It's her choice."

Her eyes met mine, widening slightly. The pleased light dancing in them made my stomach flip, a mix of relief and desire coursing through me.

"I'm flattered," Sienna said to the men, her lips curving into a smile. She reached behind the bar, the movement drawing my gaze to the graceful line of her arm. "But I'm going to pass." She produced a sheet of paper with a flourish. "Here's all the color coding to help you choose someone who will be a better match."

"Thank you." The taller man's eyes flicked to me, a knowing look in them as he nodded. I felt my jaw clench, but I forced myself to nod back, acknowledging the unspoken understanding between us.

I watched the couple retreat, their disappointment noticeable. As I stepped into the space they'd vacated, I moved closer to Sienna, hope fluttering in my chest. But when her eyes met mine, that hope shriveled. The fire in her gaze wasn't desire - it was anger.

Swallowing hard, I tried anyway. "Can we go somewhere and talk?"

Her eyes narrowed, lips pursing into a thin line. "That's a good idea. Come on."

I trailed after her, my mind racing. In her office, she motioned for me to close the door. As it clicked shut, she whirled on me, her fury scorching.

God help me, but her passion - even directed at me in anger - was intoxicating.

"What was all of that about?" she demanded, voice low and dangerous.

"All of what?" I asked, genuinely confused.

"Out there, with those guys."

I shrugged, aiming for nonchalance. "I said it was your choice if you wanted to go with them or not. Would you rather I went all caveman and threw you over my shoulder, dragged you back here, and bent you over your desk?"

The moment the words left my mouth, I regretted them. A vivid image of doing just that flashed through my mind, and I struggled to focus.

A blush crept up her neck, but her eyes still blazed. "I mean, why were you even there at the bar, anyway? Eavesdropping on me?"

"I came here to talk to you," I explained, frustration creeping into my voice. "When I saw you, I came over. But you were talking to someone, so I didn't want to interrupt. I'm not sure why you're pissed at me about that."

"I'm not," she snapped. "I'm pissed at you because you didn't tell me that Gavin wanted to sell Club Privé."

I took a step back, caught off guard. "Where did you hear that?"

She crossed her arms, her posture radiating tension. "He had a meeting today with Mr. Dalton, who made it very clear that he already looked at the club like it was his property. And he was not happy when Gavin told him he wouldn't be selling."

"Okay, if Gavin's not selling, why are you mad?"

"Because I had to find out the same way everyone else did, when I know for a fact that you already knew what Gavin was going to do and you didn't tell me."

I ran a hand through my hair, exasperated. "It wasn't my news to tell. Yeah, Gavin asked me about Dalton, but it's his business to do with what he wants, and that includes what he tells his employees and when he does it."

Her eyes flashed dangerously. "So it's okay for you to poke your nose in my business? Why is that?"

Something inside me snapped. I threw my hands into the air, words tumbling out in a desperate rush. "Because I can't stop thinking about you, okay? I came here to find out if you've been thinking about me too and I see you being propositioned by two men. Of course, I wanted to know what you were going to say. And, yes, I wanted you to send them away and choose to come with me. You drive me crazy in a million different ways, but I can't get enough of you." My voice cracked with raw emotion. "All right? Is that what you wanted to hear? That you're in my head? That I need you so badly that it hurts?"

Sienna stared at me, her eyes wide in surprise. My

confession hung in the air between us, heavy and charged. For two agonizing heartbeats, neither of us moved.

Then she launched herself at me.

Her mouth crashed against mine, hungry and desperate. I caught her instinctively, my arms wrapping around her. She fit perfectly against me, like she was made to be there. Like she belonged.

Chapter Sixteen

SIENNA

His words hit me like physical blows, staggering me. I'd had plenty of men tell me they wanted me, how attractive I was, but this wasn't the same. This wasn't a man who thought he had some sort of claim on me or that I owed him something. This was a strong, powerful man who could have any woman he wanted with a snap of his fingers, and I'd captured him. The way he said it, the pure need in his voice, it was as if he was my prisoner.

I only had one reaction that could let him know how his words made me feel.

I threw myself at him, knowing that he'd catch me, and crashed my mouth into his. He groaned, the hands now on my ass squeezing. I pushed my tongue between his lips, flicking against his teeth and tongue as I dug my fingers into his hair. The ache I'd been trying so hard to ignore was back stronger than ever. I knew all too well what he'd meant when he'd said that he needed me so badly that it hurt. I felt that pain now and knew there was only one cure for it.

It was probably irresponsible, unprofessional, and just a bad idea, but I didn't care. The last few days had been an emotional rollercoaster, and he promised something better than some fake, fairy tale romance. He offered forgetfulness. Complete and uncomplicated bliss.

Breaking the kiss, I pulled back far enough to meet his eyes. The intensity I saw there made my breath catch.

"I need you inside me," I whispered, my voice husky with desire.

A flicker of hesitation crossed his face, and I caught it immediately. My heart raced as I tried to guess what had him unsure.

"What is it?" I asked, running my fingers through his hair. "Talk to me."

He swallowed hard. "Sienna, I... I want this so badly. But are you sure? I mean, Gavin and-"

I pressed a finger to his lips, silencing him. "Shh. I'm sure. More than sure." I trailed my hand down his chest, feeling his muscles tense under my touch. "Unless you don't want to?"

His eyes darkened. "God, I want to. You have no idea how much."

I smirked, grinding my hips against him. "Oh, I think I have some idea."

He groaned, his hands tightening on my waist. "You're killing me, you know that?"

"That's not my intention at all," I purred, nipping at his earlobe. "Quite the opposite, actually."

The heat returned, and he set me on my feet. "You're gonna fulfill a fantasy I've had since the moment I met you."

Not giving me the chance to ask what that was, he spun me around to face my desk and put his hand against the small of my back. I didn't need a diagram to tell me what he wanted. I leaned forward, bracing myself on my elbows even though I knew I'd probably end up with my face against the cool, smooth surface at some point.

"You look good from any angle, but I have to say, this is definitely one of my favorites."

Cool air caressed my skin as he flipped up the back of my dress, exposing the black lace thong I wore underneath. He made a sound a lot like a growl and then gave one cheek a smack, hard enough to sting, but not even close to what it'd take to make me protest.

His hand slid down between my legs, moving aside the damp fabric to touch my sensitive skin. Without giving me a warning, he shoved a finger inside me, and I cried out, clenching around the intruding digit.

"Tell me if it's too much." The rough edge to his voice told me that even though this wasn't fueled by anger, he would not be gentle.

"It's good." The words came out breathless, but I couldn't find it in me to be embarrassed because at that moment, he added a second finger and my brain short-circuited.

My head fell forward, my eyes closing as I blocked out everything but the sensation of his fingers thrusting and twisting inside me. The first time we'd had sex, I'd been worked up from arguing, making me wet enough that it'd only been the pressure from his size that'd put a little pain into things. That wasn't the case right now. I was turned on by the kiss and his words, but my body hadn't quite caught up to where the rest of me was and even his fingers caused enough friction to burn as he worked to get me ready.

Just as I approached the point of actually hurting, his knuckles pushed against my g-spot and my entire body jerked. He chuckled and rotated his hand so that he could rub against that spot inside me. I hadn't realized that he'd gone to his knees until his mouth was on me, tongue soothing even as his fingers kept up their relentless motion inside me.

When I came, my lungs emptied into a soundless scream. My knees almost buckled from the force of it and my arms gave out, the upper half of my body collapsing on the desk. I felt a sharp sting from what felt like teeth, but then his fingers were gone, giving my g-spot one final stroke before they left me empty. A mini orgasm rolled through me, and I shuddered. Every bit of me was tingling and I knew we weren't done yet.

Somehow, Fury kept me on my feet and still get a condom from somewhere and roll it on. While we'd covered the fact that we didn't necessarily need it, I appreciated he hadn't assumed that it was okay this time.

That fleeting thought was all I had time for because he was positioning himself at my entrance. He leaned over my back and put his mouth to my ear.

"Say *yes*."

I wiggled my ass, trying to push back against him, some part of me wanting to resist even though I definitely still wanted him to fuck me.

"Say *yes*, Sienna, and I'll give you what you want." The teasing note in his voice was low, sensual. "A good, hard fucking."

I made a mewling sound that turned into an annoyed growl when he chuckled. "Just do it already."

He made a tsking noise and nipped my earlobe. "Not until you say *yes*." He scraped his teeth against the side of my neck. "And then I'll make you scream. Take you so hard that you'll feel me for days."

Fuck.

My competitive nature was no match for my libido. "Yes. Okay? I said it. Yes. Just fuck–"

He drove the last word from my mind as surely as he drove the air from my lungs. I was suddenly, impossibly, full, stretched around the thick length of him. He held himself there as he wrapped my braid around his hand and pulled my head back.

"This is going to be hard and fast," he warned. "Tell me if it's too much."

And that was all the warning I got before he started moving, slamming into me hard enough to make my desk shake. As I got my feet underneath me, I pushed back against him, refusing to passively take what he was giving me. With every withdrawal, I tightened around him, earning an extra tug on my hair and a muttered curse from my partner, both of which just added to the pleasure racing across my nerves.

I was getting close … and impatient.

Sneaking my hand beneath me, I slipped my fingers beneath the tiny triangle of the front of my panties. I'd barely brushed against my clit before Fury was bent over my back again, his hand closing around my wrist.

"Fury," I ground out his name.

"I get to make you come," he said, squeezing just enough to make me catch my breath.

Then, instead of pulling my hand away, he slid his fingers between mine so that we were teasing my clit together. The new position kept him from going too deep, but there was something about the way he covered me, surrounded me, that spoke to the mental part of what we were doing.

When he pressed his lips to the bare skin at the top of my spine, it sent a shiver through me that was more than just physical. I whimpered his name, my breathing quickening as I felt the familiar build-up. I was so close.

"Need ... need ... Fury..."

"That's right," he said. "Got what you need."

Pushing himself deep, he pulled my head back to a nearly painful angle. As he fastened his lips to the side of my throat, my breathing stuttered. I felt the pull of his mouth and the sting of his teeth, and knew he was leaving a mark, but I couldn't tell him not to. Not when it was that realization that tipped me over the edge.

I came with a wail, Fury's and my fingers pressing against my throbbing clit to draw out my climax. My pussy was still pulsing around him as his hips jerked against me once, twice, and on the third time, he let out a groan that sounded a lot like my name.

We stayed there for a minute, catching our breath and

letting our pulses return to normal. He was just starting to get too heavy when he let out a sigh and straightened. I made a strangled sound when he pulled out and barely caught myself before my wobbly legs completely gave out.

I heard him rustling around in my desk but didn't have the strength yet to look up. By the time I managed to stand, he held out some hand wipes. I thanked him quietly, but that was all either of us said as we cleaned ourselves up. The silence wasn't awkward between us, but charged, as if we hadn't been using up the attraction between us, but ramping it up.

He was the one who finally broke the silence. "I've got to go. It's a weeknight and I have a meeting fairly early tomorrow."

I nodded. "Yeah, okay."

I knew I still sounded a little dazed, but having two toe-curling orgasms would do that to a girl. He flashed me a slightly arrogant smile—one that he'd more than earned—and went to the door. Instead of leaving, though, he paused, turned, and came back to me. With a familiar hunger in his eyes, he grabbed the back of my neck and yanked me to him, covering my mouth in a fierce, scorching kiss.

It lasted only a few seconds and then he was gone, with me staring at the doorway, trying not to panic. I'd frozen when he'd kissed me, but thanks to years of needing to hide my emotions to survive, I managed to relax and kiss him back enough that he didn't notice that anything was wrong. Only after he closed the door behind him did I let out the breath I'd been holding, and sank down to the floor.

I could hear my teeth chattering and feel my body shaking, but those things felt very far away. Everything was far away as my mind took me back several years, back to a time I really didn't like to think about too much.

But sometimes, I didn't have a choice.

His fingers dug into the back of my neck, pulling me to him for a kiss I didn't want. He pushed his tongue into my mouth, making me gag.

"If you gag on my cock like that, I'll cut your fucking tongue out."

I squeezed my eyes shut, as if that could stop what I was seeing, even though it was in my head.

His hand on my neck was familiar now, as was the pain from his grip. I'd have bruises the size and shape of his fingers by the time he was done. As he used his hold on me to keep me from backing off when he shoved his cock between my lips. I focused on trying to breathe whenever I could, but the black spots dancing behind my eyelids said I was probably going to pass out. Again.

My breathing was ragged, coming in gasps as if I was being choked, even though I knew that wasn't happening.

Logically, I knew I was having a panic attack and flashbacks. It had happened to me before. But I could only ride it out. I'd never been able to stop them before. Just like I'd never been able to stop him.

I'd begged not to go with him, but had only gotten a slap as an answer. Now I was cringing away from him, even though I knew it'd just piss him off. And I couldn't escape. The moment I felt that hand on my neck, I froze, all hope draining out of me.

Tears streamed down my cheeks as the images finally stopped coming. Once able to breathe, I took in large gulps of air and waited for the nausea that always came with one of these attacks. They usually only happened as nightmares now, but the moment Fury had grabbed the back of my neck, it was like I was back there again.

I couldn't do this. I couldn't risk having another one of those attacks. I had too much going on, too much at stake. I couldn't be distracted. If I could've guaranteed that I could avoid all triggers, maybe it would've worked, but I couldn't control every aspect of our lives. Fury wasn't that sort of man. And if I was being honest with myself, I wouldn't have wanted him if he was that sort of guy. But wanting him didn't mean I could be with him.

Chapter Seventeen

FURY

I couldn't remember the last time my heart had raced with such anticipation for a weekend. Back in Palo Alto, work had consumed my Saturdays and Sundays, and while I'd squeezed in family time and the occasional date, this feeling of excitement was entirely new.

And all for what? Just more time at Club Privé.

A horn blared behind me, jolting me back to reality. The light had turned green. My fingers twitched, tempted to flip off the impatient driver, but I reined in my temper.

As I continued my drive, my mind wandered again.

At the next stop, Sienna's face swam into focus. If I'd hoped our encounter earlier this week would quench my thirst for her, I was sorely mistaken. If anything, she occupied my thoughts even more now. But the tone had shifted. Beyond my lingering desire, worry had crept in.

Every time I'd visited the club, I'd seen her, but our interactions had been brief and distant. No repeat of our passionate encounter. I'd tried to rationalize it - she was busy, just like I would be if she'd spent all day in my office. But my gut twisted, knowing that something was off. Her smile didn't quite reach her eyes, which now held a guarded look. As if she didn't trust me anymore.

What drove me mad was not knowing why. When did things change between us? It hadn't been anything dramatic - I would have addressed it immediately if it had been. But thinking back, I pinpointed the moment. During our intimate encounter, everything had been electric. She'd matched me passion for passion, giving as good as she got. But just before I'd left, something had flickered in her eyes. So fleeting, I'd almost missed it.

Now, that moment haunted me. Had I said something to anger her? Had I been too rough? The thought that I might have hurt her, made her feel she needed to hide her true feelings, made bile rise in my throat.

Gavin's warning about Sienna's baggage echoed in my mind, tempering my self-blame. I didn't know the extent of her past trauma. It could have been a messy break-up, or it could have been something far more sinister. Rage boiled in my veins at the thought of someone hurting her. The feeling was all too familiar, reminding me of when we'd discovered what had happened to my step-cousin, Maggie. If her abuser hadn't already been behind bars when we found out, the McCrae-Carideo-Gracen family might have ended up there ourselves.

If someone had hurt Sienna like that, if that was why she now seemed wary of me, I wasn't sure I could control myself.

But I needed to know. If she simply didn't want me anymore, I could handle that. But if I'd done something to frighten her, I had to make it right. The question was, how could I broach such a delicate subject with her?

As I pulled into the parking garage attached to my office building, I had to admit that this might've been exactly what Gavin had tried to warn me about. I still believed Carson was right about letting Sienna make her own decisions, but now I wondered if I should've taken Gavin's warning more seriously. I would have still wanted her, but instead of just jumping into sex, maybe we should have actually talked first.

I just didn't think clearly around her. Too much blood rushing to other places, apparently.

And I didn't think that was going to change soon. Even though she'd basically been giving me the cold shoulder for the past few days, it didn't change how I felt about her. If anything, it made things worse because I just wanted to know what was wrong and how to fix it. I didn't want to walk away from her because it might be hard or because she might have issues to work through.

As I rode up the elevator to our floor, I tried to figure out the best way to clear my head enough to focus on work, but all of that went out the window when I stepped onto the thirty-seventh floor and saw what awaited me.

The first thing that registered was that I wasn't alone despite the early hour. Jules stood just a few feet away, as if she'd started walking before her brain had processed what she was seeing and had frozen in place. The second thought that went through my head was that I needed to find out if whoever had done this was still here.

This was total and complete vandalism. Every chair was overturned, every computer monitor on the floor destroyed. The office doors were all open, some broken as if the vandal had found them locked and had kicked them in. Keyboards and other equipment were scattered all over the floor, broken. Papers were everywhere, some shredded, some just thrown around. And there were holes in the walls. Based on the debris in the same area, it looked like whoever had done this had picked up chairs and slammed them into the walls. Vulgarities and slurs were scrawled across desks and walls alike, making me see red.

A choked sound from Jules pushed back my rage. Her safety was what mattered most.

I hurried toward her. "Jules?"

She spun around, her face pale. "Fury. I just got here and... I didn't touch anything. I didn't know what to do."

"You did the right thing," I assured her, my mind racing. "Have you called the police?"

"Not yet," she admitted. "I was waiting for you. I didn't want to make that call without your permission."

I nodded, already pulling out my phone. "I'll call them now. Can you get in touch with building security? We need to know how this happened."

As Jules hurried off to make the call, I dialed 911, my eyes still scanning the wreckage of our office. Who would do this? And why? We were new in town, barely making waves yet. It didn't make sense.

The next hour passed in a blur. Jules and I waited in the lobby, watching as a parade of police officers and crime scene techs made their way up to our floor. I answered what felt like a million questions, my frustration growing with each repetition.

"Mr. Gracen?" A tall, broad-shouldered officer approached me, notepad in hand. "I'm Officer Richardson. I'd like to ask you a few more questions, if you don't mind."

I suppressed a sigh. "Of course, Officer. What else can I tell you?"

Richardson flipped open his notepad. "Can you think

of anyone who might have a motive to do this? Any business rivals or personal enemies?"

I ran a hand through my hair, wracking my brain. "Honestly, no. We're new in town, still getting established. We haven't made any enemies that I know of."

"You said your other office is in California. What about back there?" he pressed. "Anyone who might have followed you here?"

I shook my head. "I left things on good terms there. This doesn't make any sense."

Richardson nodded, jotting something down. "What about your employees? Anyone recently been fired or passed over for promotion?"

"No, nothing like that," I said firmly. "We're still building our team here. Everyone's new."

The officer's eyes narrowed slightly. "Mr. Gracen, I have to ask. Is there anything you're not telling us? Anything that might shed light on this situation?"

I bristled at the implication. "Officer, I want to find out who did this as much as you do. If I knew anything that could help, I'd tell you."

Richardson held my gaze for a moment, then nodded. "Alright. We'll be interviewing all your employees and reviewing the security footage. In the meantime, I'm afraid you won't be able to use the office today. But I'd appreciate it if you could stay nearby while we question your staff."

I nodded, frustration bubbling up inside me. "Of course. Whatever you need."

As Richardson walked away, I slumped into one of the lobby chairs, my head in my hands. This was not how I'd imagined my day going.

Chapter Eighteen

SIENNA

I DRUMMED my manicured nails against the polished surface, syncing with the pulsating rhythm barely audible to my sultry performers. It was unusual for me to keep the volume so low, but with a fresh face gracing our stage tonight, I needed to ensure my commands could cut through if necessary.

My new dancer, Annie, was absolutely killing it. She'd mastered Venus's part in a heartbeat and took direction like a goddamn pro. Never once did she get her panties in a twist when I pointed out her rare missteps, and she powered through repetitive drills without so much as a peep. If only all my dancers had her can-do attitude.

Her presence had lit a fire under JJ's perfectly toned

ass, too. She'd never been a slacker, but Annie's arrival made me realize that before, this had just been another gig for JJ. Now she was savoring every sensual movement. I couldn't give two shits if they were hooking up or not from a professional standpoint. Personally? If they were getting freaky, more power to them.

One thing I loved about Club Privé was our "you do you" mentality. We had each other's backs, whether you wore your heart on your sleeve or kept that shit locked down tight.

Of course, we occasionally had to deal with some overbearing big brother/sister crap. Not the possessive kind—I'd sooner have a root canal than tolerate that here. No, just your garden-variety protective vibes. As someone who grew up without siblings, I actually appreciated it. Most of the time, anyway.

As my dancers' bodies intertwined on stage, executing their transition with the grace of synchronized swimmers, I nodded my approval. Dana, despite her laser focus, flashed me a victorious grin. I was relieved to see her back in the groove. Though this routine differed from the one she'd previously botched, her renewed concentration was as clear as the sweat glistening on her taut abs.

Ironically, I was the one struggling to concentrate this afternoon.

I'd been grappling with emotions ever since Fury and I had our steamy encounter. The crushing realization that I could never be with him again slammed into me like a ton of bricks. He'd shown up at the club the following night, and the one after that, persistent as hell. I'd kept my lips sealed about the panic attack and those gut-wrenching flashbacks, let alone what he'd unknowingly done to trigger them. Fury was the kind of stand-up guy who'd beat himself up over it, and I didn't want that on my conscience.

There was also the matter of my checkered past. He might've pieced together some bits based on my occasional slip-ups, and Gavin might've accidentally spilled some beans. But knowing I'd worked as an "escort" years ago was a far cry from hearing the gritty details.

The last thing I wanted was for Fury to look at me with that same pity everyone else did when they heard about the assaults. Pity... and that unspoken blame. Sure, he had no qualms about getting down and dirty at a sex club, so I doubted he'd slut-shame a woman. But whether that open-mindedness extended to sex workers? I wasn't about to roll those dice.

Unable to explain any of this to him, I'd resorted to ghosting. Or at least, I'd been trying to. It wasn't easy to ghost someone who kept showing up at the club like clockwork. I did my damnedest to ignore him, but he seemed oblivious to the fact that my lukewarm responses were more than just being swamped with work.

But last night, for the first time, Fury was a no-show at the club. Maybe he'd finally gotten the message.

Fury had been rolling in like clockwork the past few nights, but when his usual arrival time came and went without a glimpse of those broad shoulders, I got antsy. My neck was getting a workout from constantly looking over my shoulder, hoping to catch sight of him striding towards me with that cocky grin.

But he never showed.

I tried to convince myself it was a relief to do my job without him hovering over me, but the gnawing ache in my gut wouldn't let up.

He'd thrown in the towel.

Which was exactly what I wanted. Right? Or what I should have wanted, for christ's sake. After all, I'd been giving him the cold shoulder ever since we'd fucked that second time. I'd figured hooking up twice would've been enough to satisfy Fury's curiosity.

I'd never been the type of woman anyone fought to be around. Even after I got out of the life, guys only wanted me for one thing. Working here had at least given me a safe way to scratch an itch without having to figure out if some dude was going to turn out to be a psycho. I was content with that arrangement. I wanted nothing else.

I should've been relieved that Fury had moved on like every other guy. So why did it feel like someone had punched me in the gut?

"Can we get a water break?" JJ's voice cut through my thoughts and brought me back to what I was supposed to be doing.

"Yeah." I stood up and stretched my arms over my head, hoping the movement would help clear my mind. "Everyone, take a couple minutes and then we'll run through it one more time at full volume."

"Annie's looking good," Darcy said as she came up beside me. "Not as good as Venus, but there's potential there."

"Have you heard from her?" I asked. "Venus, I mean."

Darcy shook her head. "We weren't close or anything, so I didn't really expect her to reach out to me." Darby frowned. "I am surprised she hasn't come back here at all."

"What do you mean at all?" I asked.

"I overheard Laila saying that Venus still hasn't come to get her last check."

"Laila didn't mail it?"

Darcy shook her head. "I guess there's something in the file about not mailing it because she didn't want her roommate taking it."

Dammit. I rubbed my forehead. While I'd thought of Venus a few times this week, I hadn't been searching for her as hard as last week. If she'd moved, she should have called to have her check mailed to a new address.

My head hurt.

"Let me know if you hear anything about her," I told Darcy.

"Will do." Darcy nodded at me and headed back to her seat.

Deciding water was probably a good idea, I headed to the bar to take a bottle from the fridge as my thoughts turned back to Fury and his absence.

This was the problem. Over and over, I'd concluded about what I should want with Fury and I'd tell myself that I'd accepted it, but then I'd start going over things again, worrying at it like some dog with a bone.

And this time, I actually hoped he hadn't given up on me. Because what I really wanted, deep down in the darkest corners of my soul, was someone to fight for me. Someone who'd respect my boundaries when I set them but who could see through my smoke and mirrors to know that if they stuck around, proved that I could trust them to be there through thick and thin, something could change. Something electric and raw and real.

The sounds of my dancers returning gave me the distraction I needed to stop thinking about things that would never happen. Taking my water with me, I went back to stand in front of the stage.

"Places," I called out when everyone had returned.

I signaled for the music to start at full blast, my pulse quickening as the dancers took their positions. The first ninety seconds of the routine unfolded flawlessly, just as I'd choreographed it. But as we approached the climax of the piece, my string of bad luck made a dramatic encore.

With only a few ominous creaks as a warning, the lighting rig came crashing down.

Pandemonium erupted as dancers frantically hurled themselves out of harm's way, bodies colliding and tumbling across the stage in a desperate scramble for safety. Glass from the shattered lights exploded everywhere, razor-sharp shards raining down. Then, for one heart-stopping moment, an eerie silence fell over the club.

It didn't last long. Screams of terror and pain pierced the air, jolting me into action.

I bolted for the stage, the crunch of glass under my heels barely registering. Every instinct screamed at me to vault onto the platform, but some last shred of sanity prevailed, reminding me that slicing my palms open wouldn't help anyone. Taking the stairs two at a time, I surveyed the scene with a mixture of relief and horror.

Thankfully, there weren't any massive pools of blood, but scattered crimson droplets and many cuts painted a grim picture. I moved from dancer to dancer as other staff members flooded in, their frantic questions adding to the cacophony of chaos.

What the hell happened?

Who's hurt?

How bad is it?

What the fuck do we do now?

When I reached JJ, I got my answer to at least one of those burning questions. The gash on her shin, while nasty, wasn't life-threatening thanks to Annie's quick thinking with a makeshift scarf tourniquet. But JJ's wrist... Jesus Christ. No bones were sticking out, thank God, but the unnatural angle told me it'd be a miracle if it wasn't shattered.

JJ's face had taken on a sickly grayish-green hue as she white-knuckled Annie's hand, clearly fighting back waves of pain and nausea.

"We need to get you checked out, stat," I said, praying I sounded more in control than I felt. I'd never felt so inadequate for this job as I did at that moment.

"Sienna!"

Laila's voice cut through the chaos. "I'll be right back," I assured the two women. "We need to figure out if it's better to call the paramedics or haul ass to the ER ourselves."

"How bad is it?" Laila asked in a hushed tone as I crouched at the edge of the stage.

"Mostly minor stuff, except for JJ," I replied grimly. "Her wrist is bad."

Laila cursed colorfully. "It'll be faster if you take her to the ER yourself. Someone just plowed into a bodega two blocks over."

"Got it," I nodded, taking the keys she offered. "You'll handle everyone else and fill Gavin in?"

Laila's expression was grim but determined as she nodded. "We'll sort this out and clean up the mess."

With a plan of action crystallizing, I returned to JJ and Annie. As we carefully helped JJ to her feet, they anxiously inquired about the night's performances.

"Don't even worry about it," I said firmly. "You're more important than some show. And before you fret about what Gavin's going to say, I know he'll back me up on this one hundred percent."

I might not have understood why he'd been talking to some suit about selling the club, but if there was one thing I knew with absolute certainty, it was that Gavin always put our well-being first. I trusted him implicitly in that regard.

Hell, he was the only man I did trust, and I didn't see that changing anytime soon. No matter how incredible the sex with Fury was.

Chapter Nineteen

FURY

After finding my office vandalized, I thought my week couldn't get any worse. Then the cops upstairs, snapping pictures of the chaos, asked if I had any idea why someone would decide to dump the contents of the breakroom fridge and cabinets all over my office—like the halffull container of tuna and mayo that had been festering on top of the refrigerator for two days.

And that was why it was Saturday afternoon, and I was still working from home. I'd hired a cleaning crew to handle the mess and had given everyone the rest of the week off. Now, that plan hinged on whether they could banish the stench of spoiled fish. I wasn't about to force anyone to work in a place that reeked like a seafood market gone wrong.

Fortunately, a lot of our work could be done remotely. Like the research I was currently diving into for a potential client. Or, at least, that was my intention.

My mind kept wandering.

More specifically, it was drifting toward a certain raven-haired beauty with a sharp tongue and fire in her eyes.

A beauty I hadn't seen since Wednesday night, thanks to the recent chaos at the office. By Thursday, after dealing with the cops, calming freaked-out employees, calling Cory, and working with Jules to get our schedules sorted, I was too exhausted to do anything but shower and collapse into bed. Then yesterday, I spent hours contacting every client based out of the New York office to reassure them that their accounts were secure and that we'd be back in the same offices come next week. After all that, the last thing I wanted was to go anywhere, let alone a packed club.

And if I was being honest, a part of me had hoped that Sienna would reach out, asking where I was and if everything was okay. But she hadn't.

I knew the club usually boasted a big performance on Friday and Saturday nights, which meant she was likely buried under last-minute changes and all that jazz. She might've even had to replace a dancer on the fly, leaving her little time to think about me, let alone text. I tried to convince myself that was the case, since she hadn't outright said she didn't want to see me again. Sure, she'd been distracted when I'd seen her at work, but that spark between us was undeniably still there.

I needed to talk to her.

I sighed, tilting my head back against the couch. As I closed my eyes, numbers and names, spreadsheets, and analysis reports flashed in my mind, but soon they were replaced by a familiar face—a face that brought with it a rush of other sensations.

The subtle coconut scent of her skin and hair. Her soft, warm skin beneath my fingertips. The mingling sounds of pleasure and gasps. The way her pussy tightened around my cock when she came.

"Fuck." I opened my eyes and grabbed my phone. I needed to reach out, even if it was just a text.

Hey, I know you're probably busy, but I just wanted to see how you were doing.

I sent it off before I could second-guess myself, hoping it sounded as casual as I intended. Then I turned back to my laptop, feigning productivity while I waited for a response.

Saturdays are busy. This one, more than usual. Lots to clean up.

I frowned at her vague comment. *Someone made a mess?*

Her reply came back faster than the first one. *More like something. Lighting rig fell yesterday in the middle of practice.*

A flash of panic jolted me upright, but I resisted the urge to call her and opted for a text instead. Nice and casual. *Are you okay?*

That was casual, right?

I'm good. One dancer messed up her wrist, but that was the worst of it.

I let out a breath. I felt bad for the dancer, but I was relieved Sienna was okay. Probably a little too relieved, honestly.

Watching practice, or do you have a minute to chat?

I didn't know why I was asking. It's not like we had long, deep conversations. We bickered, we fucked, we bickered again—that pretty much summed up our entire relationship.

I'm in my office listening to music to find something for next week. I'm guessing you're at your office using talking to me as an excuse to not work.

I grinned. *Wrong. I'm at home.*

Then you're working there.

I laughed. *Got me. And I'm only working from here because my office smells like tuna.*

Three dots appeared, then vanished for several seconds before reappearing. A series of emojis followed, all conveying the same thing: *what?*

Settling back into my seat, I explained what had happened at my building, and she filled me in on the chaos at the club. Seemed like we were both having less-than-stellar weeks.

Sounds like we could both use a chance to relax with a nice Scotch or a glass of wine. I've always been partial to Shannon's.

Gavin told me your brother makes it.

As our conversation shifted from business to personal, I sprawled on the couch, work forgotten, all my attention focused on our text exchange.

Is good Scotch the only way you like to relax?

My eyebrows shot up at her question. Maybe I was imagining it, but that sounded a little... flirty.

There are other things I enjoy just as much. Sometimes more.

I hoped I wasn't reading too much into it, but if I was, I figured she'd set me straight. One thing I knew for sure about her was that she had no qualms about voicing her opinions.

Yeah, those other things don't suck.

Or sometimes they do. My cock twitched at the

thoughts that paraded through my mind, and I reached down to adjust myself as I waited for her reply.

You wish. The two words were accompanied by eggplant and mouth emojis.

"Shit," I muttered, palming my cock through my jeans. "Yeah, I do wish."

I didn't tell her that, though. Instead, I played it cool. *If you were here, we could both* and I ended it with a mouth emoji.

Very cool.

That is something we haven't gotten to do yet and I can't say that I haven't thought about it.

My eyebrows shot up. Was she really going there?

What, exactly, is that you've thought about?

For the moment, I resisted the temptation to reach into my pants, but I couldn't stop the blood from filling my cock. I waited, anticipation twisting in my stomach. If she didn't want to do this, it was okay with me, but if she did, I wasn't going to pass it up.

I've thought about going to my knees and taking you in my mouth.

I guessed that answered my question. As I read the rest of her message, I undid my jeans, needing to ease the increasing pressure there.

Lick from root to tip, tracing every vein with my tongue. Take that drip of precum at the tip and swallow it.

Fuck me.

What would you like to do to me?

Hundreds of ideas flooded my mind, but I stuck with the current subject.

I'd go to my knees, pull your legs over my shoulders, and bury my face between your legs. Lick you from ass to clit. Plunge my tongue inside your sweet pussy.

I groaned at the mental video my words created and shoved my hand into my pants, gripping my swollen cock. How the fuck had I gone from completely soft to achingly hard in such a short period of time? I stroked myself, wishing it was her hand, her mouth.

Are you touching yourself?

I sent back a thumbs up, the easiest thing for me to type one-handed.

Proof or it's not happening.

This was a bad idea. A very, very bad idea. While I trusted Sienna, I knew that sending any sort of sexual picture could have serious consequences if the wrong person got hold of it.

And I simply did not give a damn.

I snapped a picture of me holding my cock at the base, and then another with my fist at the top, making it clear exactly what I was doing.

Your turn.

I lazily moved my hand up and down, waiting to see if

she'd return the favor. It almost didn't seem real. Like I'd fallen asleep at the computer and was dreaming this. I could honestly say I hadn't been expecting this when I'd texted her. Maybe a little flirting or some innuendo. Dirty talk and pictures hadn't even been on my radar.

I'm pretending it's your fingers.

The message came through a few seconds before the picture and I nearly came right then and there. She was sitting behind her desk, skirt bunched up around her waist, panties at her knees, and she had two fingers buried deep inside her pussy.

I turned on speech to text, too turned on to take my hand off my dick and too impatient to type with one hand.

"Fuck yourself on my fingers, baby. Take 'em nice and deep in that tight, hot cunt of yours. Play with your nipples, too. Show me your tits. I want to see how hard your nipples are."

My hips were moving in time with my hand, fucking my fist the way I wanted to fuck her mouth. I took another picture and sent it since I'd asked for another one of hers.

Several messages dinged in, one after the other.

Her hand cupping her breast, pinching one pert nipple between her thumb and forefinger.

Fingers spreading her lower lips to show the pink flesh they concealed.

Her thumb on her clit even as she sank a third finger inside her.

I want you to suck on my clit. Give me a little bit of teeth. Shove a fourth finger in my pussy to get me ready because your cock is so fucking thick.

"Are you gonna come for me? I want you to come. Want to think about you screaming my name while I imagine you taking my cock all the way, take me into your throat so deep."

I sent the message even as another one came in.

I'd swallow you down. Every fucking inch. And I wouldn't spill a drop.

That did it for me. My eyes squeezed shut as I came all over my hand. I was somewhat aware that I was making a mess, but all I could see in my head was what Sienna would look like with her lips stretched around the base of my cock as I pumped my load into her.

My body went limp, my breathing ragged. Only the signaling of an incoming message made me force my eyes open again.

Two pictures. One of her hand squeezed between her thighs, which I knew meant she'd come. The other was of her, with two of her fingers in her mouth. I groaned and my cock twitched, wanting to harden again at that sight. Instead, I took a picture of my spent cock in a pool of cum.

Then another message.

That was fun. I gotta get back to work now.

I smiled as I sent back, *me too.*

It was another minute before I had the energy to get off the couch and clean myself up. Fortunately, I had at least kept my cum off the furniture.

I'd just returned to sit in front of my laptop when a phone call came through. Seeing Gavin's name on the screen brought a flash of guilt, but I reminded myself that Sienna was an adult who could do what she wanted, and then I answered the phone.

"Hey, Gavin."

"You will not believe what just happened to me." He sounded furious. "I got swatted."

"Fuck." All the good I'd felt from my exchange with Sienna disappeared under worry. "Is everyone okay?"

"No one was hurt, but the kids and Carrie are all rattled."

"Wow." I couldn't even imagine what that must've been like for them. The idea of having SWAT officers bursting into my home, thinking I was someone dangerous, was frightening on its own. I couldn't think of how I'd react if I had a family, and that happened. "Do they know who did it?"

"No, but I don't think it's random," Gavin said. "Did you hear about the lighting rig falling?"

"Yeah." Knowing he wouldn't want to know any of the details about that, I gave him something else. "My offices were vandalized on Thursday."

Gavin was silent for a moment. "I think we both should start looking into this stuff."

I agreed. I almost suggested we go to the cops with it, but I knew I couldn't make that decision for Gavin. I'd involved the authorities in what'd happened with me, but the rest of it was his to decide about. His business, his family. If he asked my opinion, I'd give it, but I'd keep my mouth shut otherwise.

A part of me hoped it was just a run of bad luck, but the sick feeling in my gut said that this was just the beginning.

And that things were going to get worse before they got better.

Dammit.

Chapter Twenty

SIENNA

I DIDN'T KNOW WHY, but it always seemed like the club patrons got rowdier when a holiday loomed on the horizon, as if they were still in school and couldn't wait for the break. Maybe it was because we were always closed on Thanksgiving, Christmas Eve, and Christmas Day, leaving people feeling like they needed to expel all their pent-up energy before those three days of absence. Whatever the reason, these two days leading up to Thanksgiving would not be any better, which was why I was sprawled in bed, staring at my ceiling, even though I was well past the time I usually got up for work.

I wondered if Fury would stop by the club tonight, and that thought finally propelled me into action. Not that I was thrilled to rush to work hoping to see him; rather, I was desperate to stop obsessing over him. After our unexpected sexting session on Saturday, we'd exchanged a few messages, but they'd been limited to mundane small talk. I wasn't entirely sure how I felt about that; it had a relationship vibe that made me uneasy, yet I enjoyed our conversations enough not to dwell on it. I decided to roll with it, do my thing, and see where it led.

Right now, 'my thing' meant tackling the mountain of dirty dishes that had accumulated in my sink since Sunday. I was wrist-deep in soapy water, cursing the stubborn pan I'd used to make macaroni and cheese the day before—one I'd forgotten to soak overnight—when a loud knock echoed through my apartment, jolting me from my thoughts.

No, it wasn't just a knock. It was a frantic pounding, the kind someone would do if they were in dire trouble and desperately needed help.

"Shit." I grabbed a towel, drying my hands as I hurried to the door. Peeking through the peephole, I caught a fleeting glimpse of a face, but when I heard a female voice call my name, I quickly undid the locks and flung the door open.

The woman who stumbled inside was around my age, with shoulder-length ebony waves and striking coal-black eyes. At six feet tall and slender, with stunning dark skin,

Lulu Parr always struck me as the type who should've been modeling instead of turning tricks.

Except now, she couldn't have modeled for anything. She looked like she'd been beaten to a pulp. Her face was swollen, one eye completely shut and the other barely open. Her nose appeared broken, and I spotted a patch where a chunk of her hair had been yanked out. Her bottom lip was split, revealing at least one chipped tooth as she breathed through her mouth. Despite the chill in the air, she wore nothing but a pair of shorts and a tank top, which showcased the bruises already forming on her limbs. The way she clutched her side suggested she probably had bruised and cracked ribs, if not broken ones, and possibly internal injuries.

I had no idea how she'd ended up in such a condition, but I didn't ask her yet. Instead, I kicked the door shut and helped her over to my couch. Once she was settled, I rushed to the bathroom and grabbed the first aid kit stashed under the sink. We remained silent as I went to the kitchen and retrieved a bag of frozen fries.

Only after I was sitting at the table, facing her and carefully cleaning the blood from her face, did I finally ask the question that had been nagging at me since I first laid eyes on her.

"Was it Ralf?"

She nodded, the slight movement causing her to

wince. I didn't press her for details. If she wanted to share, she would. I knew all too well that Ralf Crosse didn't need a reason to beat the hell out of one of 'his girls.'

Lulu and I had met because of Ralf. In his mid-forties, with thinning brown hair and three inches shorter than me, he had never looked like someone to be feared. It was that deceptive impression that had drawn me in, along with plenty of other girls.

I'd met Ralf when he called himself an "entrepreneur," but let's cut the bullshit - he was just another pimp. The sleazeball ran RC's Escorts, a so-called "high-end service" peddling "classy women" for dates with loaded, big-shot clients. Only two parts of that steaming pile were true: he did run RC's Escorts, and most of the johns were indeed filthy rich and important. As for the rest? Some of us were better at faking "class" than others, but when the only "date" those horny bastards wanted involved us getting naked, it didn't mean jack shit. Those of us with a knack for acting got trotted out in public, but don't think for a second that meant we weren't expected to fuck 'em too. We just got paraded around like prize ponies first, before the real show began.

If I hadn't been one of those trophy girls, I never would've ended up at Club Privé with a client trying the place for the first time. He had taken me into one of the private rooms and decided he didn't like the hard limits I'd established. I fought back fiercely, reaching the emergency button that the club had in every room. Gavin had come in, intervening and throwing my client out.

Then Gavin had offered me a new job—one where I wouldn't be paid to have sex with people I wasn't attracted to, but where I could do whatever I wanted, with whomever I wanted, however I wanted, without judgment.

Ralf hadn't taken the news well, but when I dropped the name of the club and the man who'd offered me a job, he backed off, telling me that when I got tired of working there, I could always return to him.

Lulu and I hadn't been close. She'd struggled with a drug problem, and that was one vice I'd managed to avoid, but I'd liked her well enough. I had heard from a mutual acquaintance that she'd had a child shortly after I'd left, but aside from that, I'd lost track of her. Which led me to the one question I needed to ask.

"How did you find me?"

"You gave a card to Lillian and wrote your address on the back." Lulu's words were a bit slurred, but I understood her.

After a few minutes of silence, during which I bandaged her as best as I could, she began to speak.

"I almost OD'd a few months ago. My mom said she'd take care of my boy if I went to rehab, so he didn't end up in the system. I just got out a couple of days ago." She attempted a smile, but the effort was short-lived, the pain clearly overwhelming her. "Ralf heard I was out and showed up at my place, but I couldn't afford to keep it while I was in rehab. I'm at my mom's now, but he left a note with the manager saying he expected me back at work today."

"You decided you weren't going back," I murmured softly.

She shook her head. "I knew that if I started working again, it wouldn't take long before I'd be using again. I can't get through that shit without something to take the edge off." A look that resembled shame crossed her face. "I never understood how the others did it without being high or drunk."

"Hey, we all had our ways of coping," I replied. "Just because you couldn't see it doesn't mean we weren't doing anything."

"I can't go back to my mom's like this," Lulu said, her voice laced with despair. "I'll scare my kid. And I don't have anywhere else to go. You were the only person I could think of who wouldn't judge me for any of this."

"Damn right I won't," I stated firmly. "We're going to figure out what needs to be done to get you through this, okay? Get you back to your boy and keep Ralf away from you."

"I don't know, Sienna. He doesn't take no for an answer. I could never figure out how you did it—got him to leave you alone."

"It wasn't me," I admitted honestly. "It was the people who had my back."

Lulu shot me a questioning look.

"This job I have, the guy who owns the club—he has a reputation." I smiled, warmth spreading through me. "A good one for employees, but I guess he scares the hell out of people who aren't so good."

"Must be nice," she said. "Having someone like that on your side."

"It is," I agreed.

My initial instinct was to tell her he could help her, too. I could call Gavin, and he'd help us devise a plan to fix things. He had connections with powerful people. Granted, I had some connections too, but Gavin had the relationships that allowed him to ask for favors and know who to approach about certain issues.

But before I could even reach for my phone, I remembered Gavin was at the club, dealing with some electrical issue.

Fuck.

If I just wanted to offer Lulu a job, I could've called Laila since she was Gavin's second-in-command, but I needed more than just a job. We needed someone to make Ralf back off.

Fury.

The moment I thought of him, I realized I wanted him here for this. I could lean on him, and he'd do whatever was necessary to help. He wouldn't judge Lulu, either. The only potential downside I could foresee was him discovering my past as an escort, but I couldn't let that stand in the way of helping her.

"I have someone I'm going to call," I said firmly.

"Your boss?"

I shook my head. "No, he's caught up in something at the club. But I've got someone who will help."

And as I spoke the words, I knew they were true. He would help.

Chapter Twenty-One

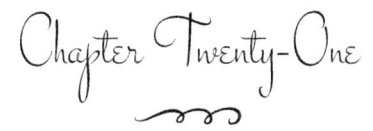

FURY

I was deep in a conference call with our West Coast office when my phone buzzed. Sienna's name flashed on the screen, and my heart skipped a beat. We'd been texting back and forth since our steamy exchange, but this was the first time she'd called.

"Sorry, guys, I need to take this," I said, cutting off Cory mid-sentence. "Jules can fill you in on the rest."

I didn't wait for a response before ending the call and answering Sienna's.

"Fury?" Sienna's voice quivered, sending a chill down my spine. "I need your help. Can you come to my place?"

"Of course," I blurted out, already on my feet. "What's going on?"

She paused, her breath catching audibly. "It's... it's my friend. She's been assaulted. Badly."

My chest constricted, her vulnerability piercing through me. This wasn't our usual flirtatious dance. She was reaching out to me—not Gavin—in a moment of crisis, and the weight of her trust settled heavily on my shoulders.

"Did you call the police?" I asked, my voice low and steady.

Another pause, longer this time. "No. Not yet. I need you. Are you coming?"

"I'm on my way," I assured her, my heart racing. "Text me your address. I'll be there as soon as I can."

I snatched my jacket off the back of my chair and fumbled for my keys, calling out to Jules as I strode towards the door. "I've got to go. Family emergency. Can you handle things here?"

Jules looked up, her brow furrowing with concern. "Of course. Go. I've got this."

I rushed out of the office, my mind racing. As I navigated through the busy New York streets, I debated my next move. My instincts told me this was serious, and we might need backup.

Making a split-second decision, I dialed 911.

"I need to report an assault," I said as soon as the operator answered. "I'm heading to the victim's location now. Can you send officers to meet me there?"

After giving them Sienna's address, I focused on getting there as quickly as possible. I arrived before the police, rushing up to Sienna's apartment and knocking urgently.

The door swung open, revealing Sienna's worried face. "Fury, thank God you're here."

As I stepped inside, I saw a woman on the couch, her face battered and bruised. My stomach churned at the sight.

"Lulu, this is Fury Gracen," Sienna introduced as I followed her to the couch. "Fury, this is Lulu Parr."

My heart clenched as I took in Lulu's battered face. "It's good to meet you," I said, the words feeling hollow in the face of her suffering. "I wish it had been under better circumstances."

Lulu's lips quivered as she attempted a response. "Thanks for coming." Each word seemed to cost her, her voice barely above a whisper.

I hesitated, then decided to be upfront. "Oh, you mentioned you hadn't called the police, so I did that on my way over."

The moment the words left my mouth, the air in the apartment grew thick with tension. Lulu's eyes widened in panic, her body beginning to shake uncontrollably.

"What the hell did you do that for?" Sienna glared at me as she sat beside Lulu, wrapping her arm around her friend. "I asked you to come over, not to take charge and do something foolish."

"Look at her, Sienna." I gestured to Lulu. "She's scared and hurt. She needs to press charges, and if it's a matter of needing cash to get back on her feet, I'll cover it."

Sienna shook her head, the disappointment and irritation written all over her face hitting me like a punch. "You don't understand. You didn't bother to find out what she wanted. You just did what you thought was best."

I felt confused, and a bit irritated. "No, I did what anyone would do if they heard someone had been beaten up. I called the police so they can take a statement and nail the bastard responsible."

Sienna let out a laugh that was so bitter it was practically a snarl. "That's not how it works."

"I know I'm new to the city," I replied. "And I'm sure there are corrupt cops here like everywhere else, but I think the odds are in our favor. The ones who came when my office was vandalized were extremely professional."

Sienna and Lulu exchanged glances I couldn't quite decipher, and when Sienna turned back to me, there was a look that resembled pity in her eyes.

"Trust me, Fury, it's not the same."

I was on the verge of asking if there was an issue with

this precinct, because I'd have no qualms about trying to pull strings to ensure we got the best they had. But just then, someone knocked on the door.

"I'll get it," I said, moving toward the door before she could protest. It was her apartment, but if the cops were here, I was the one who'd called them, and if it was the guy who'd hurt Lulu, I'd plant myself between him and her.

A quick glance through the peephole revealed two officers: a woman in her mid-forties and a man in his mid-thirties. I let them in and introduced myself.

"I'm Officer Perrault," the woman said as she shook my hand. "This is my partner, Officer Putnam."

"You told the operator you were reporting an assault, is that correct?" Officer Putnam got straight to the point.

"That's right," I said. "Not mine, obviously, but the assault of a friend of a friend."

Officer Perrault's gaze flicked to Lulu and Sienna. "So you don't know anything about what happened?"

I shook my head. "Sienna called me, and on my way here, I called you guys. Hands-free, of course."

"I'm guessing you are Sienna," Officer Putnam said, taking a few steps toward the women.

"I am," she replied, remaining firmly seated next to Lulu. "Sienna Marquez."

"And how do you know this gentleman?" Perrault inquired, positioning herself next to her partner.

"From work," I said. "And a mutual friend."

"Are you the mutual friend?" Putnam asked, pointing his pen at Lulu.

She shook her head, her eyes cast down. "I never met him before."

"It's not really important who I am," I interjected. "I don't have any information about the assault. I'm just here as moral support."

The look exchanged between the two cops suggested they found something about my statement amusing.

"What's your name?" Perrault asked Lulu.

"Lulu Parr." Her voice trembled as she reached for Sienna's hand.

"Are the two of you ... together?" Putnam gestured toward their clasped hands.

"We're friends," Sienna said with a scowl. "Not that it matters."

"So you're not a client?" Putnam asked, his tone dripping with disdain. "Yeah, I've seen you before, Lulu."

Even though Perrault didn't seem to grasp what her partner was implying, she didn't ask for clarification. Instead, she turned to Lulu and said, "Tell us what happened."

I glanced at Sienna, completely bewildered by the current situation, but she wouldn't meet my gaze. I set my questions aside and focused on what mattered: helping Lulu.

With faltering speech, the battered woman recounted how her former boss had beaten her up because she had told him she wouldn't return to work for him. It seemed straightforward until Perrault dug for more details, specifically where Lulu had worked for this guy and why she wouldn't want to return.

"I had a drug problem," Lulu finally admitted. "I just got out of rehab, and I know that if I go back to that ... job, I'll use again."

"Does your dealer work with you?" Perrault probed. "Or is he the one who did this to you?"

"She's a whore, Perrault," Putnam finally interjected, clearly annoyed by his partner's line of questioning. "Her pimp beat her up. That's all this is."

Lulu looked down, and Sienna shot daggers at the cops.

"Don't be an ass," she snapped. "Yes, Lulu worked for RC's Escorts. But she wanted to leave that line of work, and that's why Ralf assaulted her. Happy?"

Putnam scowled at Sienna, and I had to restrain myself from stepping between them.

"Sounds to me like you're taking my questions a little personal," Putnam retorted, his voice sharp. "Maybe you're a little more involved than you're letting on."

"I came to Sienna because I knew she'd help me," Lulu said, her voice steady.

"And how did you know that?" Perrault asked. "You said you are friends, but you're talking about protecting someone from a clearly violent pimp."

"Isn't it obvious?" Putnam added, a condescending smirk on his face.

I wanted to knock it off.

"They *work* together," he finished, clearly relishing his so-called cleverness.

I opened my mouth to tell him he'd crossed a line, but then I caught the look on Sienna's face, and the words died on my tongue.

"Worked," she corrected, lifting her chin and pointedly avoiding my gaze. "Ralf Crosse trafficked me and Lulu and tons of other women, labeling us high-end 'escorts' while our clients were just 'dates.' He tries to make it sound like we choose that life, but it's bullshit because we can't choose to stop." She gestured to Lulu. "At least, not without consequences."

"You said 'worked,'" Perrault noted. "Past tense."

"Yeah, because I got out."

"Did you look like this when you told him?" Perrault pressed. "Something that shows he's done this before?"

Sienna shook her head, and I felt a surge of relief. "I think he was too scared of the man who offered me a new job. One where I really could choose what I wanted to do."

"Where do you work now?" Putnam asked, his skepticism noticeable. "I can't imagine there are many high-paying jobs that require your particular ... skill set."

"My job has nothing to do with what happened to my friend," Sienna said, standing up with a fierce expression. "But *your* job is to investigate her assault. That's what you need to focus on."

Putnam's face flushed crimson. "Listen to me, you little—"

"You're going to want to reconsider how you end that sentence," I warned, advancing a step.

I fought to rein in my anger. I wanted to slam him down, but I knew that would only escalate the situation. Not only would I get arrested for assaulting an officer, but I had a feeling my actions would draw more attention from them than the actual crime they'd been called to investigate.

"I don't know who you—"

This time, it was Perrault who cut in. "Ease off, Wyatt. You don't want to tangle with a guy wearing a watch that costs more than both of us make in a year."

Sienna's eyes darted to my wrist, and I could sense the weight of her scrutiny.

"This watch is a family heirloom." I kept my gaze fixed

ahead, refusing to meet her eyes, but I could feel her stare drilling into me. "But you should listen to your partner. I'm not someone you want to mess with."

"I think we have enough," Putnam said, flipping his notebook closed and stepping back, his posture exuding bravado. "Let's go, Cassie."

"Before you leave," I said, positioning myself between the officers and the apartment door, keeping my hands relaxed at my sides to appear as non-threatening as possible. "I sincerely hope you're planning to take this assault seriously. Because if you don't, I can assure you that several influential members of my family - including a certain judge and a well-known civil rights attorney - would be very interested in hearing about your conduct here today."

Perrault's eyes widened, but she remained silent. I had no idea what she would have said if she'd had a different partner, but if she was a decent cop, I was giving her some leverage to make Putnam behave.

"Are you threatening us?" Putnam demanded, his bravado faltering.

"I'm ... encouraging," I said. "Encouraging you both to view Lulu here not as the mistakes she's made but as a brutalized woman who's—"

"A mother," Sienna interjected quietly.

"A mother," I echoed, "who has a lot of powerful people standing behind her."

Perrault nodded. "We understand. We'll do our job."

"Good," I said. "That's all we're asking for."

Both cops looked uneasy as they left, but I refused to feel even a twinge of guilt about it. I wasn't the type to seek special treatment, whether through connections or cash, but when I witnessed an injustice I could rectify, I didn't hesitate to assert my influence.

I just had no idea how Lulu or Sienna would react to it.

Chapter Twenty-Two

SIENNA

I loved my roommate, and I knew she would've been totally cool with Lulu being here. Hell, Vanessa would've marched right up to that asshole cop and scared him just as much as Fury had. Still, I was relieved that Vanessa was spending a few days with her parents in Brooklyn to help her mom with all the Thanksgiving prep. I didn't think Ralf knew where I lived, but I wasn't about to risk him showing up here and hurting Vanessa because of me.

While Lulu was in the shower, I texted Vanessa to let her know what had happened and to ask if one of us could use her bed tonight. She immediately asked if I wanted her to come home, but I insisted she stay put and promised to wash all her sheets and things, hoping she'd focus on that and not press about whether we were in danger.

I had left Fury in the living room while I set up Vanessa's room, and I hadn't checked on him before re-bandaging Lulu's injuries. By the time I was satisfied she was asleep, I fully expected Fury to be gone. After all, it was the Tuesday before Thanksgiving, and the evening hadn't even settled in yet. I figured he'd need to catch up on whatever work I'd pulled him away from.

That, and the fact that he now knew about my ugly past. He was the kind of man who could have any woman he wanted. Who would choose someone with my kind of baggage when there was an entire city full of better options?

But when I stepped into the living room, there he was, sitting on the couch, scrolling through his phone as if he had nothing better to do than wait for me.

"You're still here." The words slipped out before I could stop them, and instantly I regretted it.

"I am," he replied easily, looking up at me. "Is that all right?"

His tone was even and polite, but his expression left me guessing about whether he truly meant it. I prided myself on my ability to read people, especially men, but he was a puzzle. Maybe it was because he wasn't as shallow as the others I'd encountered, or maybe it was the way my stomach tightened whenever I saw him. Whatever the reason, I didn't know how to steer the conversation, so I just spoke my truth.

"You don't have to stick around to prove you're not a jerk," I said. "Now that you know about my past, it's fine if you want to walk away. I won't be offended if you choose to leave."

"I don't care about that." He stood and closed the distance between us.

The physical distance, anyway. There was a vast chasm separating us in other ways.

"I care about you." He reached up, resting his hand lightly on my cheek. "Are you okay?"

I nodded. "Worried about Lulu, but I'm fine."

"I'm sorry I called the cops," he said, his expression tightening. "I didn't think they'd be like that."

I shrugged. "I'm used to it. Most people treat me differently once they find out. If we'd been out to eat and something happened that required us to talk to cops, they probably would've been great. I know it's not all of them, but it's enough that people like me and Lulu, when it's about being an escort, we don't want to gamble on getting someone decent."

"I'm sorry." He brushed his thumb against the corner of my mouth. "It shouldn't be like that. They shouldn't act like that."

The edge in his voice made me scrutinize him more closely, and I saw what I'd missed before.

He was furious.

Not at me or Lulu for wasting his time here, and while I was sure he was pissed at Ralf because Fury didn't seem like the type to take assault lightly, it wasn't that rat bastard he was furious with right now. Fury was angry at the cops for how they'd handled everything.

"No matter what those idiots do, I'm going to help you," he promised. "We'll get justice for your friend, and we'll make sure she's safe. Ralf's not going to touch her again."

His words were powerful, but what made my heart race was the undeniable sincerity behind them. And even though he hadn't said it outright, I knew he'd be there for me, even if nothing ever happened between us again.

If that wasn't the sexiest thing in the world, I didn't know what was.

I grabbed the front of his shirt and rose on my toes to bring my mouth to his. I felt his surprise, but it didn't freeze him for long. His lips softened, teasing the seam of my mouth with his tongue. As I opened my mouth to deepen the kiss, I moaned, and his hands found my waist, his fingers brushing against the bare skin there.

The need that had been simmering inside me roared to life, and I wrapped my arms around his neck. He dropped his hands and lifted me, my legs wrapping around his waist.

He broke the kiss to ask where my bedroom was, and I pointed to the open door, breathless and unable to form words. But then his tongue was stroking mine, and I didn't care about speaking. I just wanted him to keep touching me, keep kissing me.

After pushing the door shut with his foot, he lowered me onto my bed with a gentleness that surprised me. His eyes were dark with desire as he straightened, and I felt his gaze like a physical caress. Then his hands moved to the buttons on his dress shirt, and I zeroed in on that. As he peeled off his shirt, exposing those hard muscles, I licked my lips, and he groaned.

"I want to be inside you," he said as he sank to his knees next to the bed. "But I've been dreaming about tasting you since the first moment we met. Please say yes."

I'd had sex with men who didn't pay me, and I'd had men go down on me before, but it had always been with the understanding that I would reciprocate. I wouldn't mind giving Fury a blow job, but the way he was looking at me made it clear that me returning the favor was the furthest thing from his mind.

"Yes." The word escaped in a whisper, anticipation twisting in my stomach.

"If you want me to stop at any time, just say the word. If you're the least bit uncomfortable, tell me."

He'd said something similar before, but there was a new weight to it. It felt like he was talking about more than just me enjoying myself or not wanting him to do something specific. It took me a moment, but then I realized he was worried about triggering me. Not only did he not blame me for having been an escort, but he was also acknowledging that the things I'd experienced might've left me with the kind of baggage that could rear its head during sex.

Or even during a kiss.

That was when I saw it in his eyes. The understanding that my behavior after we'd had sex in my office had something to do with my past. And instead of dragging that up to satisfy his curiosity or placing his own need to know above mine, he simply let me know it was safe to tell him when something bothered me.

I nodded, hoping he could read everything in my eyes and on my face because I couldn't articulate any of it. He must've sensed it because he didn't push, but instead reached for the waistband of my pants. His fingers skimmed over my legs as he pulled off my shorts and tossed them aside. Before he moved to take care of my underwear, I quickly discarded my shirt, relieved that I hadn't bothered with a bra yet. Judging by the way the muscle in his jaw clenched, I guessed he was glad for it too.

Then he started kissing his way up the inside of my leg and I let everything else fade into the background. His hair was soft against my skin as he turned his head to lavish attention on the other leg. Only after he'd kissed that one too, he hooked my legs over his shoulders and focused in on his goal.

Just as I was going to start feeling awkward, he grabbed my hips and pulled me to the edge of my bed. With one last smoldering look sent my way, he buried his face between my legs.

"Oh!" I couldn't stop the exclamation that came to my lips as he licked me, the flat of his tongue hot and wet on my flesh.

He laughed but didn't even pause what he was doing, letting the contact between us send all of those delicious vibrations through me. As he dipped his tongue inside my core, his nose nudged my clit, and I shivered, the light touch almost ticklish. His grip on my hips tightened, and he moved his tongue higher, tracing circles around that little bundle of nerves. Dancing, teasing touches that told me he'd paid attention during our other times together, and not just to getting his rocks off. His circles grew tighter and higher, moving from the base of my clit to the top where he flicked back and forth with feather-light touches that made me squirm, my desire for more feeding the almost desperate need inside me that was clawing its way out.

Speaking of clawing, my hands moved restlessly on my blanket, trying to find a place for me to sink my nails, to release some of this pressure in some way other than exploding.

Then he wrapped his lips around my clit, and I came apart at the first pull of his mouth. My back arched and my mouth opened in a silent scream.

I barely had the presence of mind to grab my pillow and put it over my face as he kept sucking and I kept coming. Wave after wave crashed into me, rolling me under and over with shocking intensity.

All those times I'd gone down on a guy after he'd given me a few licks, I was beginning to think that I'd been cheated.

It wasn't until I reached down to push his head off of my aching clit that he finally stopped. I tossed my pillow away and looked down in time to see him wiping his face on his shirt. I'd come so hard I couldn't even get up the energy to be embarrassed by how wet I was.

"That ... wow." My voice was hoarse. "Give me a minute and I'll..." I flapped my hand in his direction.

To my surprise, he shook his head. "Don't get me wrong, I want your lips wrapped around my cock, but I want to be inside you when I come and if you put your mouth on me, I won't be able to stop myself."

He quickly shed his pants and underwear, his cock springing free, already swollen and leaking. After climbing onto my bed, he stretched out on his side and then pulled me up to lay in front of him, my back to his chest.

"I'm guessing your clit's too sensitive to much friction," he said.

I nodded, wondering how many more times he could surprise me.

"Shit. Forgot the condom." He leaned over so I could see his face without hurting my neck. "We went without before. You okay with that again, or do you want me to get one?"

I frowned, confused. "You now know what I used to do."

He shrugged. "You said you were clean. I trust you."

Okay, so at least one more surprise from this man. I reached up to put my hand on his cheek and he leaned into the touch, his expression softer than I'd ever seen it.

"Thank you." My chest felt strangely tight, and I shifted the tone back to the sexual one that I preferred to this tender intimacy. "I like you bare inside me, so as long as you're good with it, so am I."

He curled his body over mine to give me a sweet kiss before positioning my leg at just the right angle to let him slide into me with one smooth stroke. We both let out sighs, the sort that had to do with a contentment, a peace ... a coming home. That last thought struck me just as he began to move, and I couldn't catch my breath, emotions mixing with physical sensation until I felt like every cell in my body was ready to explode, to change into something new, something that could contain everything I had churning inside me.

As he set a fast, but steady, pace, one arm slid around my waist and up to allow his hand to cup one of my breasts. Each thrust was angled so that he rubbed right over my g-spot every time. His fingers played with my nipple, light tugs and pinches that never crossed the line into pain, and I closed my eyes as I tried to absorb it all. It was a different pleasure than I'd experienced with his mouth, but no less intense, no less incredible.

I rose toward another climax and started pushing back against him, my teeth sinking into my bottom lip to hold in my cries. His rhythm faltered, and I knew he was fighting for control, fighting to hold back until I came one more time. He hadn't been joking when he'd said he would've gone in my mouth if I'd tried to blow him, and that was the mental push I needed to let go.

As I soared, he was right behind me, groaning my name against my skin as he pressed his mouth to the side of my throat. We kept moving together in strange little jerks and twists, lost in that primal connection that didn't need elegance and grace to be deep and meaningful.

And then he was wrapping his arms around me, his cock still inside me as it softened, and I snuggled back against him. I didn't know what this meant or how it had changed things between us, only that it did. At some point, I knew that would terrify me, but right now, I felt safe and I was going to hold to that for as long as I was able.

Chapter Twenty-Three

FURY

I wasn't sure who was more surprised when I spontaneously asked Sienna to join me for Thanksgiving with my New York family—her or me. Honestly, I think it was me who felt the shock most acutely when she said yes. She hadn't canceled, and now, standing outside her building, my heart raced at the prospect of taking her to Maggie and Drake's for dinner. I could almost taste the anticipation mingling with the aroma of roasted turkey and family chatter.

When Sienna opened the door, my jaw nearly hit the floor. I'd seen her in dresses before, but holy shit, nothing like this. The deep crimson red made her eyes sparkle like diamonds, and I swear my heart skipped a beat. It hugged her body without being too revealing, accentuating her lithe figure and making her legs look a mile long. The heels she wore brought her to just shy of six feet tall, the perfect height for me to ravish those luscious lips of hers. Damn, I was in trouble.

I played it safe, though, and just kissed her cheek before giving her the flowers I'd brought. My first instinct had been to go all out, to make one of those grand, extravagant gestures like filling her apartment with roses, but it had taken me only a few seconds to dismiss that idea. First, because our relationship wasn't traditional, and second, because that would've felt too much like trying to buy her, and she'd had enough of that in her life.

So, I'd opted for a dozen orange and yellow chrysanthemums.

"Thank you." A pleased smile curved her lips, and I knew I'd made the right decision.

"Apparently, they're the official flower of November."

As Sienna turned away to head to the kitchen, I mentally kicked myself. *The official flower of November?* I was usually great at charming women, spinning words like an artist. Hell, it had practically been in my job description when Cory and I launched our company, since he was the one who got tongue-tied around women. So what the hell had happened to me?

"They're beautiful," Sienna said as she placed the

flowers in water. "And different from the usual sort. I like that."

"You look beautiful," I said. "I mean, you're always beautiful, but you look even more stunning today in that dress and ... shit." I shook my head.

She laughed softly, coming over to me and taking my hand. "I know what you mean. And thank you. You look very good today, too."

I smiled and lifted our joined hands to brush my lips across her knuckles. "This is new for me."

She raised an eyebrow. "Really? You don't exactly strike me as a monk."

I laughed, feeling the tension within me ease a bit. The nerves were still there, but they weren't as overwhelming. "I mean taking someone to Thanksgiving. I had some semi-serious relationships when I was younger, and sometimes they'd come over for dinner or a birthday party, but I never brought anyone over for the big holidays."

"So, no pressure, right?" Her tone was teasing, but I caught a hint of concern in it.

I laced my fingers between hers and tugged her into the hallway. "It'll be fine."

"Sure," she said. "Former escort, now working at a sex club, living in an average New York apartment with a roommate, mingling with a well-known fashion designer, a violinist with the Philharmonic, and some other people I assume are as rich as you."

I bit back a groan, realizing it was probably for the best that I'd kept my mouth shut about London and Spencer. Those two had flown in yesterday and would grace us with their presence at dinner. Christ, Spencer's royal family connections could make anyone's knees weak.

"My cousin Carson," I said, "the designer? His fiancé grew up in a cult. My other cousin Alec is engaged to a teacher. All perfectly normal people."

Sienna nodded, but she didn't appear completely convinced. At least I knew I could count on my family not to treat her weirdly. Like any family, we had our issues, but there were some things I always knew for sure. They'd always have my back unless I was being an idiot, in which case they'd give me a kick in the ass if I needed it. And they'd always treat people with respect and compassion, no matter where they stood in life.

The drive to Maggie and Drake's place was slow, but I'd factored in the traffic when I'd told Sienna the time to be ready, so we arrived right on time. Sienna's eyes widened the deeper we went into the swanky neighborhood, and when we pulled up to the curb in front of a two-story, four-bedroom house, she let out a low whistle.

"I know your family has money, but damn."

"Well, it's not just Maggie's money," I said. "Drake has

plenty of his own. He comes from a wealthy Scottish family."

"Right." Sienna shot me a sideways look. "Are we going to be having caviar and lobster? Flakes of gold in our champagne? Servants at our beck and call?"

I opened and closed my mouth a couple of times, unsure how to respond to her questions. Hell, I didn't even know if they were genuine or if she was just messing with me.

She let me flounder for a few seconds before bursting into laughter. "I'm impressed, but I'm not an idiot. You'd probably have wine and Scotch instead of champagne."

I joined her in laughter, hoping this meant she was feeling more at ease. Still, I took her hand as we approached the door.

Maggie opened it before I even knocked, beaming as she greeted both Sienna and me with hugs. "Come on in. Carson and Vix are already here. London and Spencer are on their way. Rose is just putting down the twins for their nap, so everything should be perfectly timed for us to eat while they sleep."

"Boys, girls, or one of each?" Sienna asked as we hung up our coats.

"One of each," Maggie said, her face lighting up even more. "Shannon and Carlyle. And be forewarned because you'll be hearing about them all evening. Drake will probably break out pictures, too."

"I look forward to it," Sienna said sincerely.

I knew it was too soon for the image that popped into my head, but I couldn't help it. My mind immediately conjured up a tantalizing picture of Sienna cradling a baby, her luscious body curving around the tiny bundle. I stood behind her, my hand possessively gripping her shoulder, feeling the warmth of her skin beneath my fingers. I tried to shove the enticing vision away, but I had a gut feeling it would return with a vengeance. The more time I spent with this intoxicating woman, the further ahead I could see our future unfolding—a future I'd had no clue I craved until she waltzed into my life and turned everything upside down.

I heard footsteps on the stairs and looked up, smiling, when I saw Rose coming down. She looked a lot better than she had the last time I'd seen her, but there was still a shadow in her eyes as she hugged me. I didn't ask her about it, though. I knew my sister, and she wouldn't want me to call attention to her feelings. Instead, I turned toward Sienna.

"I know the two of you have met briefly before, but that was under some weird circumstances." I reached for Sienna's hand, loving the way her face lit up with pleased surprise. "Rose Gracen, meet Sienna Marquez. Sienna, my little sister, Rose."

"It's nice to officially meet you." Sienna extended her free hand, her cheeks pink. "And I'm sorry if I was short with you the other day. I ... misunderstood your connection to Fury."

"You were lovely," Rose said. "And thank you for joining us today."

I loved my sister. She wasn't an idiot. She knew Sienna had been jealous, and she chose not to focus on that, just like she wasn't asking about me and Sienna holding hands, even though I knew she was curious.

The doorbell interrupted us, and we all moved forward to give London and Spencer some room as they entered, Spencer carrying their one-year-old son, Alexander. We went through additional introductions as Maggie herded us toward the living room, where Drake, Carson, and Vix waited.

Living on the opposite coast from these cousins, I hadn't gotten to know their significant others very well, and one thing I'd been looking forward to when I moved here was spending more time with them. Having Rose here was just a bonus.

They were all just as warm and kind to Sienna as I'd expected. They asked her the kinds of questions anyone in this setting would ask and shared their own anecdotes and stories with ease. Not a single one of them pushed for more information when she gave vague answers, either. By the time we finished dinner, I felt like the day was already a success.

It wasn't until Maggie brought the twins downstairs and we were all watching them and Alexander doing their baby thing that I realized Sienna had been unusually quiet for a while. Trying to be discreet about it, I glanced at her, but it was impossible to read anything from her expression.

The fact that she wore that too-familiar mask told me enough. Something was wrong. When she excused herself a couple of minutes later, saying she needed to use the restroom, the subdued way she left the living room confirmed my suspicions.

I was still mulling over the issues when Drake came over and sat down next to me.

"Your lady friend is quite beautiful," he said, his Scottish brogue as thick as my Uncle Patrick's. He smiled, his eyes softening as he looked over at Maggie giving Carlyle a toy. "Not as beautiful as my love, but still lovely."

"She is," I agreed.

"And like my Maggie, your Sienna seems to have had some ... darkness in her past." Drake placed a hand on my shoulder, his expression serious. "Women like that, they take time to let you in, and it takes time for them to heal.

She may push you away, but if you really care about her, lad, don't let her."

Carlyle flapped his arms and started making "da-da-da" sounds, prompting Drake to smile and head for his son without another word to me. In the little time I'd spent with him, I knew he wasn't the type to mince words, so I appreciated what he'd said and planned to ask Sienna if she was okay when she returned.

Except ten minutes passed, and she still wasn't back. Then fifteen minutes. I began to worry.

When I saw everyone's attention was on a story London was telling about something Alexander had done to one of Spencer's sisters, I quickly got up and headed in the direction Sienna had gone. I didn't need to search far to find her. She was standing by the door of the guest bathroom, leaning against the wall and looking at something on her phone.

"Hey, I was starting to think you got lost," I teased, sticking my hands in my pockets to appear more casual as I approached her.

"Oh, no." She raised her head but didn't meet my eyes. "I was just checking on Lulu and didn't want to be that rude person on my phone while everyone's visiting."

She sounded like she was telling the truth, but my gut said it wasn't the whole truth. Still, it was concern for Lulu

—not trying to catch her in a lie—that made me ask, "How's she doing?"

"Good," Sienna replied. "Her mom, son, and she went to Albany to see some cousins for the holiday, and she thinks they'll stay there until Ralf's been arrested."

"So the police haven't caught him yet?"

Sienna shrugged. "Lulu said that one cop, Perrault, called her yesterday evening to tell her they were still looking for Ralf, but that he'd either gone underground or completely left the city altogether."

I suddenly realized she'd just shared more with me in this little exchange than she'd said to anyone since dinner, and I couldn't, for the life of me, figure out why. I knew she'd been nervous about being here with my family, but I'd thought their clear acceptance from the start had eased those concerns. Unless someone had said something to her, but I couldn't even think of anything that could've been misinterpreted.

"So everything's all right?" I purposefully made my question vague, hoping she might either answer about Lulu or reveal what had her acting so reserved.

"Yeah." She pushed off the wall and seemed to gather herself, lifting her chin defiantly. "Why wouldn't it be?"

As she walked past me, I instinctively reached out, but she flinched slightly, pulling away just enough to evade my touch. It was a subtle movement, a mere shift of her body that, had I not been attuned to her, I might have missed entirely.

But I caught the fleeting flash of pain that crossed her face, and it struck me hard, echoing Drake's warning that she would likely push me away. If she genuinely wanted me to back off, I'd respect that. Yet I refused to let her retreat simply because she harbored misguided doubts about our connection. I hadn't officially called her my girlfriend yet, but I was more than willing to explore that possibility.

I realized I had finally found a woman worth fighting for.

Chapter Twenty-Four

SIENNA

It had almost a week since Thanksgiving, and avoiding Fury hadn't become any easier.

After he dropped me off at my place following his family dinner, I claimed to have a headache. For the next two days, I responded to his incoming texts with one- or two-word replies before cutting communication altogether. I let his calls go straight to voicemail, deleting them without a second thought. I was honest enough with myself to understand that hearing his voice might shatter my resolve.

Work had been a nightmare. Since he was Gavin's friend and everyone had seen Fury and me together multiple times, no one thought twice about letting him come to my office. So, I couldn't hide there. He also knew all my usual spots around the club where I directed performances, which meant I had to change those up too.

I was just grateful that no one had asked about my erratic behavior, even though I knew they noticed. I wasn't sure if the concerned looks Gavin cast my way were because he had picked up on my changes or if Fury had reached out to him, but either way, he hadn't brought Fury up, and I was genuinely thankful for that.

Just the thought of Fury stung, but even that couldn't prevent him from invading my thoughts constantly. Especially at the worst times. Like when I was supposed to be choosing new music and realized I'd gone through six songs without remembering a single one because my mind was too busy trying to figure out what features Fury and Rose shared. Or how Laila had to repeat herself three times about a costume order because I was lost in thought, staring at a candy bar and thinking about how the color had matched Fury's eyes.

It was driving me insane. Crazy and miserable—what a delightful combination.

But I'd done the right thing.

I shuffled into the kitchen, yawning as I tightened the belt of my robe. I was halfway to the fridge to grab the milk when I noticed Vanessa at the stove, pouring pancake batter onto a pan.

I frowned. "It's Wednesday, right?"

"It is," she replied.

"I thought you had a meeting this morning." I turned away from the fridge and reached for a mug.

"That's next week. Which you'd know if you'd paid attention to our one-sided conversation yesterday. Or the day before."

I winced. "Sorry."

I stared at the coffee I'd just poured, debating whether adding sugar and creamer was worth the effort to retrieve either. Nope, I decided. It'd be better just to sit and sip the bitter liquid.

Vanessa's sympathetic gaze lingered on me as she flipped the pancakes. "What's going on?"

I shrugged.

"Uh-uh." She shook her head, pointing the spatula at me. "I'm not accepting that. I'll be more specific. What's going on with you and Fury?"

I closed my eyes and dropped my head into my hands. "I don't want to talk about it."

"Too bad. Because if I have to spend one more morning watching your sorry ass trudge around in that ratty robe, looking all sad and pathetic, I'm going to march right over to Mr. Bigshot's office and ask *him* what's wrong."

My head shot up so fast that it spun, but I didn't wait for it to stop before blurting out, "You can't do that."

Vanessa's eyebrows shot up, her expression shifting as she slid the pancakes onto a plate and brought it over to me. As she retrieved butter and maple syrup, she said, "You like him, Sienna. I know you do."

"I do," I admitted, reaching for the knife and fork she'd set before me.

Her kindness piled on a fresh layer of guilt; this was how she handled her worry—by taking care of me while trying to figure out the problem and how she could fix it.

She returned to the stove to prepare her own breakfast, giving me a moment to think as I ate. I knew there was no way I could avoid sharing, not when she'd made those funny-shaped pancakes. I'd never been able to resist those, and she knew it.

"It's not about whether or not I like him," I finally said.

"He likes you," she countered. "Don't even try to tell me he doesn't. Men like him don't bring girls flowers and invite them to spend holidays with their family if they don't like them."

"I know he does," I said, setting down my fork and letting my shoulders slump. A heavy sigh escaped my lips. "How we feel doesn't matter. Not when we don't... move in the same circles."

"Move in the same circles?" Vanessa echoed. "What the hell does that mean?"

"Remember that story last year about the Broadway star who fell in love with some British noble, ended up having his kid, and won a Tony? Everyone was calling it a Cinderella story?" I asked.

She nodded. "Yeah, they presented at the Tonys together this year, right?"

I shrugged. "I don't know about that, but the actress? She's one of Fury's cousins."

Vanessa's eyes widened as she sat down across from me. "No way!"

"They were both there," I said. "Tony-winning Broadway star and British nobility."

"Well, I mean, people like that have family, so a new girlfriend or whatever is bound to be surprised at a holiday dinner, right?"

"I guess," I agreed. "But that's not all. He also has a cousin who plays in the Philharmonic, another who's a famous designer. I heard there's an archeologist, someone who makes really expensive whiskey, and a professional soccer player." I shook my head. "And no matter what the rest of them do, they're rich. These people have money coming out of their ears."

"That sounds painful," Vanessa said dryly.

"They don't flaunt it," I continued. "I mean, the

house we were at was big, but not a palace. Nice cars, but no Ferraris or whatever. No massive diamonds or crazy electronics."

"Well, did any of them treat you badly?" she asked. "I mean, you don't seem pissed, which is what the Sienna I know would be if someone looked down their nose at her."

"No," I blurted. I might've had my issues, but they were mine. I wouldn't let anyone think Fury or his family had done anything wrong. "They were all great. Nice, and they weren't faking it."

Vanessa set down her fork and leaned back, folding her arms as she gave me a hard look. "So you're saying that the rich, well-known family of your smoking-hot man—who likes you and whom you like—was genuinely nice when you came to Thanksgiving dinner as a last-minute addition… and you're staying away from him because you 'don't move in the same circles'? Do I have that right?"

I was going to regret answering her, but when she got that look on her face, there was no point in trying to avoid it. She'd keep at me until she said her piece.

"Yes," I said, mimicking her pose. "That's right."

"Then you need to stop being an idiot."

I wished I could say I was surprised by her words, but nope. She had no problem being polite and kind to people, but if she thought someone needed the truth, she'd deliver.

"Look." She leaned forward, her expression softening. "He's a good man, and you said he knows about your past and doesn't care. He wants to be with you. Don't let your self-worth issues make you give up someone like that."

I bristled at her 'self-worth issues' comment, but deep down, I knew that was the truth. That didn't mean it annoyed me any less.

My irritation grew as Vanessa took her dishes to the sink and then headed back to her room. I wasn't truly mad at her; I just didn't want to think about what she'd said. I didn't want to confront the reality that I was doing something I'd promised myself I'd never do.

I was seeing myself through the lens of how people like those cops viewed me. A whore. Someone beneath others. Not worthy of time or attention.

"Dammit, Vanessa," I muttered as I pushed back from the table.

I needed to escape.

Instead of doing chores around the apartment like I usually would until it was time to head to the club, I got dressed and went straight in. I told myself it was to get a jump on some work because, with Christmas less than a month away, it was wise to work ahead. I just hoped that if I repeated that enough times, I'd start to believe it.

Except, thirty minutes later, when I told Laila why I'd come in early, I knew it was a lie. And when she followed me to my office, I realized she didn't believe me either. So, I gave her the truth.

Sort of.

"My roommate and I are having a bit of a disagreement," I said as I sat down behind my desk. "I thought it'd be a good idea to come here and let things cool down."

"Anything I can help with?" Laila asked, concern lacing her voice.

I shook my head. "It'll blow over."

I fully expected Laila to either leave or start talking about work, but she lingered in the doorway, as if she wanted to say something but wasn't sure she should.

"Is there something else I can help you with?" I forced my voice to stay polite. No need to snap at her because I was having a bad day.

"Look, feel free to tell me to butt out and mind my own business," she began, "but I can't help noticing that things seem to have changed between you and Fury Gracen."

I stiffened. "What do you mean?"

"He seems to do an awful lot of sitting and waiting for you or watching you, and you've been ignoring him."

Irritation surged within me. First Vanessa, now Laila? While I respected and liked Laila, I felt like she was crossing some kind of line. I was getting my work done, and that's all she should've cared about.

I swallowed all that down. The thing I liked about the club—the way we all looked out for each other—was exactly what she was doing. I couldn't let them have my back in one instance and then get pissed when they tried to get involved in another.

"I know Gavin and Fury are friends, but I don't really know him, so I'm going to ask you if he's done something. If he has, I'll tell Gavin we need to bar Fury from the club, no matter their friendship."

"No," I said quietly. "He didn't do anything. I'm fine. I just want to focus on my work."

Laila stood there for a few more moments before nodding. "All right. But if you need anything, even just a listening ear, you let me know, okay?"

I agreed, even though I never planned on taking her up on her offer. But I appreciated the sentiment.

Yet, as the day dragged on, the restlessness I felt overwhelmed any positive emotions I'd experienced that day. I hated this. My mind felt scattered, and I couldn't concentrate on anything. I kept scanning the crowd for Fury or glancing at my phone, wondering if he'd try to reach out again. While I should've felt relieved when I reached the end of the night without seeing or hearing from him, I didn't. I was left only with annoyance over how the day had unfolded.

As I made my way down the sidewalk toward the

subway, I took a couple of deep breaths, using the chilly November air to clear my head. That's when I realized that I'd been hearing something behind me for the last two blocks. I didn't want to glance back and give anything away, but I quickened my pace, checking my wrist as if I had a watch.

Ahead of me, people were moving toward the entrance of the subway. If I could reach the stairs, there'd be enough people around to look back and see if my imagination was running wild.

I never got that far. When I was still a block away from my goal, pain exploded across the back of my head, and I felt a dim sensation of falling before everything went black.

Chapter Twenty-Five

FURY

The last time I looked at my phone, it was two forty-seven in the morning, but I had no idea how much time had actually passed as I drifted in that hazy space between sleep and wakefulness. I'd always despised that feeling more than the inability to sleep at all because it felt like I was neither productive nor truly resting. I was just kind of existing—neither asleep enough to dream nor awake enough to think.

That had been my reality since I turned in after the late-night news finished.

As the piercing shriek of my phone shattered the tranquility, I jolted upright. Despite the ungodly hour, relief washed over me. Finally, a reason to be awake. The darkness beyond my tightly drawn curtains hinted at pre-dawn, but I snatched up the phone anyway, squinting at the unfamiliar number.

"Hello?" My voice was thick.

"Fury?"

A woman's voice, unfamiliar and tense, crackled through the speaker.

"Yes. Who's this?" I scrubbed my face with my free hand, fumbling to switch on the bedside lamp. Harsh light flooded the room, making me wince.

"Vanessa Rodriguez. I'm Sienna's roommate."

My stomach dropped, every muscle tensing. "What's wrong?"

"She's been mugged."

Ice flooded my veins. "Where is she? Is she okay?"

"She's here," Vanessa said, exasperation clear in her tone. "She's refusing to go to the hospital."

"I'm fine!" Sienna's voice rang out in the background, slurred but defiant. "I just need to sleep."

"That's the last thing you need to do," Vanessa snapped, her patience clearly fraying. "And if you won't listen to me, maybe you'll listen to him."

I didn't bother telling her that I doubted I could make Sienna listen any more than Vanessa could; honestly, at this point, the roommate probably had a better chance. Still, I wasn't going to give Sienna a reason to turn me away. I was already throwing off the covers and scrambling to find clothes.

"If you can't get her to go to the hospital, she needs someone to stay with her for a while. Make sure she doesn't start throwing up or pass out or anything."

"I just have a headache," Sienna muttered, her voice quieter this time but still audible. "I don't need a babysitter."

"Normally, I'd stay with her," Vanessa continued, ignoring Sienna. "But my sister just called to say she's in labor. Her husband's overseas on deployment and won't be back until next week. I'm her backup birthing partner."

"I'm on my way," I said. "If you have to leave, go ahead."

"Thanks," Vanessa replied. "I have a little time before I have to go, but if I'm gone before you get here, I'll let Sienna know she can't lock you out."

Something in the way she said that made me think she knew that Sienna was being weird with me, maybe even knew why. If she did, and had still called me, it meant she was rooting for me, and that felt good. Really good.

"I'm heading to my car now," I said as I locked my door behind me. "I'll text you when I'm at your building."

We ended the call, and I focused on getting to their place as quickly and safely as I could. Less than twenty minutes later, I hit the buzzer, and Vanessa let me in, but didn't linger. When the door closed behind her, leaving Sienna and me alone for the first time since I'd dropped her off here on Thanksgiving night, I turned to Sienna.

"I'm fine," she said before I could even speak.

I raised an eyebrow and walked over to where she sat on the couch, holding something to the back of her head. I perched on the low table in front of her, close enough for our knees to brush, but I resisted the urge to reach for her. I had no idea what had been going on with her, and I wasn't about to assume my touch was welcome.

"What happened?"

"I was mugged." The words came out flat, and her eyes darted everywhere but at me.

"Then why won't you go to the hospital to get that looked at?" I gestured toward her head. "A mugging is hardly something you need to hide."

"You saw how the cops treated Lulu and me," Sienna shot back. "Do you really think they'd give a damn about me getting mugged? Hell, that one asshole would probably claim I made it up."

"Then we find another cop."

"You don't get it," Sienna snapped. "No one gives a shit about people like me, so why should I waste my time trying to get them to care? I'd rather just sit here with ice on my head and wait for the ibuprofen to kick in."

"I give a shit," I shot back, unable to hold back. "I thought I'd made that pretty clear."

"Oh, yeah, your whole savior complex makes it crystal clear." Sienna rolled her eyes. "You just love swooping in and saving damsels in distress, right? And that's what I am. How you see me. And while you might think it's better than how those cops saw me, it's not."

"You think I've been trying to 'rescue' you?" I stared at her, waiting for a punchline. When none came, I had to accept she was serious, and it did nothing for my temper. "You're one of the strongest people I know. How the hell would I rescue *you*?"

"Oh, come on." Sienna laughed, but it was bitter. "You really expect me to believe that *you* see me that way? With all the money and power and your perfect family and everything you have? Why would you ever see me as anything other than a project?"

And that's when it hit me—the reason she'd been pushing me away. I didn't know the exact trigger, but understanding her struggle was enough to find the words.

"I was nine when my parents died in a car crash." I looked down at my hands, unable to face her expression. "My older brother, Blaze, was eleven, and Rose was just one. She doesn't remember them." I took a deep breath. "I'm not telling you this so you'll feel sorry for me, or trying to compare our shit."

"Then why are you telling me?" Her voice still had an edge, but it felt forced now.

"Because you said my family was perfect," I explained. "I love them, and I know how lucky I've been. My siblings and I could've been split up and sent to foster care. Instead, we were taken in by my aunt and her new husband, both wealthy enough to care for their own kids —some from their first marriages and three from the two of them—but also for three orphans. So I call them my cousins and my step-cousins, but we were raised more like siblings."

"Sounds like you're all close."

"We are," I said. "Maybe not the way some people think, but in the ways that matter." I glanced up at her. "Like being there for each other. Not because we think anyone is weak, but because that's what we do for those we care about."

"It's not the same," she protested.

"One of my cousins, Eoin, was in the army. He nearly died in an IED attack, and he wasn't the same when he came home. But we didn't give up on him or tell him he should just get over what happened to him. We loved him, supported him. And he got through it. I'm not saying everything's perfect for him, but he's a husband and a dad. Damn good at being both, too."

"He was lucky to have support," Sienna said, her tone wooden. "Too many of our veterans don't."

She wasn't getting it, but I had a feeling I knew whose story would resonate with her. It wasn't an easy one to share, but she needed to understand that I didn't view her as weak.

"My cousin, Maggie? That beautiful, talented violinist with the doting husband and the two darling kids?" I locked eyes with Sienna. "She spent years in an abusive relationship with an asshole who used her as a punching bag. I'm pretty sure he did other things to her, too."

Horror spread across Sienna's face. "She…"

"Understand me, Sienna." I took the risk and grasped her free hand. "Absolutely nothing about your past or your present makes me pity or look down on you. I don't rescue you. We rescue each other. That's how this works."

I saw it then—the longing in her eyes, how desperately she wanted to believe me.

"When I met everyone last week, in that house, and heard about all the things they'd done and who they were…" She set down the bag of frozen peas and took my other hand. "I couldn't see a place for me there. I only saw how much we didn't make sense."

I brought our hands up to my mouth and kissed her knuckles. "I don't care if we don't make sense, and neither will my family. Trust me, all of them could list a hundred ways why they don't make sense if people think too hard about it."

"But people are going to think hard about it, Fury," she insisted. "They're going to wonder why someone like you is with someone like me. And if anyone finds out about my past..."

I shook my head. "I don't care."

"You say that now," she replied, "but wait until someone looks at you the way those cops looked at me. Well, not exactly the same way, since a guy buying a whore never gets the same criticism that the whore does."

"Stop," I said firmly. "First of all, you're not a prostitute anymore. And second, if anyone says anything about you like those cops, I guarantee I won't be as polite to them as I was to the cops."

"Fury..." she began.

"No." I squeezed her hands. "Listen to me, Sienna. I don't know when it happened, but at some point after you showed up at the airport, I realized how much you mean to me. More than that, I realized we belong together."

Her eyes widened, as if she hadn't expected such a declaration, and I didn't blame her. I hadn't expected to say it either. But since I had, I felt compelled to see it through.

"If you really don't want me," I said, "if you can look me in the eye and truly tell me you don't care about me, don't want me in your life, then I'll let you go. I won't force you to be with me. You'll only ever see me when I come to the club, and it'll only be in passing. We can be polite to each other and go on with our lives." I leaned closer, not enough to invade her space, but enough to hear her sharp intake of breath. "But if you can't say that, then I'm going to keep fighting for you."

She swallowed hard, but didn't pull away.

"Because you are worth fighting for, Sienna Marquez. Do you hear me? You are worth everything."

Chapter Twenty-Six

SIENNA

"Because you are worth fighting for, Sienna Marquez. Do you hear me? You are worth everything."

Most of his words had struck a chord deep within me, but that last declaration knocked the breath clean out of my lungs. I locked eyes with him, a swell of emotion building inside me to the point where I could barely breathe, barely think. My heart thudded against my ribs like it was desperate to escape, a wild animal seeking freedom.

That nagging voice at the back of my mind insisted I couldn't trust him, that he must be lying—how could someone like him possibly want someone like me? But that voice was nowhere near as loud as it had been lately. Other whispers drowned it out, suggesting he genuinely cared, that if he saw me as worthy, then maybe I truly was. They warned me that if I let this man slip away because I couldn't accept how he viewed me, I'd regret it for the rest of my life.

I reached for him, my fingers brushing against his cheek. "Thank you."

A flash of relief flickered across his face just before I kissed him, a soft, gentle press of my lips to his. A heat ignited within me, both familiar and foreign. Familiar because his touch always sparked a fire, but foreign because this wasn't a roaring inferno, blazing bright and hot, yet unsustainable. No, this felt like a fire smoldering deep beneath the surface, sending cracks through the barriers that kept us apart. It enveloped me completely, growing more intense until I finally pulled away, gasping, my body throbbing in a way that had nothing to do with the bump on the back of my head.

I made another decision at that moment and stood, extending my hand to him. "Come to bed with me?"

He smiled, taking my hand with a warmth that sent shivers down my spine. "I'll go anywhere with you."

When we reached my bedroom and closed the door behind us, I turned to Fury and reached up to kiss him again. Surprising me, he caught my wrists in one hand and put them on his chest between us.

"Are you sure you feel up to this?" The obvious concern in his eyes kept me from thinking he was second guessing his feelings about me.

"I think that the perfect medicine for my headache is orgasms," I teased. "I could take care of it myself, but it's more fun when you do it."

He cupped the side of my face with his free hand, thumb brushing the corner of my mouth. "I should refuse, but I want you too damn much to be selfless."

I turned my head and flicked my tongue against the pad of his thumb. "I'm very glad to hear that."

"If you start to feel sick or anything hurts, you tell me and we'll stop," he added. "Got it?"

I nodded. "Got it. Now get naked."

He laughed, which was what I wanted. And then he let go of my wrists to reach behind him and pulled his shirt over his head, which was also what I wanted. I'd already changed out of my work clothes as part of my argument against going to the hospital, so I slipped my robe off my shoulders, and stood there in just my bra and panties for a moment before following Fury's lead and taking those off two.

The silence between us as we undressed and got onto the bed wasn't weird or uncomfortable. It just felt like we'd already said what we needed to say, and now we needed this physical connection.

I parted my legs as he stretched out over me and a little thrill went through me at how perfectly the two of us fit together. Resting on one elbow, he ran his hand from my hip to my breast, leaving my skin tingling every place where he touched. Plumping up my breast, he leaned down and ran his tongue around and over my nipple. When he lightly blew on it, the skin pebbled and I let out a breathy sort of moan and squirmed underneath him. Then he took it into his mouth and sucked, hard. My back arched and my eyes closed, a direct line of pleasure straight through me, so bright that it almost hurt.

As his mouth worked its magic on my breast, he moved his hand between my legs, stroking my sensitive skin with just the tips of his fingers for a moment before slipping a single finger inside me.

"Fuck," he groaned, his lips moving against the skin on my breast. "You're already wet for me."

I slid my hand down his chest and over those amazingly defined abs to wrap my hand around the thick cock jutting out of the dark curls around the base. He uttered a low curse, his body stiffening. I pulled my fist up the length of him, rubbing the tip with my thumb and smiling when he swore again.

"Seems like I'm not the only one ready to go," I said.

His mouth came down on mine with a fierceness that would've taken my breath away if I wasn't already trading breathing for kissing. Our tongues tangled together, and he worked his finger into me with a steady deliberation that had me rocking my hips against his hand, wanting harder and faster, but he denied me that, keeping his hand gentle even as his mouth ravished mine.

Fury was being careful, treating me like I was fragile, and I didn't know how I felt about it. He wasn't doing it because he thought I was weak, that I knew for sure. He just wanted to take care of me, and that was what had my heart twisting in my chest even as it raced.

It wasn't until I was right on the edge of coming that he pulled out his finger, but before I could protest, something considerably thicker took its place. The tip pushed inside me, just an inch, but the angle caused the shaft to press against my clit, sending a ripple of pleasure through me.

"So tight." He gritted his teeth as he raised himself off me and squeezed his eyes closed.

I slid my hands along his sides, wanting nothing more than to dig in my nails and demand that he fuck me, but I resisted, instead enjoying the emotions playing across his face. Desire and barely restrained passion. The need to put me first. A mix of ecstasy and pain.

He pushed in a little more, drawing a gasp that had his eyes flying open. "Are you okay? Did I hurt you?"

I gave him the only response that I thought would get

through to him. I moved my hands over his hips to his ass and dug in my nails as I tugged him closer. Another inch stretched me and I shifted, bending my legs to put my feet flat on the bed and give myself some leverage.

"I'll tell you if I'm hurt," I said. "Trust me."

I was fairly certain I'd never said those words to a man before, not even Gavin. Asking someone to trust me was opening myself up to them asking me the same in return, and I'd never wanted to give that power over to any man. Even when I'd done some kinky shit and used safe words, I'd never said the words *trust me*, and honestly, it'd never been the man I'd fucked that I'd trusted. It'd been the rules of the club and the fact that I'd seen Gavin take them seriously the first time we'd met.

All of this went through my head in an instant, but it must have also shown on my face before Fury's expression softened and he leaned down to brush his lips across mine. Something about it seemed to have eased the strain he was under because he slid the rest of the way home in one smooth stroke, holding himself there just as his gaze held mine.

We didn't stay like that for very long, both of us giving in to our bodies' more primal needs, but something felt like it changed in those few intimate moments. We were joined in the closest way two human beings could be joined and yet it was the precious seconds when our eyes met that made something click between us. When we started moving, it was in perfect synch with each other, as if this had been as carefully planned and practiced as one of my routines.

The world faded away until nothing existed but us and our dance. No pain from my head. No sounds through the too-thin walls of my apartment. Not the complications of work and life that threatened to pull us apart. It was only the dance and the heat we generated with it. Heat that turned from smoldering embers to a full-out inferno, burning us until we combusted together. Combusted and then rode the waves of pleasure until they finally faded, leaving us panting and our skin slick with sweat.

And, for the moment, at least, satisfied and content.

Chapter Twenty-Seven

FURY

I'd never understood it when people said they wanted to spend all day in bed with someone. Even with my former girlfriends, the only time I lingered in bed after sex was during those rare moments when we fell asleep together. I wasn't an asshole who'd finish and kick my partner out, but this wasn't aftercare or cuddling or whatever people called it.

This was something else entirely.

"Are you sure I'm not keeping you from work?" Sienna asked as she rolled onto her side, facing me. Her cheeks were still flushed from our third round of lovemaking, and although I'd come three times in two hours, my dick stirred back to life.

"Believe me," I tucked some escaped hair behind her ear, "there's no place I'd rather be than right here with you."

And it wasn't just a line to ease her guilt. It was a Thursday afternoon, and I was lounging in bed, feeling no urgency to do anything else. Not only was there no restless need, but I *didn't want* to be doing anything else.

She sighed, catching my hand and kissing my palm. "Unfortunately, I have to go to work soon. My boss is a great guy, but I can't very well tell him I'm calling off because his friend has fucked me upside down and sideways."

I raised an eyebrow. "I remember the sideways, but I must've missed something because I don't recall anything upside down."

She grinned at me, humor dancing in her eyes. "Maybe that's something we can try out next time."

Next time.

I liked the sound of that.

I liked it so much that I was tempted to persuade her to skip work. I wouldn't do it though. That'd be too much like trying to control her.

When my phone rang, I groaned and rolled over, stretching out to grab my pants from the floor. I laughed when I saw Gavin's name on the screen and turned my phone toward her so she could see it. Sienna's eyes went wide, and a new color flooded her face.

Her phone rang just as I answered mine. "Hey, Gavin. What's up?"

"Someone broke into the club. Can you come by? If you're too busy, that's fine, but—"

I cut him off before he could offer me an excuse. "I'm on my way."

I turned back to Sienna just as she hung up her phone. Seeing her pale face and shaken expression, I felt pretty confident I could guess that she'd just heard the same news I had. She looked like I had felt when my office had been vandalized.

That thought gave me pause. Both my place of business and Gavin's had been messed with, and Sienna had been 'mugged,' all within a short period of time.

"That was Laila," Sienna said as she threw back the covers. "I'm guessing Gavin told you that the club was broken into."

"Yep." I followed her lead, quickly redressing. "Want to ride together or separately?"

She gave me a surprised look. "Do you really think I have a car?"

I shrugged. "Didn't want to assume." I adjusted my shirt. "Guess that turns my question into 'Would you like a ride instead of taking the subway or a bus or however you normally get to work?'"

"You're a brave man," Sienna said, braiding her hair with that quick efficiency that I'd seen in some of my cousins. "Few non-natives keep driving in New York traffic after the first couple of weeks here."

"It probably won't come as a shock to you that I prefer being in control as much as possible." I grinned, hoping to recapture some of that lightness we'd shared before our phones rang.

The soft curve of her lips wasn't a full-blown smile, but the look in her eyes suggested she understood my attempt to lighten the mood and appreciated it.

"Do you really think you can get us there quicker than taking the subway?" she asked. "I want to get there as fast as we can."

"I'll do my best."

I must've done pretty well because as we pulled up to Club Privé, Sienna told me I'd made it five minutes faster than her usual commute. But I didn't feel like celebrating when I saw the two police cars parked nearby.

"Shit. If they sent two cars, it's got to be bad inside," Sienna said.

"No ambulances mean no one was hurt," I pointed out. "That's good, at least."

"Yeah," she agreed, a distracted expression on her face.

A part of me wanted to delve into what was going on in her head, but we both needed to get inside more than I needed to satisfy my curiosity. I parked my car, and Sienna and I headed for the employee entrance around the back. As we walked inside, she reached over to take my hand, her fingers cold as they laced between mine.

I gave her hand what I hoped was a comforting squeeze, and as we stepped into the main club area, I was immediately glad I was here for her.

I didn't know if it looked worse than my office because there'd been different stuff to break and throw around or if whoever did this had just been angrier than the person who trashed my place.

Again, that little thought tugged at the back of my mind, wondering if maybe the two were connected or if this was just a coincidence.

Then the smell of alcohol hit me, and I nearly gagged. Next to me, Sienna stared at the destruction, the hand covering her nose and mouth the only sign that the eye-watering stench affected her at all.

It looked like every bottle from behind the bar had been hurled against a wall or the floor, leaving glass everywhere. Tables and chairs were flipped and broken, some with enough force that the pieces were scattered across the room. The lighting on the stage had been torn down, all the glass parts shattered, wires cut, metal bent out of shape. Like in my office, food was everywhere, but it also seemed like whoever had done this had dragged in trash from outside and dumped it.

"Sienna!" Laila hurried over from where she'd been talking to a tall, lanky cop. The manager's eyes were red-rimmed, but they flashed with anger more than anything else. "Thanks for coming in so quickly. The cops wanted to talk to all the employees right away, so Gavin and I decided to start with management and then work down through each department."

"Of course," Sienna said, accepting a hug from Laila before stepping back next to me. She didn't, however, take my hand again. "Is it just this room, or did anywhere else get hit?"

"Just this room," Laila said. "All the offices and private rooms were locked up pretty tight."

"Wasn't the club itself locked?" I asked.

"Yeah," Laila nodded. "And the alarm was set, but it didn't go off."

"The offices and private rooms have separate alarm systems," Sienna said, frowning. "But not as many people have access to those codes."

"Do they think it's an inside job?" I asked.

Laila shrugged. "If they do, they're not saying. It's mostly been them talking to Gavin, Carrie, and me while a couple of their CSI guys do their thing."

It wasn't until she gestured toward a pair of men on the stage that I realized the four uniformed officers weren't the only members of the NYPD here. I counted at least two detectives and a couple of crime techs.

My office getting trashed hadn't merited this kind of manpower, which made me wonder just how many strings Gavin and Carrie could pull in this concrete jungle.

"Was anyone here when it happened?" I asked, forcing myself to bring my thoughts back under control. Everyone was tense enough. They didn't need my irritation adding to an already volatile situation.

"We always have at least one member of security on the premises at all times," Laila said. "Today, that was Lamar Fulton."

She pointed to a dark-skinned man who looked to be in his early twenties. He was talking to a stocky man in a bad suit but didn't look injured.

"He's okay?" Sienna asked.

"Apparently, around eight this morning, he did his rounds and then used the men's restroom. While he was in there, someone barricaded the door, trapping him inside. He was stuck until Gavin got here about an hour ago." Laila's hands shook, and she shoved them into her pockets. "If Lamar hadn't been in the bathroom…"

"Maybe that's what they were waiting for," I suggested. "If he follows the same routine, someone could've known that and waited for when he usually goes to the bathroom before breaking in."

"Which would mean it wasn't just some random thing," Sienna said.

"I honestly don't know which would be worse," Laila said. "Random means it's more likely to go unsolved, but someone connected to the club means that someone we know did this."

I watched as Gavin strode over to us, his jaw clenched with barely contained fury. "Laila," he said, his voice tight, "can you handle the next round of calls? Make sure to let everyone know we're closed tonight, but they'll receive full pay."

As Laila nodded and moved away, I caught wind of a nearby conversation that made my blood boil. One of the uniformed cops had the audacity to mutter to his partner, "That's a helluva lot easier for these whores than having dudes shoving dollar bills down their g-strings."

Gavin's head whipped around so fast I thought he might get whiplash. "What the fuck did you just say?" he snarled, advancing on the officer with predatory grace.

The cop stumbled back, his face flushing. "S-sorry," he stammered. "Didn't mean nothin' by it."

"Like hell you didn't," Gavin spat, his eyes flashing dangerously. "I think you've taken quite enough statements for one day, jackass."

"But I was just—"

"Are you seriously gonna make me spell this shit out for you?" Gavin's voice had gone arctic cold. "Get your bigoted ass out of my club and don't you ever fucking dare show your face here again."

"But... but this is my job," the officer sputtered pathetically.

Gavin leaned in close, his voice dripping with menace. "If you don't drag your sorry ass out of here in the next thirty goddamn seconds, I'll make damn sure the only job you can land in this city is scrubbing toilets at some roach-infested hourly motel. Now move it!"

Something about Gavin must've convinced the cop he was serious because the officer scurried away with his tail between his legs, mumbling something under his breath that I was sure wasn't complimentary.

"Sienna," Gavin turned back to us, his tone returning to his usual, albeit a little more stressed, professional sound. "The detectives need to know where you were today and if you have any idea who could've done this. When you're finished with that, could you call your dancers? The ones who aren't servers too? We'll need them to come in and do the same."

"Of course," she said. "How's Carrie?"

Gavin looked over to where his wife was talking to one of the detectives. Neither one of the pair looked happy.

"Pissed as hell and making sure the boys in charge know that she has deep connections in the DA's office, and if they treat any of our people with disrespect, they'll be riding the desk in evidence lockup for the rest of their careers."

Carrie called for him then, and he walked away. I looked down at Sienna. "You go make your calls, and I'll call Carson. Gavin and Carrie should know that we have their back."

Sienna's expression was grim but determined. The shock had worn off, and now she was a woman preparing for a fight. "They might own the club, but it's special to a lot of us."

"Let's get this done, then," I said before dropping a kiss on her cheek and moving off to talk to the first officer I could find.

After I finished giving my statement—which was basically just me saying that the only person I knew of who was pissed at Gavin was Arthur Dalton, and yes I had an alibi, and no I didn't have a motive.

I stepped away from the chaos to call Carson. As soon as I explained what had happened, he didn't hesitate.

"Vix and I will be there as soon as we can," he said. "We'll help however we're needed."

I felt a wave of gratitude wash over me. "Thanks, man. I appreciate it."

By the time Carson and Vix arrived, the police were packing up their gear and heading out. Most of the club's employees had stuck around, determined to get the place back in shape.

"Holy shit," Carson muttered as he took in the destruction. "This is way worse than what happened at your office."

Vix nodded, her eyes wide. "It looks like a tornado hit in here."

I ran a hand through my hair, feeling the weight of everything that had happened. "Yeah, it's pretty bad. But everyone's pitching in to clean up."

Carson rolled up his sleeves. "Well, let's get to it then. Where do you need us?"

"Can I have everyone's attention?" Gavin called from the stage. When everyone turned to him and quieted down, he continued, "First, thank you all for coming in, some of you on your day off, and some of you who don't even work here. Obviously, we're going to be closed today, but I'm hoping we'll be able to reopen tomorrow. That wouldn't even be a possibility if not for you guys. Carrie and I really appreciate all of you."

After thanking everyone, he gave us all instructions, assigning groups to various parts of the club, and then stepped down from the stage to talk to Laila.

"So you guys don't know who did this?" Carson asked as he and Vix each pulled on a pair of leather gloves.

Sienna and I exchanged looks that said we'd been thinking along the same lines, even if we hadn't talked about it yet.

Carson caught the exchange. "Or do you know?"

I shrugged. "I have an idea, but no proof."

"That doesn't sound ominous at all," Carson said dryly. "Spill."

"There's a guy who's pissed at Gavin."

Sienna nudged my arm and raised an eyebrow.

"Okay, yeah, he's pissed at me too. And my office kind of got the same treatment."

"I'm assuming you told the cops this," Carson said.

"I did," I said. "Whether or not they believe it is a whole other story."

"Are you talking about Arthur?" Gavin asked as he came up on the other side of Sienna.

"I figured you'd already made the connection," I said, shoving two handfuls of alcohol-soaked paper towels into the bag Sienna held.

"Yeah, when our two places of business get trashed not long after he storms out of here, angry with both of us, it wasn't too much of a leap to put him at the top of the suspect list." Gavin nodded at Vix and Carson. "Thanks for coming to help."

"When family asks for help, you give it," Carson said simply.

I felt a familiar twist in my heart. Logically, I knew the McCrae part of the family who weren't biologically related to me and my siblings didn't distinguish between any of us regardless of what we called each other, but when they said things like that, it reminded me just how lucky I was.

"I don't think it's going to be a matter of whether or not the cops believe you," Sienna said quietly.

"What do you mean?" Gavin asked.

"I think it's going to be more about whether Arthur Dalton has connections high enough to get the cops to focus on other leads."

Even as she said it, I knew she was right. It was going to come down to who had more pull: Gavin and me or Arthur and his business partners.

Chapter Twenty-Eight

SIENNA

I'D BEEN awake for fifteen minutes and still hadn't quite mustered the energy to get out of bed. It was late Monday morning, and for the first time since Fury and I had been interrupted by the news that Club Privé had been vandalized, I didn't have anything demanding my attention. Thursday had been a late night, ensuring the place was clean and safe, while Friday and Saturday had rolled by with regular hours at the club, not even a pause in our usual schedule.

Some people might've thought it was about Gavin not losing money, but those who knew him understood it was more about flipping off the people responsible, showing them he wouldn't be intimidated. I didn't know if Arthur had gotten the message, but everyone else sure had.

Yesterday should have been another relaxing day off, but instead, I'd spent it at the club, setting up all the replacement equipment Gavin had ordered.

I felt like I'd been running non-stop for days, which hadn't exactly aided in my healing from the assault last week. Still, I refused to use that as an excuse to neglect my job, so I kept pushing through. Now, my body protested all the ways I'd abused it over the past few days, making it that much harder to drag myself out of bed.

Honestly, if I hadn't needed to pee, I probably would've stayed there until I dozed off again. But once I emerged from the bathroom, I heard the unmistakable sound of Vanessa in the kitchen. She'd had a busy weekend too, but I wasn't surprised she was up and cooking. That was her favorite way to unwind, and she was definitely more of a morning person than I was.

"Hey," I mumbled before yawning. "What are you making?"

"Four-cheese omelets." She was far too cheerful for this time of day. "Do you want ham in yours?"

I shook my head and headed for the coffee pot. "Can I have extra cheese?"

She laughed, a bright, happy sound. "Already added

the extra cheese to yours. Not mine, though. All of that would go straight to my ass."

I rolled my eyes. "Please. You've got one of those asses that someone could bounce a quarter off of."

"Because I do things like avoid death by cheese."

I laughed before taking a long sip of my coffee.

"Before I forget, there's a letter for you on the table." She gestured with her spatula.

"A letter? Doesn't our mail usually come in the middle of the afternoon?" I glanced at the clock on the microwave, making sure I hadn't misread the time.

"Someone slipped it under our front door," Vanessa replied with a shrug. "No return address or stamp or anything. I'm thinking it's from someone in the building. Maybe that cute guy one floor up?"

"Really? A letter from a cute guy?" I asked as I sat down. "What are we, Jane Austen characters?"

"Letter writing can be romantic," Vanessa said earnestly.

"It's also how horror movies start," I pointed out, glancing at the front of the envelope where my name was printed in block letters.

I tore it open and found a single sheet of computer paper with a typed message on it. It wasn't long, but it got straight to the point.

Convince your boss to sell or you and your roommate are

the first to pay for his stupidity. And if I can find you, I can find anyone else who works there. Find and make them disappear. No one will miss a bunch of whores. You got twenty-four hours to get it done. After that, I start with the redhead.

My stomach lurched, and I bolted to my feet.

"Sienna?" Vanessa turned, concern threading through her voice.

"I, uh, need a tampon," I blurted, the first thing that popped into my head, and practically ran to my bedroom, shutting the door behind me.

My mind raced as fast as my heart, and I slid down the door to sit on the floor. I stared down at the paper still clenched in my hand, and one thought struck me: I should let go so I wasn't potentially messing up evidence.

That was quickly followed by the memory of how little the cops had cared about Lulu being assaulted. Chances were, they'd take one look at this letter and laugh. They might even accuse me of writing it myself to get attention or some other bullshit like that.

Except I knew this was connected to Arthur Dalton and what he'd done to Club Privé and Fury's office.

And a part of me suspected that my 'mugging' hadn't been about stealing fifty bucks from my purse.

Knowing it and proving it, however, were two different things. Because I knew about the vandalism and about who my boss and my ... whatever Fury was, the accusation of me making it up could still stand. And it could take attention off finding the real culprit.

But I couldn't just ignore the threat either. Not when it wasn't just me being threatened.

"Sienna, are you okay?" Vanessa knocked softly on my bedroom door.

"I'm fine." I forced the words out. "Just cramps. I'll be out in a few minutes."

"Okay. Let me know if you need anything."

I squeezed my eyes closed and rested my forehead on my knees. What was I going to do about her? I didn't want to tell her about the letter, especially since she didn't know about anything else except me getting hurt, and she thought that was just a run-of-the-mill sort of city crime. But I'd never forgive myself if she got hurt because of me.

Then another thought hit me.

It wasn't because of *me*. I hadn't done shit to deserve this. Gavin and Fury were the ones who'd pissed Arthur off. I'd just been collateral damage because of my connections to both men.

I was calling Fury before I even realized I'd gone to him instead of Gavin, even though his employees were being threatened.

He picked up on the first ring.

"Hey, I was just getting ready to call you."

Something in his tone told me he wasn't talking about a personal call. "What happened?"

"You first."

I wasn't going to waste time arguing. "I got a letter threatening Vanessa, me, and my co-workers if I don't convince Gavin to sell the club."

"Dammit." He sighed. "Gavin and I each got one too. Delivered to our homes without a return address or postage."

"Same," I said. "They threatened your families?"

"Yeah," Fury replied. "Gavin's ready to go burn down anything connected to Arthur Dalton."

"Probably not the best idea," I said. "Tempting though."

"The three of us need to come up with a plan," Fury said. "Something that'll protect our people without giving Arthur what he wants, but giving us enough time to figure out how to take him down."

"Is Gavin with you?" I asked.

"No, he's at home with Carrie and the kids," Fury said. "Let me conference him into the call instead of us trying to figure out the best place to meet. The sooner we get this taken care of, the better."

"Yes, please." I closed my eyes and rubbed my forehead. "This is crazy."

"That's a good way to describe Dalton," Fury said dryly. "Give me a minute, and I'll get Gavin on the line."

A few seconds later, I heard Gavin's voice. "Hey, Sienna. You okay?"

"Freaking out a bit," I admitted. "Probably the same as you guys. I mean, I don't have a spouse or kids or anything, but—"

"People you love are being threatened," Gavin interrupted. "Doesn't matter who they are. It's … a lot."

"So how are we going to do this?" Fury asked. "I'm assuming that hiring a hitman to kill Dalton isn't a real option."

"Don't tempt me," Gavin said.

"I can tell Vanessa to stay with her parents, but I don't know if that would end up putting more people in danger since they just live in Brooklyn. They'd be easy to find," I said.

"She can stay with someone in my family," Fury offered. "All of them have top-of-the-line security, and I guarantee they'll all be locking down once I tell them what's going on."

"She can also stay with my family if she doesn't want to stay in the city," Gavin said. "I'm sending Skyler and her grandparents, along with Carrie and the kids, to our vacation home for a while. Vanessa's welcome to join them."

"Thank you." A rush of gratitude warmed me. "I'll let

her know she has options and find out what she wants to do."

"Family protects each other," Gavin said, as if it were that simple.

As if I'd ever had a family willing to do for me a fraction of what Gavin had.

"We take care of that first," Fury said. "Get our people safe, and then we go after Dalton."

"How do we do that?" I asked. I felt completely out of my league here.

"We go on the offensive," Gavin said.

"I'll dig deeper into his finances," Fury said. "See if there's any way to squeeze him that way."

"And I'll reach out to my connections, see if anyone knows anything about him we can use for leverage," Gavin added.

And suddenly, I knew what I could do.

"I've got connections too," I said. "In some ... different parts of the city. I'll ask around, see if there's anything there I can use. Maybe we'll get lucky and he'll have a coke addiction or something."

Even as I said it, though, I knew it wouldn't be that easy. Nothing ever was.

Chapter Twenty-Nine

SIENNA

I watched Vanessa toss another pair of socks into her suitcase, visibly frustrated. "I fucking hate the idea of you being stranded here alone while I'm whisked away with your boss's family to some swanky summer retreat," she griped. "If Gavin's family has space for my ass, they sure as hell could accommodate you. Christ, you're the one who actually works for him."

I shook my head, feeling the weight of responsibility on my shoulders. "I've gotta stay put, collaborate with Fury and Gavin to ensure that bastard Arthur Dalton doesn't harm another soul."

"Why is that your problem?" Vanessa whirled to face me, her eyes blazing with a mixture of anger and concern.

"Why should you be the one to deal with this shit? Aren't your boss and Fury able to handle this crap? Let them and the damn cops sort it out. I know you're devoted to your job and your work buddies, but for Christ's sake, Gavin doesn't pay you enough to risk your life."

"I have to do this," I insisted, my voice firm despite the knot in my stomach. "I know it's hard to comprehend."

Vanessa's eyes narrowed dangerously. "If you get so much as a scratch doing this bullshit, I swear to God I'll beat their asses to a pulp," she warned. "You make damn sure they know that, you hear me?"

"I'll pass along the message," I promised, feeling a rush of affection for her fierce protectiveness. My phone buzzed, interrupting the moment. I glanced at the screen. "Are you all set? The car's arrived."

"Jesus, I wish you'd at least stay at Fury's place," Vanessa grumbled, hefting her suitcase with a resigned sigh that spoke volumes about her frustration.

"I'll be fine, babe," I assured her as we trudged down to the lobby, my heart clenching at the worry etched across her beautiful face.

I continued to believe that when I said goodbye to her and made my way back upstairs. I still believed it when I stretched out on the couch to catch a couple hours of sleep before work.

When someone's banging at my door jerked me out of

sleep, I was disoriented enough to think Fury was here to take me to work. Then I saw the time and realized I'd only been asleep for about an hour. Confused, I sat up and made a few steps toward the door before the person on the other side shouted my name.

It was like someone had dumped a bucket of ice water over my head. Instant wakefulness, ice in my veins, and fear so sharp and bright it made it hard to breathe.

"Sienna, answer your damn door! I know you're in there, bitch! Open up!"

Holy shit. It was Ralf.

I wanted to squeeze my eyes shut and pretend this was just some fucked-up nightmare, but I couldn't tear my gaze away from the door, utterly terrified that he would find a way to break in. That he'd do to me what he'd done to Lulu, or something even more horrific.

"Sienna!" Ralf roared, his voice dripping with menace. "Open this motherfucking door before I kick it in, you sorry-ass bitch!"

Then I heard something worse.

"Excuse me, young man." It was Mrs. Goldstein, my elderly neighbor across the hall. "If you can't keep a civil tongue in your head, you need to leave."

"Who the hell are you? I'll beat your ancient ass, too. Don't think I won't."

His threats against a woman who'd been nothing but

kind to me got me moving. I would not put one more person in danger for knowing me.

So I opened the door a crack and came face-to-face with my former pimp for the first time since I'd told him I was leaving. In his mid-forties now, he hadn't aged well. His thinning brown hair was worse now despite his obvious attempts to cover it up. His eyes were bloodshot, and the smell of cigarettes and weed clung to him. His athletic build, however, remained, which wasn't good for me because when he slammed his shoulder into the door, I couldn't stop it from flying open.

I stumbled backward, struggling to stay on my feet. I knew if I fell, it was all over. Standing, I could at least try to avoid any punches, but on the ground, he'd kick me, and I knew from personal experience how bad that could be.

"Where is she?" he demanded, advancing toward me.

"Where's who, Ralf?" I played dumb, knowing he wouldn't fall for it.

"Lulu, bitch." He glared at me. "Is she hiding in one of those back rooms? Or are you two setting up your own place? Turning tricks without giving me a cut?"

"I don't do that anymore," I said. "You know that. I told you when I went to work for Gavin Manning that I wasn't hooking anymore."

"You gotta be doing something worthwhile to get a place like this," he sneered. "You think you and Lulu could double up, maybe bring in even more? Or did your new 'boss' tell you to start recruiting? You are getting older. Things maybe not so high and tight anymore?"

"She's not here, Ralf," I said, trying to keep the desperation out of my voice.

"But you know where she is, right?"

He took two more steps toward me, and I moved back until my legs hit the couch.

Shit.

"I know she came to you," he said. "I got eyes and ears everywhere."

It was on the tip of my tongue to snap back that if that was true, then he'd already know where she was. But I knew better than to smart off.

"She's not here," I repeated.

"Don't lie to me, you stupid cunt."

I held up my hands, as if that would keep him away. "She was here, but she left the next day. I don't know where she went after that."

That was technically true. I left out the part where I'd given her the means to get out of the city and that I had a phone number to reach her. We'd both agreed it was smarter for me not to know her whereabouts, just in case something like this happened.

Ralf's lips twisted into a scowl as a too-familiar light came into his eyes. My stomach dropped and my brain raced, trying to find a way out. But I knew there wasn't one. He was between me and the door, and he'd catch me if I tried to go around him. I had nothing within reach to use as a weapon. If I ran to either bedroom or the bathroom, he'd break down those doors.

I was totally fucked.

"You know something," he said. "And I'm gonna enjoy getting it out of you."

He closed the distance, his arm going back to get as much force into his blow as possible. I could only hope it'd be a slap, not a punch.

It never came because, suddenly, someone was between Ralf and me. A huge body I knew intimately. I had no idea how Fury had gotten from the door to the few feet separating Ralf and me, but I wasn't going to question it. I was just glad he was here.

"Who the fuck are you?" Ralf tried to sound big, but I knew that tone too. It was how he sounded when he realized he wasn't the biggest bully in the playground anymore.

"I'm the one who's going to throw you out on your ass in about three seconds." Fury's hands curled into fists.

"Wait a minute. I know you. You're the boyfriend." Ralf sounded far too pleased, warning me that whatever came next would piss both Fury and me off even more. "You got some bigwig job, don't you? Working with other people's money. Rubbing elbows with the rich and famous."

"Just go, Ralf." I put my hand on Fury's back, feeling the tension radiating off him as he fought for control of his temper.

"I will," Ralf said. "As soon as your boy here writes me a nice fat check. And give me whatever cash he got in his wallet. I like the watch too."

"Fuck off," Fury growled.

"Don't be like that," Ralf said, almost enjoying himself. "It's just a business transaction. You give me what I want, and I don't tell people you're fucking a whore."

Fury went impossibly still.

"Sorry to burst your bubble," Ralf continued, as if he didn't realize he was poking a very angry bear. "She learned all those bedroom skills to impress the upper crust."

"I know what you made her do," Fury said quietly.

The calm in his voice was somehow scarier than his rage.

"Okay, but you're not gonna want anyone else to know. I mean, who's gonna want you handling their money with the same hands you handle someone who's fucked half of Manhattan?"

"I don't care what you tell people," Fury said. "What I do care about is you harassing her. So you're going to leave this apartment and stay away from Sienna."

"And if I don't?" Ralf asked. "If I decide she has information I want and I intend to get it one way or another?"

"Then I'm going to make your life a living hell," Fury said evenly. "Because what you apparently didn't figure out about me is that I have the means to destroy you. Make you disappear off the face of this earth, and we both know not a single person will miss your sorry ass."

"You can't—"

"I can," Fury interrupted. "And more importantly, I will. For this woman, I'll do a hell of a lot. Now, get out before I have to make you."

As I peeked around Fury, I saw the fear on Ralf's face before he tried to cover it up with his usual bluster and swagger. Shooting me a glare, he slinked out, not turning his back on Fury until he was in the hall and on his way.

I was fairly certain that Fury's threats were the hottest things a man had ever offered to do for me.

Chapter Thirty

FURY

I waited until Ralf disappeared before closing her door, locking it, and turning back to Sienna. Only a supreme effort on my part kept my hands from trembling as I reached for her, lightly touching her cheek.

"Are you okay? Did he hurt you?"

She shook her head, pressing her lips together, the silence heavy with unspoken fear.

"Was that Ralf? The guy who assaulted Lulu?" I asked, my voice rough with the whirlwind of emotions swirling inside me.

She nodded, swallowing hard as she struggled to pull herself back together. The terror I'd seen etched on her face hit me hard. She was strong, but for him to have shaken her so deeply revealed just how much power he'd once held over her.

"It's okay," I said, cupping the side of her face. "You're safe. I've got you."

I didn't know if it was my touch or my words that sparked something within her, but suddenly, she seemed to snap free from whatever had a grip on her. Her wide eyes locked onto mine, and she practically threw herself at me, crashing her mouth against mine. I barely had time to brace myself before she pushed her tongue between my lips, a heady mix of desperation and urgency radiating from her.

I kissed her back, surrendering to the intoxicating bliss that enveloped me as I drowned in Sienna. Just as my grip on her tightened, she took a step back, leaving me momentarily disoriented. When she grabbed my hand and spun me around, confusion washed over me. With a gentle push to my chest, she sent me tumbling back onto the couch, and I stared up at her, utterly bewildered.

Until she sank to her knees in front of me.

If I hadn't gotten it then, I would've figured it out when she reached for the button of my jeans. I wanted to protest, tell her she didn't need to do that, but the moment I opened my mouth, she gave me a stern look that both shut me up and turned me on.

She tugged my pants and underwear down to my

thighs, then made a pleased sound as she looked down at my cock, half-hard and getting harder. She wrapped her hand around the base and stroked from the bottom of the shaft to the tip. I groaned at friction that was just this side of painful, then sucked in a breath when she ran her tongue over the head.

"Sienna."

"Shh." She lightly blew on my wet skin and I shivered, my fingers curling into fists at my side. "No talking."

"Why–" I started to ask, but the rest of my words came out in a garbled mess as she engulfed the top few inches in the wet heat of her mouth.

She bobbed her head up and down, moving a little lower each time until the head of my cock was part way down her throat and her lips were sealed around the base. My control was stretched to the point of snapping, my entire body humming with electricity. Every breath was ragged as it rasped in and out of my lungs, the sound mixing with the thumping of my heart and the rush of blood in my ears.

As the pressure built to a critical point, I reached for her head, trying to warn her I wouldn't be able to hold back much longer.

Then, suddenly, the suction I'd been enjoying disappeared and cool air took its place. The change in temperature had my eyes flying open, my impending climax easing off as my brain struggled to keep up with what was happening.

Considering it took me a minute to process that she'd just stripped off her leggings and panties, I was fairly certain she'd scrambled my brains with the blow job. But then she was climbing onto the couch, straddling my thighs with a knee on either side. Putting her hands on my shoulders, she paused for a moment, looking down with a question written on her face.

I put my hands on her hips and let her read my answer in my eyes. Then, with our gazes locked, she lowered herself onto me, taking me inside her in one steady motion. We both sighed as she settled on my lap, rocking back and forth as our bodies adjusted to being joined.

No matter how many times we did this, I couldn't get over how perfectly we fit, like we'd been made as two parts of the same whole. I ran my hand up her spine, holding the back of her neck as she began to ride me. Sensing her desire to keep control, I let her set the pace, focusing only on helping, touching her, soaking in the sight of her.

I'd already been so close that it took little to race back toward the tipping point. Needing her to be there with me, I leaned forward and caught one of her tight nipples in my mouth. I worked over the sensitive skin with my teeth and then sucked on it with harsh pulls until she started writhing, the sexiest mewling sounds falling from her lips.

"Fury," she whimpered my name as she reached up to bury her hand in my hair, holding me closer to her breast. "Close."

I released her nipple only long enough to say two words, "Me too."

As I went back to lavishing attention on the now-swollen bud, her pussy started tightening around my cock, shooting jolts of exquisite pleasure across my nerves. Then, between one breath and the next, I came. Her breast muffled my shout and my teeth clamped down harder than I'd intended, but it must've been what she'd needed because then she was coming too, calling out my name even as her fingers twisted in my hair.

She slumped into my arms, her body quivering as I wrapped my arms more tightly around her, both of us slowly coming down from our highs, waiting for our breathing and pulses to return to normal. My cock softened inside her and when she finally shifted to get her legs in a more comfortable position, I slipped out. I half-expected her to climb off, but she didn't. Instead, she sat on my lap and rested her head on my shoulder.

My fingers traced patterns up and down her arm as we sat in comfortable silence for a while. Finally, I broke it, unable to resist the urge to ask a question.

"Not that I'm complaining, but what prompted that?"

I brushed some hair back from her face. "I mean, I thought you'd be pissed at me doing my 'savior' thing."

I felt her smile more than I saw it, and a bit of the tension that had built up within me as the question arose dissipated.

"You didn't even flinch," she said, her fingers dancing across my chest. "Ralf threatened to tell people that you're sleeping with a former prostitute, and you didn't care. You didn't sugarcoat it with the whole 'that's not who she is anymore' crap that most people would say. I mean, it's true, but sometimes it sounds like I wouldn't have been worth your attention back then."

Something about the way she said it hit me, twisting my heart. In that moment, I knew I needed to tell her what I'd slowly been accepting since before Thanksgiving.

I caught her chin and tilted her head up to meet my gaze. "I meant every word. This isn't just me sleeping with you. I don't know when it happened, only that it did." I brushed a soft kiss across her lips. "I love you, Sienna."

The surprised joy that lit up her face flooded me with a happiness I hadn't thought could be any more intense.

Until she spoke.

"I love you, too."

The intensity of the emotion swelling within me was almost overwhelming, and I did the only thing I could do.

I kissed her again.

Chapter Thirty-One

FURY

I'D NEVER BEEN fond of having people invade my space, despite being a social person in my day-to-day life. I'd always attributed it to the transition from having my own room and sharing a house with just my parents, one brother, and one sister, to suddenly living in a house with more than a dozen people. Sure, I had my own room there too, but I never truly felt like I had much in the way of alone time.

So when I finally secured my place in Palo Alto, I discovered I preferred spending time with others anywhere but my apartment.

Yet here I was, sitting in my home office, a smile

creeping across my face because Sienna was sleeping down the hall, curled up in my bed as if she'd always belonged there. And this wasn't just a one-night thing. After the whole mess with Ralf, I had convinced her to stay with me. Having two separate people threatening her safety had been enough to sway her. Well, that and my promise not to mention Ralf to Gavin unless the idiot showed up at Club Privé.

According to Sienna, she could handle only one over-protective man at a time, and since she loved me, she preferred it to be me rather than her boss.

That thought made me chuckle softly. She loved me. I loved her. It felt like some sort of dream. I hadn't been searching for it, nor had I really wanted it, but I found I couldn't stop it.

For the first time, I truly understood everything the paired-off members of my family had been raving about over the past couple of years, and I braced myself for the inevitable harassment when they found out. Technically, my family in New York already knew I was involved with Sienna, and I assumed that meant everyone else had at least heard of her. But once they learned that this was serious, I knew it would be a while before I heard the end of it.

While I was thrilled to have Sienna here with me, her safety weighed heavily on my mind. I couldn't do anything about Ralf at the moment, but I convinced Sienna to accompany me to the police station to file a complaint against him, hoping it would reach the same people investigating Lulu's assault. Assuming they were still looking into it, anyway. If nothing came of it, I might consult Drake to see whom he thought I should approach about it. After all, if the cops weren't willing to take a known pimp off the streets just because they looked down on his victims, who the hell would they arrest?

I sighed and shook my head. I was doing it again. Even knowing she was perfectly safe and content, Sienna was a distraction—one I was more than happy to have, but I still needed to focus.

An alert flashed on my computer screen, yanking my attention back to my work.

Days had passed, and neither Gavin nor I had unearthed anything about Arthur Dalton that we could use to bring him down. Since neither of us liked the idea of Sienna reaching out to her connections, she hadn't found anything either. He was the one problem I should tackle, and yet here I was, unable to do a damn thing.

That was why I was trying something different.

Yesterday, I had exhausted my legal resources. I'd called in favors, reached out to old classmates, and even had Cory asking around back in California, but I was coming up empty. So finally, I decided it was time to take a risk. Break the law a little.

I'd asked Jules if she knew anyone who could help us dig deeper into Arthur's finances. As luck would have it, she'd gone to college with a computer wiz, Gianni, who was also freelancing as a competent hacker. After a brief conversation and a substantial payment, Gianni agreed to help us out, no questions asked.

The alert on my screen was from him. I opened the encrypted message, my heart racing as I read through the information he'd uncovered.

Considering all the shady dealings Arthur had been involved in for years, it was a little embarrassing how easily Gianni had accessed his accounts. Arthur had chosen one of the least secure banks in the city, an institution I'd barely heard of and didn't think existed outside of New York State, but I supposed he assumed that a bigger bank would scrutinize his transactions too closely.

Like the two large electronic payments made the day before, and the day after, the club was vandalized. And he hadn't done it with a check he could claim was stolen and forged; no, it was right there as an electronic transfer completed from an unsecure computer. Gianni had traced the IP back to an address that belonged to Arthur.

Idiot.

It didn't take Gianni much longer to access the account that received those payments and confirm not only that the two large ones originated from Arthur but also that a series of smaller payments had as well. Once he did that, he searched for the account's owner.

Dodd Espenson.

Finding that name explained a lot. Getting into my building wouldn't have been easy, but all someone had needed to do was bribe a person who worked there. Club Privé was a different story. As I'd seen when employees showed up to help clean, Gavin's people were fiercely loyal to him. At one point, I would have claimed they all were, but the name in front of me proved otherwise.

It wasn't a surprise once I thought about it.

Gavin had demoted Dodd Espenson from head of security to bouncer, and Arthur's payments had started the day after. Now I just needed Sienna to confirm that Dodd still could have gained access to the club after hours.

I hated waking her up, but this was something she needed to know, and we required that confirmation as soon as possible.

After brewing a pot of coffee, I made my way back to my bedroom and crouched beside the bed. Seeing her lying on her stomach, the blanket barely covering the swell of her ass, the bare skin of her back practically begging to be kissed, I was tempted to crawl in beside her and wake her in the most torturous way. But I knew her well enough to realize she'd be furious if she found out I'd lingered.

Reminding myself that we had plenty of time for such indulgences, I brushed some hair from her face and lightly touched her cheek.

"Sienna, time to wake up." She stirred but didn't wake, so I tried again. "Sienna, sweetheart, you need to wake up. I have something important to tell you."

Her breathing changed, and even with her eyes still closed, her expression shifted. I waited until her eyes fluttered open.

"Get dressed and meet me in the living room. I'll have coffee ready for you." I leaned forward and kissed her forehead before heading back out to the kitchen.

By the time she stumbled into the living room, still looking half-asleep, I had a cup waiting. She smiled gratefully at me and took the drink, sipping it as she settled on the couch, tucking her feet under her in a casual gesture that made my heart swell.

It might have been too soon, but I loved seeing her feel at home here.

But I couldn't dwell on that. We had work to do.

"I found something," I said.

Her eyebrows shot up. "Don't keep me guessing."

"First, a question just to be sure," I said. "Would Dodd Espenson be able to get into the club on his own?"

I watched realization dawn on Sienna's face with every word I spoke after his name. I didn't even need her to respond to know I was right.

"What did you find on Dodd?" she asked.

"So that's a yes?"

She nodded, setting down her coffee, her expression serious. "Why were you looking into him?"

"I wasn't," I said with a sigh as I sat down beside her. "I was investigating Arthur Dalton and with the help of Jules and her hacker friend, Gianni, we discovered two large transfers he made around the time the club was vandalized. Gianni traced those to an account that also had regular deposits from Arthur's account. It belonged to Dodd, and those deposits began the day after he was demoted."

She closed her eyes, rubbing her forehead. "Shit."

"Yeah." I allowed her some time to process.

After a minute, she looked up, resolve etched on her face. "He's the weak link."

"What?"

"Dodd," she clarified. "The guy likes to talk big, but he's all about himself. If he thinks he's in trouble, he'll sell out Dalton."

I rubbed the back of my neck. "Well, the thing is, what

we did to find that information wasn't exactly legal. We can't go to the cops with it."

She grinned at me, as if my admission only made her like me more. "Dodd's not the brightest bulb in the box. We can make him believe it."

"Okay." I nodded. "Now we just need to find him."

Her smile widened. "I can help with that. I have his employee file on my computer. It'll list his address."

"All right then," I said. "Let's grab some breakfast, then we'll head over to Dodd's place and see if we can get him to spill on Arthur."

She stood up. "How about we grab something on the way? Traffic's going to be a nightmare, so we might as well eat while we wait."

I agreed, and she went to change clothes. Thirty minutes later, we left my car in a public parking garage and walked a block to the building Dodd lived in.

Neither of us spoke as we ascended two flights of stairs and made our way halfway down the hall to apartment 2C. Since Dodd had flirted enough with Sienna for us to figure out she'd be our best way in, she knocked on the door while I hung back.

"It's unlocked," Dodd called from inside. "Bring the food in and leave it on the counter."

Sienna and I exchanged glances, and I recalled her earlier words about him not being the sharpest tool in the shed. Anyone who'd leave their apartment unlocked in New York City was asking for trouble.

Then she opened the door, and we stepped inside, realizing he was even dumber than we'd anticipated.

And we'd definitely missed something.

Because Dodd was sitting at a small table a few feet away ... and next to him was Ralf Crosse.

Chapter Thirty-Two

SIENNA

I COULD COUNT on one hand the number of times I'd been shocked speechless. This was one of them.

Both Ralf and Dodd stared at Fury and me long enough for Fury to close the door behind us, but they recovered much quicker than I did.

"If it isn't the highest earner for RC's Escorts." Ralf smirked. "How about a private demonstration of your best moves?"

I heard Fury growl behind me, but I was already moving, breaking free of my shock. I didn't think, didn't consider whether this was smart. I just acted. My fist connected with Ralf's nose, and I smiled at the satisfying crunch.

He yowled, jerking away hard enough to tip over his chair and send him crashing to the floor. Out of the corner of my eye, I saw Dodd bolt for the door, but with Fury there, he wouldn't get far.

"Get up, Ralf," I ordered.

"Sit down, Dodd," Fury said, shoving him back toward the empty chair. "You two have answers we need."

Then Fury stepped back, crossing his arms over his muscular chest. When I shot him a questioning look, he nodded at me to go ahead. My heart gave an unsteady thump as I realized what he was doing. Even though he had as much at stake in this as I did, he was letting me take the lead because he knew how powerless I felt with Ralf.

"You first." I pointed at Dodd. "You've been taking money from Arthur Dalton."

He glared at me.

"That wasn't a question," I said. "We know you've gotten money from him, and we're pretty sure we know what he got out of it. I want to know how far you went."

"What's that supposed to mean?" His voice was thick, nasally.

I took a step toward him and was gratified to see him flinch. "Did you just let him or his goons into the club, or did you join in? Help them trash a place where your friends worked?"

"I don't have any friends there," Dodd said petulantly. "Everyone just stood there and let Gavin treat me like shit."

"You let guys with guns into the club and nearly got people killed!" I shouted. I took a step back, inhaling slowly, then letting it out just as slowly. "Okay, so that's where it started, right? Gavin demoted you, and then what? Keep in mind that since Fury and I aren't cops, we can beat the shit out of you, and nobody's going to care."

I could see the wheels turning in Dodd's head and wondered if he would believe me. While it'd been very satisfying to break Ralf's nose, I didn't think I was up to torturing Dodd for information. I'd do it to protect the people I loved, but I was hoping he'd spill before that became necessary.

"Yeah, that's when it started," he finally said. "I don't know how Dalton found out about what happened, but when I got home from work the next day, he was there, waiting for me. He said he needed eyes and ears in the club, that he'd not only pay me, but he'd make sure I had any job he wanted when he took over the club."

"What did you do as his 'eyes and ears'?"

"I let in some guys for him, and they trashed the club," Dodd admitted. "And they did some other shit, like messing with the lighting rig, that sort of thing."

"That crashed during the middle of a practice, you idiot," I snapped. "What else?"

"He said he needed to test the employees, see who he'd want to keep around when he took over." Dodd shifted uncomfortably in his chair. "And he wanted to know if anyone was looking for Venus."

My heart nearly stopped in my chest. "What about Venus?"

Dodd looked at Ralf, but I slammed my hand down on the table to get his attention.

"Arthur got her personal info from somewhere. I don't know where. He didn't tell me. But he had some people grab her."

"What for?" I didn't think I wanted to hear the answer, but I needed to know.

"He's selling her to traffickers," Dodd finally said. "And he said he needed to know who the people would be that'd look for her, because he couldn't have nosy people working in his club."

I glanced at Fury, the clenching of his jaw telling me he was just as furious about this as I was. "What else?"

Dodd shook his head. "That was it."

"Dodd," I warned.

He held up his hands. "I swear. I don't know anything else." He pointed at Ralf. "But he knows more. He's been working with Dalton longer than I have."

I turned to Ralf, pushing aside the flutter of nerves that came with being near him. The fact that they were a flutter and not a full-on panic attack was an accomplishment, and I knew it was because I had Fury with me. Not in some sort of 'I needed a big strong man to defend me' way, but rather just knowing I wasn't alone, that someone had my back, gave me the courage to face off with a man who'd exploited me for years.

"It's your turn to talk," I said to him. "And don't think for a minute I won't break more than your nose."

Ralf looked at Dodd, then at Fury, and finally turned his attention back to me. He folded his arms, and for a moment, I thought I'd have to follow through on my threat. While it was tempting, my hand hurt already. But he started talking instead.

"Dalton never would've found me if he hadn't been digging up dirt on you."

I took a step back at that. "What are you talking about?"

"Exactly what I said. Arthur was looking into all the managers and shit at that club, and you led him to me. I was, after all, your previous employer." He leered at me, rocking his chair back on two legs.

"If you want to break something else but don't want to hurt your hand, I'm sure we can find something to hit him with," Fury said mildly.

All amusement vanished from Ralf's face, and the chair dropped back on all fours with a thump.

"What else did he say?" I asked.

"He was interested in my 'expertise,'" Ralf said.

"What the hell does that mean? Spell it out." I spoke through gritted teeth.

"He offered me a shitload of money for my girls," Ralf said. "Which is why I need to know where Lulu is. He paid for her. When I figured out she went to you, I realized that was a chance I couldn't pass up."

"A chance for what?" I asked.

"A chance to deliver you." He shrugged. "Dalton said he'd give me a bonus if I could get you for him. Said it'd piss off two guys you were important to."

"So even if I'd been able to tell you where Lulu was, you weren't going to leave me alone," I hissed.

"It ain't personal, sweetheart," Ralf said. "Just business. Like it always was."

"Must've pissed both of you off when you realized your plan failed," I said. "No money for you and no revenge for him."

Dodd snickered.

I shot him a glare. "What's so funny?"

He shrugged, and I took a step toward him. He held up his hands. "Damn. All right. You don't need to get all violent on me. I was just laughing because Arthur doesn't have anything to be pissed about. He found a better mark."

Fury and I exchanged glances, both of us confused.

"What's that supposed to mean?" I asked.

"Gavin has someone he'd be willing to pay a hell of a lot to get away from the future Arthur has planned for her." Dodd looked pleased at the idea. "And if Gavin decides to call the cops and not pay, Arthur could get a fuckton of money selling a pretty little virgin teenager."

I opened my mouth to ask for a name, but it hit me before I got the question out. "Skylar? Dodd, is Arthur going after Skylar?"

Dodd shrugged, but I didn't need confirmation. It was the only thing that made sense.

"Someone would have to be monumentally stupid to go after Gavin's kid," Fury pointed out.

"Gavin won't let anyone near his daughter," I added. "We're not idiots. All of us took precautions. Skylar's not even in the city."

It was Ralf's turn to laugh. "C'mon, you gotta know that a man like Arthur Dalton would have his ways."

When I looked at Fury this time, I saw my concern reflected on his face. He pulled out his phone and called Gavin, putting him on speaker.

"Hey, Fury. What's up?"

"Sienna and I are looking into something and we think

Arthur might try to go after Skylar. Is she still at your vacation home?"

There was a slight pause and then Gavin let out a string of curses before saying, "One of my security guys just took Vanessa and Skylar to a doctor's appointment Skylar couldn't miss. They're not here."

Chapter Thirty-Three

FURY

I TOOK the corner fast enough to make my tires squeal, and I caught a glimpse of Sienna gripping the handle above the door to keep from tumbling into me. Not a word had passed between us since I'd hung up with Gavin. We'd bolted from the apartment together, leaving Ralf and Dodd behind without a second thought, both tied up for the police to apprehend.

Just before hanging up, Gavin had shouted at Carrie to call the cops and mentioned that he was on his way too. The address he'd given me placed Sienna and me a little closer, but like everything else in the city, who got there first would probably hinge on the whims of traffic.

Right now, traffic was on our side.

"Right there." Sienna pointed up and across the street just moments before my GPS announced we'd arrived.

As I looked over, I spotted three figures emerging from the building. A bulky guy who seemed vaguely familiar, with Skylar and Vanessa trailing behind.

Without a second thought, I pulled into a No-Parking zone and leaped out of the car without even turning off the ignition. I didn't give a damn if someone stole it; I'd buy a new one. Sienna was right behind me, leaving her door wide open too.

"Vanessa!" she shouted as I called out to Skylar.

"Get back inside!" I waved my arms frantically.

"Go!"

Sienna was at my side as we dashed across the street, ignoring the blaring horns of drivers honking at us. Before we reached them, everything felt surreal, a strange blur that was both too fast and too slow at the same time.

Vanessa and Skylar looked confused, but the moment the bodyguard recognized Sienna and me, he turned. A car screeched to a halt in the opposite direction, and a man jumped from the passenger seat, heading straight for Skylar. The bodyguard shifted to shield Skylar from the approaching stranger, colliding with Vanessa, sending her crashing against the wall beside her. She crumpled to the ground, and it was impossible to tell how badly she'd been hurt.

As I changed my direction to confront Arthur's man, I saw him pull a gun from his waistband, and I pushed myself even harder. He was just out of reach when he aimed and fired at the bodyguard. People screamed, but I didn't look to see if he'd hit anyone. I lunged at the shooter from the side and tackled him to the ground.

I slammed down on him with all my weight, driving his body into the concrete with enough force to knock the gun from his grip. Without wasting a moment, I pushed myself up, pressing my knee into the middle of his back as I yanked his arms behind him.

I pushed down harder on the shooter's hands as he began to stir, the wail of police sirens growing louder.

"Knock it off, asshole," I growled. "You're not going anywhere except prison. Hope you like orange."

He twisted his head, trying to glare at me over his shoulder. "You're gonna regret this," he snarled. "I got friends."

I snorted. "Not very good ones," I shot back. "They left you behind."

The EMTs rushed past, heading straight for Vanessa and the fallen bodyguard. I caught only a glimpse of Sienna backing away, her hands stained with blood, before a swarm of people blocked my view.

"Sir, I need you to stand up and keep your hands where I can see them."

I looked up to find a young cop standing over me, weapon drawn and aimed uncertainly between my captive and me.

"This guy assaulted me," the shooter whined, playing innocent. "I didn't do nothing; he just knocked me down."

I rolled my eyes. "His gun is over there," I said, gesturing with my chin. "I'll happily get up, but you might want to secure that man before he reaches for it."

The cop's eyes darted from me to the gun, then back to the man face-down on the sidewalk. With a nod, he positioned himself between the weapon and the guy.

"I'm going to stand up now," I said slowly, not wanting any misunderstandings. "I'll keep my hands in the air and stand right here while you secure him."

"I've got him, Officer Timmons." An older cop approached from behind me. "You secure that man on the ground, and we'll start getting statements. Starting with who shot that man over there."

"Him," I said quickly, nodding at the guy I'd tackled. "And I'm not the only witness."

"Fury!"

Sienna's voice cut through the chaos. She threw her

arms around me, burying her face in my chest. I glanced at the older cop, who nodded in understanding.

Relieved, I returned the embrace and wrapped my arms around Sienna. "It's okay," I murmured into her hair. "We're safe now. It's over."

She pulled back slightly, her emerald eyes wide and searching. "Vanessa? The bodyguard?"

"EMTs are with them," I assured her. "We did everything we could."

Sienna nodded, then suddenly frowned. "Your hands... they're shaking."

I hadn't even noticed. The adrenaline was wearing off, leaving me feeling drained. "Yeah, well, tackling armed kidnappers isn't exactly my day job."

That got a small laugh out of her. "My hero," she said, only half-joking.

I cupped her face gently. "Hey, we're in this together, remember? You were pretty heroic yourself."

She leaned into my touch, a mix of emotions playing across her face. "What happens now?"

I looked around at the flashing lights, the bustling officers, the stunned onlookers. We'd thwarted Arthur's kidnapping plan and had one of his guys in custody. The cops would listen to our suspicions now and hopefully only a matter of time before Arthur was behind bars, too.

"Now? We give our statements, make sure Vanessa and Gavin's guy are okay, and then…" I met her gaze, allowing myself a small, hopeful smile. "Then we start thinking about that future we talked about. Together."

Sienna's eyes softened, a tentative smile tugging at her lips. "Together," she echoed. "I like the sound of that."

Chapter Thirty-Four

SIENNA

I shifted uncomfortably in the hard plastic chair, wincing as my back protested. Hospital waiting room chairs were really uncomfortable, but until I knew for certain that Vanessa and the bodyguard were okay, I wasn't going anywhere.

Next to me, Fury let out a soft groan as he stretched, his arm coming to rest behind me on the back of my chair. The warmth of his presence was oddly comforting.

"You okay?" he murmured, his voice low and concerned.

I nodded, offering a tight smile. "Yeah, just worried about Vanessa."

Across from us, the bodyguard who'd come with

Gavin to rescue Skylar was furiously tapping away at his phone. I caught his eye and raised an eyebrow.

"Everything alright?" I asked.

He glanced up briefly. "Just updating Mr. Manning. Calvin, the injured bodyguard, is still in surgery."

I nodded, remembering that Gavin had taken Skylar back to his place about a few minutes ago after her doctor had given her an all-clear.

"How was Skylar when they left?" Fury asked, voicing my unspoken question.

The bodyguard's expression softened slightly. "Shaken up, but physically fine. The woman who took her statement was really understanding. Didn't push too hard."

I sighed in relief. "Thank god. That poor girl's been through enough."

Fury's hand found mine, giving it a gentle squeeze.

On my other side, Vanessa's parents were huddled together, speaking in hushed tones. I'd called them as soon as we'd arrived at the hospital, and they'd rushed over immediately.

"Any news?" Vanessa's mother had asked, her voice trembling slightly.

I shook my head. "Not yet, but no news is good news, right?"

Finally, a short, slightly plump woman in a white coat entered the waiting room. The air seemed to still as all conversation ceased, and we collectively sat up straighter.

"Family of Vanessa Rodriguez?" she called out, her eyes scanning the room.

My heart leaped into my throat as I stood, Vanessa's parents right beside me. "That's us," I said, my voice barely above a whisper. "How is she?"

The doctor came over, and the smile on her face made me think things were okay.

"She has a concussion. It's more than a mild one, and we're going to keep her overnight for observation, but I'm optimistic that she won't have any long-lasting effects."

"Thank goodness," Mrs. Rodriguez said, her shoulders slumping in relief. "Can we see her?"

"Immediate family only, and two at a time. If she gets tired, you'll have to go."

I was a little disappointed that I couldn't go see her, but I knew she was okay, and that would have to be enough. I told her mother to let Vanessa know that if she needed me, just to reach out, and then I turned to Fury.

"I think I'm going to go."

"Okay." He stood up and held out his hand. When I gave him a questioning look, he explained, "The shooter might flip on Arthur, but as of right now, Dalton's still out there. You're not safe until he's caught."

He had a point.

"Come home with me," he said. "Your stuff is there, anyway. We can figure out the next step in the morning."

I took his hand and laced my fingers between his. As we said our goodbyes and headed out to Fury's car, I went back over everything that'd happened from arriving at Dodd's apartment through Fury hugging me as we realized the worst was over. So many emotions swamped me that I felt almost suffocated by them. By the time we got back to Fury's condo, the pressure of everything building up inside me had me ready to explode.

Then Fury looked at me with unconcealed heat in his eyes. That was it.

The front door wasn't even all the way closed before we started tearing at each other's clothes. All the stress and adrenaline from the day, the close call, and the relief of it being over eliminated even the possibility of taking this slow. And, fortunately, Fury seemed to be on the same wavelength because his fingers were just as busy with the button of my pants as mine were with his. Then we were down to a bra for me and socks for him, and waiting any longer to have him inside me seemed ridiculous.

As his mouth latched onto mine, he grabbed my ass and lifted me. My legs went around his waist. A little maneuvering while he devoured me and his cock was sliding home at the same time my back came up against the wall. I heard something fall to the floor and hoped it wasn't important because the only thing I really cared about at the moment was how fucking fantastic I felt being full of long, thick cock.

When he started to move, using the wall to brace us, my eyes rolled back, and I broke the kiss just so I could start chanting his name. Well, his name, the word *yes*, and a whole lot of expletives.

I clung to him as he thrust up into me; the angle putting just the right pressure on my clit, and our closeness causing my bra to chafe my nipples until they were tight buds, burning with a near-painful intensity. But it was the fact that I couldn't really move, couldn't really control my pleasure, that ramped up my arousal. It was all up to him now, and letting him have that control broke something open in me, solidified this bond that we'd been creating from the first moment we'd met.

As I raked my nails across his back, he growled low in his throat and pounded into me harder, fingers digging into my hips hard enough to leave bruises. Up and up I went, the spiral of pleasure tightening until I reached the peak. I came with a cry, each of his strokes prolonging it until I couldn't think, could see. Then he came in a rush, his teeth going to the side of my throat, giving me a nudge to spill over into a second climax, a reminder that we were alive and we were together.

And that was more than I'd ever dreamed I could have.

A man I loved and who loved me, who could rock my world physically, and be my rock emotionally. He was everything I hadn't known I'd wanted. And as we stood there, wrapped up in each other, I knew everything that'd happened from the moment Gavin sent me to that airport had been leading up to now and to the new future I saw stretching out in front of me.

Chapter Thirty-Five

FURY

I paced back and forth in Gavin's office, my mind racing with possibilities. We were pretty sure Arthur wasn't far away yet, but it wasn't enough. We needed to find out where he was located, bring him down and rescue Venus, if possible. The weight of the situation pressed down on me, but I refused to let it crush me. There had to be a solution.

"Fury, you're going to wear a hole in my carpet," Gavin said, his tone light but his eyes serious.

I stopped and ran a hand through my hair. "Sorry. I just can't shake the feeling that we're missing something."

Sienna, perched on the edge of Gavin's desk, nodded. "I know what you mean. It feels like we're so close, but…"

"But we need more," I finished for her.

Just then, a knock at the door interrupted us. Jules poked her head in, a tentative smile on her face. "Sorry to interrupt, but Gianni's here."

I felt a surge of hope. Jules' hacker friend had already proven invaluable in uncovering Dodd's connection to Arthur. Maybe he could be the key to cracking this case wide open.

"Send him in," Gavin said, straightening in his chair.

Gianni entered, his lanky frame hunched slightly as if trying to make himself smaller. His eyes darted around the room, taking in each of us before settling on me. "You must be Fury," he said, extending a hand. "Jules has told me a lot about you."

I shook his hand, noting the strength in his grip despite his nervous demeanor. "All good things, I hope."

He cracked a smile. "Mostly."

After quick introductions, we gathered around Gavin's desk. Gianni pulled out a laptop and began typing furiously. "I've been digging into Arthur Dalton's activities since our last conversation," he said, his eyes never leaving the screen. "And I think I've found something interesting."

We all leaned in closer as he turned the laptop to face us. On the screen was a satellite image of a sprawling mansion nestled in the woods.

"This is a property in upstate New York," Gianni explained. "It's registered to a shell company, but I've traced it back to Dalton. There's been a lot of activity there recently—unusual shipments, increased security measures, that sort of thing."

My heart raced. This could be it. "You think this is where he's running his operation from?"

Gianni nodded. "It's the most likely candidate. And…" he hesitated, glancing at Sienna. "Based on the patterns I've observed, I think there's a good chance this is where they're keeping Venus."

Sienna's sharp intake of breath was audible in the sudden silence of the room. I reached out and squeezed her hand, offering what comfort I could.

"How sure are you?" Gavin asked, his voice tight with barely contained emotion.

"As sure as I can be without physically being there," Gianni replied. "The data patterns match what you'd expect from a… from that kind of operation."

I felt a surge of anger, quickly followed by determination. We had a target now. All we needed was a plan. We couldn't run to the cops just yet, given how we came across this info.

"So, how do we get in there?" I asked, my mind already racing with possibilities.

Sienna straightened, a fierce look in her eyes. "I have an idea, but you're not gonna like it."

I turned to her, dread pooling in my stomach. I had a feeling I knew where this was going, and she was right—I didn't like it one bit.

"We use me as bait," she said, her voice steady despite the gravity of her words.

"Absolutely not," I said immediately. At the same time, Gavin said, "That's too dangerous."

Sienna held up a hand. "Hear me out. Arthur wants me, right? We know that. So we give him what he wants—or at least, we make him think we are."

I shook my head, my chest tight with fear. "Sienna, no. It's too risky."

"It's our best shot," she insisted. "Look, I know the risks. But I also know that place, that world. I can handle myself."

"She has a point," Gianni interjected softly. When we all turned to look at him, he shrugged. "From a tactical standpoint, it makes sense. They'll be less suspicious if they think they're getting what they want."

I wanted to argue, to find another way, but I could see the determination in Sienna's eyes. And as much as I hated to admit it, they were right. This could work.

"Okay," I said finally, my voice rough. "But we do this smart. We need a solid plan, backup, everything."

Gavin nodded, his expression grim. "Agreed. And we need to figure out how to deal with Arthur. If he's there when we make our move..."

"Actually," Gianni interrupted, "I might have a solution for that." He turned his laptop back towards himself and began typing again. "I've been monitoring Dalton's communications. He's got a meeting scheduled in the city tomorrow. If we could... encourage him to keep that appointment, it would give us a window to infiltrate the mansion."

I felt a glimmer of hope. This could work. It was dangerous, yes, but it was a chance to end this nightmare once and for all.

"Okay," I said, my mind already planning. "So we use Sienna as bait to get us in. But we need to explain our presence." I looked at Gavin. "What if we pose as Dodd and Ralf? They were working with Arthur, after all."

Gavin nodded slowly, a smile spreading across his face. "That could work. We know enough about their involvement to be convincing."

"And I can provide you with any additional stuff you might need," Gianni added. "Comm devices, fake IDs, the works."

I turned to Sienna, my heart heavy. "Are you sure about this? There's no shame in backing out."

She met my gaze steadily. "I'm sure. This is our chance to save Venus, to stop Arthur for good. I have to do this."

I wanted to argue, to wrap her in my arms and never let her go. But I knew that wasn't fair. Sienna was strong, capable, and determined. I had to trust her, to support her.

"Okay," I said softly. "Then let's make this plan bulletproof."

For the next few hours, we hashed out every detail of our plan. Gianni would provide us with the tech we needed – earpieces for communication, fake IDs, even a way to hack into the mansion's security system remotely if needed. Gavin would reach out to a trusted police contact to set up Arthur's arrest during his meeting in the city. And Sienna... Sienna would play the most dangerous role of all.

As we finalized the details, I couldn't shake the knot of fear in my stomach. I pulled Sienna aside while Gavin and Gianni discussed some technical aspects of the plan.

"Are you absolutely sure about this?" I asked, searching her face for any sign of doubt.

She smiled, reaching up to cup my cheek. "I am. I know it's dangerous, but this is something I have to do. Not just for Venus, but for myself. To face this part of my past and put it behind me for good."

I leaned into her touch, closing my eyes briefly. "I

just... I can't lose you, Sienna. The thought of you in danger..."

"Hey," she said softly, making me meet her gaze. "You will not lose me. We're in this together, remember? I trust you to have my back."

I nodded, pulling her into a tight embrace. "Always," I murmured into her hair.

As we broke apart, Gavin called us back over. "Alright, I think we've got everything hammered out. Gianni's going to get started on the tech we need. We'll reconvene tomorrow morning to go over final details and get everything in place."

We all nodded, the weight of what we were about to do settling over us.

"Get some rest," Gavin continued. "Tomorrow's going to be a long day."

As we left Gavin's office, I felt a mix of anticipation and dread. This plan was risky, but it was our best shot at bringing down Arthur and rescuing Venus. I just hoped we were ready for whatever challenges lay ahead.

Back at my place, Sienna and I tried to relax, but the tension of the upcoming mission hung heavy in the air. We ordered takeout, neither of us in the mood to cook, and settled on the couch to eat.

"Tell me what you're thinking," Sienna said softly, setting down her container of Pad Thai.

I sighed, running a hand through my hair. "Honestly? I'm terrified. Not for myself, but for you. I know you can handle yourself, but the thought of you in that place, surrounded by those people..."

She nodded, understanding in her eyes. "I get it. But Fury, we've been over this. I need to face this part of my past and come out stronger on the other side."

I reached out, taking her hand in mine. "I know. And I admire your strength, your determination. It's one of the things I love about you. I just... I can't help but worry."

"That's because you love me," she said with a small smile. "And I love you for it. But you have to trust me on this. We're partners, remember? Equal partners."

I nodded, bringing her hand to my lips and pressing a kiss to her knuckles. "You're right. I do trust you. It's just hard to turn off the protective instinct, you know?"

"I know," she breathed. "But remember, I'm not some damsel in distress. I've survived a lot, and I'll survive this too. Especially with you by my side."

Her words warmed me, easing some of the tension in my chest. "You're right."

We spent the rest of the evening going over the plan, refining details and discussing contingencies. As we finally headed to bed, exhaustion weighing heavily on us both, I pulled Sienna close.

"No matter what happens tomorrow," I murmured

into her hair, "know that I love you. More than I ever thought possible."

She tilted her head up, meeting my gaze with a fierce intensity. "I love you too. And we're going to get through this. Together."

As we drifted off to sleep, I held onto that thought. Together. No matter what challenges lay ahead, we'd face them side by side.

The next morning dawned far too early. We were both tense as we got ready, the weight of what we were about to do hanging heavy in the air. Sienna was quieter than usual, her movements precise as she dressed in clothes that would fit her undercover role.

"You okay?" I asked softly as she finished applying her makeup.

She met my gaze in the mirror, a determined set to her jaw. "Yeah. Just... getting into character, I guess."

I nodded, understanding. This wasn't just any undercover operation. For Sienna, it was a return to a world she'd fought hard to escape. I moved behind her, wrapping my arms around her waist and resting my chin on her shoulder.

"You've got this," I murmured. "And I'll be right there with you every step of the way."

She leaned back into me, drawing strength from our connection. "I know. That's what gives me the courage to do this."

We arrived at Club Privé early, meeting Gavin and Gianni in Gavin's office. The hacker had dark circles under his eyes, evidence of a sleepless night spent preparing our tech.

"Alright," Gianni said, spreading out an array of equipment on the table. "I've got everything you'll need. Earpieces for communication—they're small enough to be practically invisible. Fake IDs for Fury and Gavin, complete with backstopped identities if anyone does a deep dive."

He handed us each our respective gear, then turned to a laptop. "I've also hacked into the mansion's security system. I can't shut it down without raising suspicions, but I can create a loop in the camera feed for key areas once you're inside. That should buy you some time to move around undetected."

I nodded, impressed. "Nice work, Gianni. This is going to make a big difference."

"There's one more thing," he said, his expression serious. "I've set up a kill switch for all of Arthur's accounts and operations. Once you give the signal, I can shut everything down. It won't be permanent, but it should create enough chaos to give the authorities time to move in and seize evidence."

Gavin clapped Gianni on the shoulder. "Excellent. This is exactly what we needed."

We spent the next hour going over the last details, making sure everyone knew their roles inside and out. As we prepared to leave, Gavin pulled me aside.

"My police contact is ready," he said in a low voice. "They'll move in on Arthur the moment we give the signal. But Fury... let's be careful in there. If anything seems off, we abort the mission. We can always try again, but not if we're dead or arrested."

I nodded, appreciating his concern. "Understood. We'll be careful."

My heart raced as we stepped out to the car, adrenaline coursing through my veins. This was it. The culmination of endless cups of coffee and meticulous planning. I caught Sienna's eye, her jaw set with resolve, but I noticed the slight tremble in her hands as she reached for the car door.

"Ready?" I asked softly.

She took a deep breath, then nodded. "As I'll ever be. Let's do this."

The drive to the mansion was tense, each of us lost in our own thoughts. As we approached the imposing gates, I felt my heart rate increase. This was it. No turning back now. We only hoped that none of the guards knew Dodd and Ralf personally.

I rolled down the window, adopting Dodd's cocky demeanor as I addressed the guard. "We're Dodd and Ralf," I said as I handed him our fake IDs. "We're here to see the boss. Got a special delivery for him." I jerked my thumb towards the backseat where Sienna sat, her wrists bound in front of her.

The guard's eyes widened slightly as he recognized Sienna, then he nodded and handed back the IDs. "Go on through. Park by the side entrance."

As we drove up the winding driveway, I caught Gavin's eye. We shared a look of grim determination. Whatever happened next, we were in this together.

I parked the car, and we got out, Gavin roughly pulling Sienna from the backseat. My heart clenched at the sight, even though I knew it was all an act.

"Remember," I murmured as we approached the door, "if anything feels off, we abort. No heroics."

Sienna and Gavin both nodded imperceptibly. Then the door swung open, revealing a burly man with a gun holstered at his hip.

"Well, well," he said, eyeing Sienna with a predatory grin. "Looks like Christmas came early this year. The boss is gonna be real happy to see you."

I forced a laugh, channeling Dodd's sleazy persona. "Yeah, figured we'd bring him a little present."

The guard nodded, stepping aside to let us in. "Smart move. Follow me."

There was no turning back now. We had a job to do, people to save. And come hell or high water, we were going to see it through.

Chapter Thirty-Six

SIENNA

My chest tightened, each heartbeat a desperate cry for escape as we delved deeper into the winding manor. The guard's iron grip sent shockwaves through my arm, his fingers biting into my flesh as he shoved me forward with brutal force. I tripped, my feet scrabbling on the polished floor. Every fiber of my being screamed to fight back, to resist, but I choked down the urge, burying it in my gut. I had to play the part of the terrified, obedient captive, not a battle-hardened warrior.

I caught Fury's backward glance, his face a storm of worry. His clenched jaw betrayed his barely contained rage. His muscles coiled, ready to explode at any second. I sensed him teetering on the edge, a hair's breadth from blowing our meticulously crafted cover. With the tiniest shake of my head, I silently begged him to stay put. We'd invested too much, come too far to risk exposing ourselves now.

As we passed by an open door, I overheard two guards talking in low voices. "...yeah, the boss just left for that meeting in the city. Said he'd be back late tonight."

Relief washed over me. Arthur was gone, just as we'd planned. One less complication to worry about.

The guard leading us stopped abruptly in front of a heavy wooden door. He rapped his knuckles against it twice before pushing it open. "Got some visitors for you, sir. Dodd and Ralf. They brought a gift."

My stomach churned as we were ushered into what looked like a study. Behind an imposing desk sat a man I recognized from the files Gianni had shown us - Jackson Reeves, Arthur's right-hand man and the head of his trafficking operation. His cold eyes swept over us, lingering on me with a look that made my skin crawl.

"Well," Jackson drawled, leaning back in his chair. "What do we have here?"

Fury stepped forward, imitating Dodd's cocky swagger. "Thought we'd bring you a peace offering. Show of good faith, you know?"

Jackson's eyes narrowed. "And why, pray tell, do you think you need to make a peace offering?"

I could feel the tension radiating off Fury and Gavin. This was the moment of truth, the most crucial part of our deception. I subtly shifted my weight, drawing Jackson's attention. Time to put my knowledge to use.

"Please," I whimpered, injecting fear into my voice. "I-I'll do whatever you want. Just don't hurt me."

Jackson's focus shifted fully to me, a predatory gleam in his eyes. "And who might you be, sweetheart?"

I ducked my head, playing the part of the terrified captive. "S-Sienna. I used to work for Ralf, but then I... I ran away. He caught me and brought me here."

"Did he now?" Jackson stood, circling around his desk to approach me. He grabbed my chin, forcing me to look up at him. "And why would he do that?"

I swallowed hard, letting genuine fear bleed into my expression. It wasn't hard - the situation was terrifying enough without having to act. "B-because I know things. About the club, about... about Arthur Dalton."

Jackson's grip tightened painfully. "What kind of things?"

"Enough to cause trouble," Gavin interjected, his voice gruff as he channeled Ralf's persona. "Figured you'd want to deal with her personally. Make sure she doesn't run her mouth to the wrong people."

Jackson studied me for a long moment, his eyes cold and calculating. I held my breath, praying our story would hold up under his scrutiny. Finally, he released my chin and stepped back.

"Smart move," he said, turning to address Fury and Gavin. "Arthur will be pleased. He's been looking for this one for a while now."

I allowed myself a small internal sigh of relief. He was buying it, at least for now.

As Jackson continued to question Fury and Gavin, I took the opportunity to survey the room. My eyes darted around, cataloging potential escape routes and weapons. Maybe even Venus.

No such luck.

"...and what exactly do you expect in return for this generous gift?" Jackson was saying, drawing my attention back to the conversation.

Fury shrugged, affecting an air of nonchalance. "Just looking to get back in the boss's good graces. Maybe a cut of whatever you get for her."

Jackson's eyes narrowed suspiciously. "That's awfully generous of you. Last I heard, you weren't exactly on Arthur's favorite persons list. From what I know, you messed up. Couldn't locate some of your girls you promised."

I watched as Gavin stepped forward.

"That's exactly why we brought her," he said, gesturing towards me with a dismissive wave. "I fucked up, no denying that. But this little prize?" He smirked, and I had to fight not to shudder at the predatory look in his eyes. "This is my way of making it right. Arthur's been after her for a while now, hasn't he? Just imagine how pleased he'll be when he gets back and finds her all wrapped up with a bow."

Jackson's eyes narrowed, his gaze flicking between Gavin and Fury. I could practically see the gears turning in his head as he weighed the situation. My heart was going crazy in my chest, every instinct screaming at me to run, to fight, to do something. But I forced myself to remain still, playing the part of the terrified captive.

"Arthur has been looking for this one," Jackson admitted slowly. "She could be... valuable. But that doesn't erase your previous mistakes."

"Course not," Fury chimed in, his voice gruff. "But it's a start, ain't it? Show of good faith and all that."

I watched Jackson carefully, trying to gauge his reaction. Everything hinged on whether or not he bought our story.

After what felt like an eternity, Jackson nodded. "Alright. I'll make sure Arthur knows about your... contribution when he returns. For now, we'll get her settled in with the others."

My stomach churned at his words. 'The others.' Venus had to be among them. We were getting close.

Jackson snapped his fingers, and a guard appeared in the doorway. "Take her to processing," he ordered. "Make sure she's secured properly. We don't want any runaways."

The guard nodded, moving towards me. As he grabbed my arm, I caught Fury's eye one last time. The concern in his gaze was clear, but I tried to convey with a look that I was okay. That this was all part of the plan.

As I was led out of the room, my mind raced. We were in, but now came the hard part. We had to find a way to get Venus out, signal for backup, and get out of here alive.

The guard's grip tightened on my arm as he shoved me down a dimly lit hallway. The musty smell of damp and decay filled my nostrils, a stark contrast to the opulent study we'd just left. My heart raced as I tried to memorize the path we were taking, knowing it could be crucial for our escape later.

We stopped in front of a heavy metal door. The guard fumbled with a set of keys, the jingling sound echoing ominously in the quiet hallway. As he worked to unlock the door, I caught a glimpse of movement out of the corner of my eye.

Was that...?

Chapter Thirty-Seven

FURY

I watched helplessly as the guard led Sienna away, every fiber of my being screaming at me to intervene, to protect her, but I knew I had to maintain our cover. As she disappeared down the dimly lit hallway, I forced myself to turn back to Jackson, schooling my features into what I hoped was a convincing imitation of Dodd's cocky smirk.

"So," Jackson drawled, leaning back in his chair, "tell me more about how you two captured our elusive Sienna. I'm sure Arthur will be very interested in the details."

I exchanged a quick glance with Gavin, silently praying we could keep this charade going long enough to find Venus and get Sienna out safely.

"Well," I began, channeling Dodd's bravado, "it wasn't

easy. Girl's slippery as an eel. But Ralf here had some connections, and we tracked her down at a seedy motel on the outskirts of town."

Gavin nodded, adding gruffly, "Caught her trying to skip town. Figured we'd bring her straight here instead of risking her slipping away again."

Jackson's eyes narrowed, and I felt a bead of sweat trickle down my spine. "Interesting. And you didn't think to call ahead? Let us know you were coming?"

I shrugged, trying to appear nonchalant. "Didn't want to risk her overhearing anything. You know how crafty she can be."

"Indeed," Jackson murmured, his gaze boring into me. "Well, gentlemen, since you've gone to all this trouble, why don't I give you a tour of our operation?"

My pulse quickened. Bingo. This could be our chance to gather more information, maybe even find where they were keeping Venus and the other victims.

"Lead the way," I said, gesturing for Jackson to precede us out of the office.

As we followed him through the winding corridors of the mansion, I tried to memorize the layout, keeping an eye out for any signs of where Sienna might have been taken. The opulent décor of the main areas gave way to more utilitarian spaces as we descended deeper into the building.

"This is where we process new arrivals," Jackson explained, gesturing to a room filled with medical equipment. The clinical smell of disinfectant made my skin crawl as I thought about what "processing" might entail.

We continued on, passing by rooms that Jackson referred to as "training facilities" and "merchandise storage." Each revelation made my blood boil, but I forced myself to nod along, playing the part of the impressed visitor.

As we turned down yet another corridor, a burly guard came rushing towards us, his face red with exertion. "Sir!" he called out to Jackson. "We have a problem!"

Jackson frowned. "What is it?"

The guard's eyes darted between me and Gavin, suspicion clear in his gaze. "These aren't Dodd and Ralf," he said, his hand moving to the gun at his hip. "I just got off the phone with the real Ralf's lawyer. He's in custody."

Time seemed to slow as Jackson's expression morphed from confusion to rage. In an instant, the hallway erupted into chaos. Jackson lunged for his weapon while shouting for backup. Gavin and I sprang into action, our cover blown but our mission far from over.

I ducked as Jackson fired, the bullet whizzing past my ear. Adrenaline surged through me as I tackled him, driving us both to the ground. Out of the corner of my eye, I saw Gavin grappling with the guard who'd exposed us.

"Where is she?" I growled, pinning Jackson to the floor. "Where's Sienna?"

He spat in my face, a vicious grin twisting his features. "You'll never find her in time," he sneered. "By now, she's probably already been... processed."

Rage clouded my vision, and I slammed his head against the floor, knocking him unconscious. As I scrambled to my feet, I heard footsteps approaching. More guards were on their way.

"Fury!" Gavin called out, having subdued the other guard. "We need to move!"

I nodded, my mind racing. We were outnumbered and outgunned, with no idea where Sienna or Venus were being held. The situation seemed hopeless, but I refused to give up. Not when we were so close.

I radioed Gianni to call the cops, but Gavin and I both realized it was a long-shot they would arrive in time. We'd have to handle this shit ourselves.

"This way," I said, leading us down the corridor Jackson had been about to show us. It had to lead somewhere important.

We ran, the sound of pursuit growing louder behind us. As we rounded a corner, we found ourselves face to face with three more guards, their weapons already drawn.

"Freeze!" one of them shouted. "Hands where we can see them!"

I raised my hands slowly, my mind frantically searching for a way out of this mess. Just as I was about to make a desperate move, a deafening explosion rocked the building.

The guards stumbled, momentarily distracted. It was all the opening we needed. Gavin and I sprang into action, disarming the closest guards and using their own weapons against them. The fight was chaotic, my worry for Sienna fueling every punch and kick.

As I grappled with one of the guards, trying to wrest his gun away, a familiar voice cut through the din of combat.

"Fury! Duck!"

I dropped to the ground without hesitation, trusting Sienna's voice implicitly. A second later, I heard the satisfying thud of a body hitting the floor behind me. I looked up to see Sienna standing there, a fire extinguisher in her hands and a fierce grin on her face.

"Took you long enough," she quipped, offering me a hand up.

Relief and pride surged through me as I took in the sight of her. She was disheveled but unharmed, her eyes blazing with determination. Beside her stood another woman, one I vaguely recognized from the files we'd studied.

"Sorry for the delay," I said, unable to keep the smile off my face despite the dire situation. "Traffic was hell."

Sienna shot me a look, but I caught the warmth in her eyes. "Meet Tina. Ex-escort of Ralf's and a certified ass-kicker. She took out my guard before you showed up."

With Sienna and Tina evening the odds, we made quick work of the remaining guards. As the last one fell, I pulled Sienna into a fierce embrace, my heart filled with relief and lingering fear.

"Are you okay?" I murmured into her hair, reluctant to let her go.

She nodded against my chest. "I'm fine. But we need to move. Tina told me where they're keeping Venus and the others."

I pulled back, meeting her determined gaze. "Lead the way."

Minutes later, we reached a heavily fortified door, and Tina punched in a code. As the door swung open, we were met with the frightened faces of dozens of women and girls, huddled together in the dim room.

"It's okay," Sienna called out, her voice gentle but firm. "We're here to help. You're safe now."

I spotted Venus among the group, her eyes glazed but a spark of recognition lighting up as she saw Sienna. As we began helping the victims out of the room, I could hear sirens in the distance. Our backup was finally arriving.

The next few hours passed in a blur of police statements, medical examinations, and coordinating with various agencies to ensure the victims received proper care. Through it all, I kept Sienna close, unwilling to let her out of my sight again.

As the sun began to rise, casting a warm glow over the chaos of the crime scene, I found a quiet moment to pull Sienna aside. I cupped her face in my hands, drinking in the sight of her – tired, bruised, but alive and triumphant.

"You were amazing in there," I said, my thumb tracing her cheekbone. "I've never been more terrified or more proud in my life."

She leaned into my touch, a small smile playing at her lips. "We did it together," she replied. "Just like we said we would."

I nodded, leaning in to rest my forehead against hers. As I held her close, I made a silent vow to never let her face such danger alone again. But I also acknowledged the strength and bravery she'd shown, the fierce determination that had saved not only herself but countless others.

"So," Sienna murmured, her breath warm against my skin, "what do you say we get out of here and go home?"

I smiled, pressing a gentle kiss to her lips. "Home sounds perfect. But first..." I pulled back slightly, meeting her curious gaze. "How exactly did you manage to cause that explosion?"

Epilogue

SIENNA

I JOLTED AWAKE, my heart racing as the remnants of the nightmare faded. Fury's arm tightened around my waist, his warmth anchoring me to reality.

"You're safe," he murmured, his voice rough with sleep. "I've got you."

I took a deep breath, letting his words wash over me. Safe. It was still a foreign concept, even weeks after the raid on Arthur's mansion. But as I nestled closer to Fury, I felt the truth of it settle into my bones.

The clock on the nightstand read 3:17 AM. Another restless night, but they were becoming less frequent. I closed my eyes, thinking back to the chaos that had followed our escape from the mansion.

The sirens had barely faded when the media circus descended. Reporters clamored for details, their microphones thrust in our faces as we tried to shield the rescued women from their prying eyes. I'd given a brief statement, my voice steady despite the trembling in my hands, before Fury whisked me away from the cameras.

The following days were a blur of police interviews, medical examinations, and debriefings. I'd insisted on staying close to Venus throughout it all, watching over her as she began the long process of healing. The drugs they'd pumped her full of had taken their toll, leaving her disoriented and weak. But even in those early days, I saw flashes of the fierce woman I knew her to be.

"How is she doing?" Fury asked softly, pulling me from my thoughts.

I turned in his arms, meeting his concerned gaze. "Better," I said. "She's starting to open up in therapy. It's going to be a long road, but she's strong."

He nodded, pressing a kiss to my forehead. "Like someone else I know."

I smiled, warmth blooming in my chest at his words. It was still strange sometimes, being on the receiving end of such unwavering support and affection. But I was learning to embrace it, to believe that I deserved it.

"Have you thought more about testifying?" Fury asked, his fingers tracing soothing patterns on my back.

I sighed, the weight of the upcoming trial settling over me. "Yeah. I'm going to do it. They need to pay for what they've done."

The thought of facing Ralf, Arthur, and his associates in court made my stomach churn, but I knew it was necessary. My testimony, along with the mountain of evidence we'd uncovered, would ensure they spent the rest of their lives behind bars.

"I'll be right there with you," Fury promised. "Every step of the way."

I leaned in, capturing his lips in a gentle kiss. "I know. I couldn't do this without you."

As the first rays of dawn peeked through the curtains, we reluctantly untangled ourselves from each other and started our day. The routine we'd fallen into over the past weeks was comforting—shared showers, coffee brewed just the way I liked it, stolen kisses as we got dressed.

On the drive to Club Privé, I marveled at how much had changed in such a short time. The club itself was thriving under the new security measures Gavin had implemented. He'd hired a team of ex-military personnel to handle security, and every employee had undergone extensive background checks. The dancers felt safer than ever, and it showed in their performances.

As we walked through the club's main entrance, I was struck by the energy of the place. Even in the early morning hours, there was a buzz of activity as staff prepared for the night ahead.

"Sienna!" Venus called out, waving from behind the bar where she was restocking bottles. It was her temporary gig until she felt ready to get back on stage.

I made my way over to her, drinking in the sight of her looking so... normal. Her hair was pulled back in a messy bun, and she wore one of the club's signature tank tops. To anyone else, she might have looked like just another bartender getting ready for her shift. But I could see the lingering shadows in her eyes, the slight tremor in her hands as she arranged the bottles.

"Hey, you," I said, leaning against the bar. "How are you feeling today?"

She shrugged, a small smile playing at her lips. "Better, I suppose. Still some trouble sleeping."

I nodded, understanding all too well. "You know you can call me anytime, right? Day or night."

"I know," she said. "And I appreciate it. But I'm trying to... I don't know, reclaim some independence, I guess?"

"I get it," I assured her. "Just don't push yourself too hard, okay?"

She rolled her eyes, but there was affection in her gaze. "Yes, mom."

As I made my way to my office, I caught sight of Fury deep in conversation with Gavin. They both looked up as I approached, twin expressions of concern on their faces.

"What's wrong?" I asked, immediately on alert.

Gavin sighed, running a hand through his hair. "We just got word from the DA's office. Arthur's lawyers are pushing for a plea deal."

My blood ran cold. "What kind of deal?"

"They're offering to give up names of other traffickers in exchange for a reduced sentence," Fury explained, his jaw clenched tight.

I shook my head, anger bubbling up inside me. "No. Absolutely not. He doesn't get to wiggle out of this."

Gavin held up his hands placatingly. "I agree. But the DA thinks it might be worth considering. The information could lead to taking down other rings, saving more victims. He'll still spend decades behind bars."

I closed my eyes, trying to process this new development. On one hand, the thought of Arthur getting any kind of leniency made me sick. But if it meant saving others from the fate Venus and so many others had suffered...

"What do you think?" I asked Fury, meeting his steady gaze.

He was quiet for a moment, considering. "I think... it's not our decision to make. We should talk to Venus, to the other survivors. See how they feel about it."

I nodded, grateful once again for his level headed approach. "You're right. We'll set up a meeting, let them have a say."

As Gavin headed off to make the calls, Fury pulled me into a tight embrace. I melted into him, drawing strength from his solid presence.

"You okay?" he murmured into my hair.

I nodded against his chest. "Yeah. Just... sometimes it feels like this will never really be over, you know?"

He pulled back slightly, cupping my face in his hands. "I know. But we're making progress. And no matter what happens, we're in this together."

I smiled, leaning in to kiss him softly. "Together," I echoed.

The rest of the day passed in a whirlwind of meetings and preparations for the night ahead. As I made my final rounds before opening, I caught sight of my reflection in one of the mirrored walls. The woman staring back at me was a far cry from the guarded, defensive person I'd been just months ago. My posture was straighter, my eyes clearer. I looked... happy.

"Penny for your thoughts?" Fury's voice came from behind me, his reflection appearing beside mine in the mirror.

I turned to face him, drinking in the sight of him in his

perfectly tailored suit. "Just thinking about how much has changed," I said. "How much I've changed."

He smiled, reaching out to tuck a stray lock of hair behind my ear. "You've always been amazing, Sienna. You're just letting people see it now."

I leaned into his touch, warmth blooming in my chest. "Including myself, I guess."

As the first guests filtered in, Fury and I made our way to the VIP section.

The music pulsed around us, the energy of the crowd electric. I sipped my drink, content to people-watch for a while. Fury's arm was draped casually over the back of the booth, his fingers playing absently with the ends of my hair.

"You know," he said, leaning in close so I could hear him over the music, "we never finished that conversation we started the other night."

I raised an eyebrow, a smile tugging at my lips. "Which conversation was that?"

He grinned, his eyes twinkling with mischief. "The one about our future plans. Specifically, whether or not you'd be interested in making this arrangement of ours a bit more… permanent."

My heart skipped a beat. We'd been dancing around the subject for weeks now, both of us hesitant to push too hard or move too fast. But as I looked into Fury's eyes, I felt a sense of certainty wash over me.

"Are you asking me to move in with you, Fury Gracen?" I teased, even as my pulse quickened.

He shrugged, feigning nonchalance. "Maybe. Now that I finally got approved for that fancy penthouse. Or maybe I'm asking for something more. Like, say, a lifetime commitment?"

I blinked, momentarily stunned. "Are you... proposing?"

His expression softened, all traces of teasing gone. "Not officially. Not yet. But I want you to know that's where I see this going. If that's something you want, too."

I took a deep breath, letting his words sink in. A lifetime with Fury. A home, a family, a future built on trust and love and mutual respect. It was more than I'd ever dared to dream for myself.

"It is," I breathed, my voice barely audible over the thumping, pulsating music. "It's exactly what I want."

The smile that broke across Fury's face was radiant. He pulled me close, kissing me with a passion that made my toes curl. When we finally broke apart, both breathless, I laughed.

"What's so funny?" Fury asked, his eyes dancing with joy.

I shook my head, still grinning. "Just thinking about

how different my life is now compared to a few months ago. If someone had told me then that I'd be sitting here, planning a future with you..."

"You'd have laughed in their face?" he supplied.

"Probably," I admitted. "Or punched them."

He chuckled, pulling me closer. "Well, I'm glad you didn't punch me when I first kissed you."

"Technically, I kissed you." I leaned my head on his shoulder, watching the crowd below us.

Fury's hand found mine, our fingers intertwining naturally. I looked at him, taking in his profile. He must have sensed my gaze because he glanced back, a soft smile playing at his lips.

"What are you thinking about?" he asked, his voice low and intimate.

I squeezed his hand, a warmth spreading through my chest that had nothing to do with the temperature. "Just wondering," I said, a hint of teasing in my tone, "how soon is too soon to start planning a wedding?"

THE END

The Scottish Billionaires Series

Alec & Lumen:
When Alec mistakes a young woman's salon for a "happy ending" massage parlor, things get more complicated than he prefers. Especially when their lives become entwined in ways never imagined.

1. Off Limits
2. Breaking Rules
3. Mending Fate

Eoin & Aline:
After Aline Mercier, a young American teacher, is taken hostage in Iran, Eoin McCrae is tasked with getting her out at all cost. He never imagined falling for her.

1. Strangers in Love
2. Dangers of Love

THE SCOTTISH BILLIONAIRES SERIES

Brody & Freedom:
At his distillery, Brody McCrae crafts the finest Scottish whiskey, while Freedom Mercier is finishing her Master's degree with big plans to change the world. When the two of them are brought together at a holiday party, things heat up more than anyone could predict.

1. Single Malt
2. Perfect Blend

Baylen & Harlee:
After Baylen McFann discovers that his fiancée has left him, he escapes Scotland to find advice from his friend across the pond, Alec McCrae. As Alec presents his newest statistical analyst, Harlee Sumpter, Baylen's already smitten.

Business or Pleasure

Drake & Maggie:
When Drake Mac Gilleain lays eyes on Maggie McCrae, he believes he's seeing the ghost of his late wife and decides to follow her.

At First Sight

Carson & Vix:
When Carson McCrae, the hottest designer in Manhattan, asked me to model a new bra in a fashion show, I knew it

was a line. I'm anything but a runway model. I got more curves than Kim Kardashian.

It was definitely a line. So why did I say yes?

A Dress for Curves

Spencer & London

Spencer York, a dashing and distinguished British theater producer, arrives in Manhattan with the exciting prospects of bringing his production to Broadway's illustrious stages. Destiny steers him to a cozy, intimate pub where he encounters London McCrae, a fiery and ambitious actress with dreams of conquering Broadway's greatest stages.

A Play for Love

Blaze & Trisha

Airport closed and stranded by a Christmas storm, Blaze and Trisha embark on a cross-country road trip from Chicago to San Francisco, discovering laughter, chemistry, and challenges that test their pact to remain just travel buddies.

Mistletoe Detour

Cory & Rylee

Cory McCrae, a charming hunk yet socially awkward finance guru, clashes with Rylee Palmer, a brilliant rival,

sparking an intense, steamy romance amid a fierce rivalry and a scandal that threatens their passionate connection.
Rival Desires

Fury & Sienna
When a rugged billionaire meets a fierce talent coordinator, sparks fly and secrets unravel. As passion ignites, they're thrust into a dangerous game of love and survival. Can Fury and Sienna overcome their pasts to forge a sizzling future together?
A Dance with Obsession

Printed in Great Britain
by Amazon